Scaring the Stars into Submission

By
Adam "Bucho" Rodenberger

All Contents Copyright © 2016
Adam "Bucho" Rodenberger

Cover Art by Robert Romine

ISBN: 9781976700613

"Machineries of reason, machineries of conduct, machineries of virtue. The machine that regulates instinct, keeps one's hands free of another man's throat, free of one's own. These machines have all, as someone said, gone too long in the elements. Gummed now, rusted, bloodless. I forget who said it and I no longer care."

- Ben Marcus, *The Flame Alphabet*

" – Fire comes and the news is good,
It races through the streets
But is it true? Who knows?
Or just another lie from Heaven?"

- Aeschylus, *Agamemnon*

"Now this is not the end. It is not even the beginning of the end. But it is, perhaps, the end of the beginning."

- Winston Churchill

I've been fortunate to have pieces in this collection published first in various webzines, literary journals, and magazines.

Since their first publication, some of the stories may have been edited again for better clarity, stronger writing, or a more stringent focus on the ideas within them.

"In the Morgue" – *Up the Staircase (July 2012)*

"Photo Finish" – *Crack the Spine Literary Magazine*
(Issue 79 as "Puzzle Peace" and reprinted in the Winter 2014 Anthology)

"Scaring the Stars into Submission" – *Lunch Ticket (May 2014)*

"Black Crush" – *Ginosko Literary Journal (Issue 17, 2015)*

"Saudades& Ossuaries" – *Slice Magazine (Issue 16, Spring 2015)*

"Firebug for Hire" – Samizdat *Literary Magazine (April 2012)*

"You Are the Key Witness to the End of the World" –
Phoebe: A Journal of Literature and Art
(Issue 42.1, Spring 2013 as "Springtime for the World")

"Only So Far" – Fox Spirit's *'Girl at the End of the World'* Anthology
(2014)

"Trauerspielen (Mourning Plays)" – *Glint Literary Journal (Summer 2013)*

"New Hire Video" – *L'Allures des Mots (Issue 18, Fall 2015)*

"Sugarhouse" – *Aphelion Webzine (March 2013)*

"The Memory of a Gypsy Moth" – *Eunoia Review (July 2014)*

"Equity Lamp" – Almond Press' *'Broken Worlds:Dystopian Stories'*
Anthology*(2014)*

"Ruinous Bloom" – *Bluestem Magazine (December 2013)*

"I Waited for You" – *Sheepshead Review (Fall 2014)*

Litany

Foreword by S.K. Kalsi
"Darkness Visible: The Stories of Adam "Bucho" Rodenberger
(i-xiii)

Publication List

I. - The Beginning

II. – Altered States

III. - Keira

IV. - Interlude

V. – Dark Dawns

VI. – Hope *or* The End

Darkness Visible:
The Stories of Adam "Bucho" Rodenberger

By SK Kalsi

In the summer of 2009, I left my comfortable, caged life in Huntington Beach, CA, and drove over four hundred miles north to San Francisco, the city of bridges. Having been accepted to the graduate writing program at USF on the strength of a single short story written years earlier, I believed that discovering my identity as a writer meant redefining my value as an artist. Similarly, the author of this collection made his own journey west, leaving Kansas City to attend the same graduate program, and much for the same reasons. We both believed that being a writer meant leaving behind your comfort zone. Our *terminus ad quem* on the good days meant writing with authority and purpose, imagination and depth; and on the bad ones, learning to pause, to be grateful for the opportunity to write anything we wanted.

Writers are explorers first. As explorers, we were going to learn about our own limits and how best to transcend them. We would learn about point of view and characterization, how to develop theme, delve into the mechanics of plot, experiment with structural forms, and immerse ourselves in the works of authors whose works we admired. We would discover new writers, discard bad habits and hopefully develop good ones. Over the course of two years, we would pick apart great works of literature and discover how certain stories worked, or where they fell apart. Through professor and peer critiques, we would define and redefine our own fictional worlds, or at the very least discharge the beasts in our heads. We would develop new friendships, hear famous authors speak to our classes, and talk about writing without the fear of judgment. We had been afforded a great luxury, that of time, and our challenge was how best to utilize it.

New to San Francisco, alone, dazzled by the bustle and bright lights, we were both anxious about this new chapter in our lives. In the days leading up to the summer session, I roamed the Embarcadero, nervous about how easily I had traded security for an uncertain life of letters. Yet there I was, standing at the edge of the Ferry Building's easternmost parking lot, gazing out at water black as oil in which the lights of Oakland shimmered like shattered stars, determined to do the hard work of developing good writing habits, and just finish something for god's sakes!

Adam must have felt the same anxiety and the same commitment: we had both left behind a comfortable and caged life for a different one, for we both believed the creative life was the best kind of life. I can think of no better metaphor for our crossroads than the dueling images of the Golden Gate Bridge arching above cold, deep, shark infested water, and Alcatraz, rising silently in the center of the bay: We make our lives either bridges to the future or prisons of the past.

On an early Saturday morning in June, I ascended the several hundred steps to the Lone Mountain campus and found the banquet room where the two-day orientation was taking place. At the numerous round tables sat students of poetry, fiction, and non-fiction, and I claimed a seat for my own. As the head of the department began his opening remarks, the seat beside me stood vacant for several minutes when a man in his early thirties with close-cropped, reddish blonde hair, shaded lenses, and neatly trimmed beard stepped forward and inquired about the vacant seat beside me. He wore a gray hooded sweatshirt, khaki shorts, and sneakers on that cool summer morning. As one professor after another took the podium and spoke, we smiled to ourselves, excited by this journey and a little afraid, for to dream something for so long and then to find yourself in its palm felt a bit terrifying: would the outstretched fingers of our dream collapse around us like a Venus Fly Trap, crushing us with its pressure, or would it simply cradle us and ask us to stay?

At the break I sat outside on the front stoop and smoked. To my surprise my tablemate joined me, his backpack in tow. After brief introductions (he was German, but had he read Wittgenstein?) we talked about our origins and what led us to this famed literary city that bestowed the brave their success. We covered a range of topics—music, literature, and philosophy (he had read Herr Witt…and Kant and Nietzsche). His voice was self-assured with a low register that, when he laughed, sounded full of joy. His eyes twinkled with mischief as we shook hands, his grip firm, and we returned inside.

When he first sat down beside me, I did not believe I had found a lifelong friend, but that is what happened. I would come to know his affable manner, acerbic wit, and bawdy sense of humor. I would come to respect his opinion on my rough drafts, read his stories and attempt to reconcile the joyful, mischievous man in the khaki shorts and close-cropped hair with the utter darkness of his vision. I found his stories astonishing, like fever-dreams, so unlike the stories I would read of depressed, divorced men searching for love, or robots in a utopian/agrarian society, or party girls skipping from one empty sexual conquest to another, or Vietnamese rickshaw drivers, or *roman a clefs*, coming of age stories, or breeding chinchillas, and so on.

For two years we read one another's work and offered compliments as well as criticism. For two years we made it a point to meet during the weekends to write, offering each other writing prompts. In my apartment, after an hour of silence, him tapping away on his laptop in the far corner and me at my desktop, one of us would shout to the other, "What do you think of this? Too much?" We met for coffee at a café on Townsend Street. We met at the movie theater to watch films (like Cormac McCarthy's *The Road)*, then discussed the differences between film and book. We met for drinks (whisky, wine, vodka, or anything that put a shine on the night and loosened our spirits). At museums we expressed to one another what moved us about Expressionism and what disappointed us about Minimalism. We had our aesthetic differences: I loved James Joyce's work and Flaubert's *Madame Bovary*, and he did not. He had strong opinions about Victorian-era writers, too; Austen, the Bronte sisters. He didn't "get" Chekov or Carver's appeal. Though our reading tastes differed greatly then as they do now (so, too, our writing styles) we found in each other a commitment to the writer's creed: read deeply, widely, write honestly and every day.

Good writers are good readers. They are also varied readers. Faulkner once famously declared that writers must read everything, good or bad, because everything has something in it and the good in it makes its way into your work and the bad in it teaches you which mistakes to avoid. A voracious reader, Adam would consume as many books as he could get his hands on (he's read the *Harry Potter* series for god's sakes, but also *Leviathan*). He prided himself on having procured more books than he had time to read. We often visited City Lights Books (as much a church of literary history as a bookstore) and upon entering, drifted away. We perused the shelves and then found one another to point out certain books and authors the other might enjoy. Budget allowing, we each left with three or four books apiece.

After abandoning my first attempt at a novel, a book about tin miners in Eastern Congo, a story meant to pay homage to Cormac McCarthy's *Blood Meridian* with its strict objective point of view, I attempted psychological realism; and Adam, after taking a course in experimental fiction, became hooked on nonlinear, unconventional modes of storytelling. His first foray into such a "genre" was a novel about museum paintings that witnessed a theft of one of their own. Avant-gardists became his heroes and eclecticism his *raison d'etre*. He eschewed spherical characters for one or two-dimensional states of being, moving them against an often violent backdrop. These would become hallmarks of his style.

Whereas I focused on bridging fiction, non-fiction, and poetry, he set about creating surrealist worlds. While I focused on learning literary tropes and techniques—synecdoche, asyndeton, anaphora, complex sentence structure—Adam took a macro view. He explored magical realism and fantastical fiction. For every William Maxwell book or Rilke poem I devoured, he gulped down Juan Rulfo's *Pedro Paramo*, Blake Butler's *Scorch Atlas*, or Roberto Bolano's *2666*. For every Cormac McCarthy and William Faulkner book I deconstructed, he dismantled the works of Gabriel Garcia Marquez and Italo Calvino. While I was consumed by Marilynne Robinson's prose styles he busied himself with Barthelme and David Foster Wallace.

Over the years I have read many of the stories in this collection, offered only slight criticism, and at other moments remained silent for fear of altering Adam's unique vision. For that is the real goal of critique: Not to impose your ideas upon the author's story, but to allow your question about the nascent work to flower in the author's mind so that he may draw his own conclusions about what works and what doesn't. He might accept the critique, embrace it, or discard it. To raise too many questions about a work in progress without understanding the author's intention robs the work of its life. It's like being upset at a newborn for not having the ability to vacuum a room. Even when a work is finished, if we pursue experiencing art with the formal approach to comprehension rather than feeling, we then, as John Keats put it so eloquently, "Murder to dissect." To seek with a forensic eye explanations or causes of the state of things, the faults of characters, the treatment of landscape, etc. is reductive. It reduces a literary work to a psychological treatment. Let us point to this cause or that, and there you have it, the explanation of the text in summary form. Such explanations are idiotic at best and damaging at worst.

I respect dedication. When talent fails, dedication takes over, a furious work ethic. Behind Adam's bawdy Midwestern exterior (sometimes crass, misogynistic, and egotistic—but all meant as a bad joke, an anti-image) toils a workhorse, one whipped by self-expectation, one dedicated to improving his craft.

Even the earliest drafts that would ultimately comprise this collection felt to me fearless in their depiction of an altered world. Here was a writer who was wrestling with something, who knew what he wanted even if he hadn't yet the means to capture it. Here apocalyptic landscapes rose to the foreground and characters were swept up in its shadow; there imagery gained prominence over plot. For him, image was king. Reading his work was like watching an abstract painting unfold. This was conceptual writing, like conceptual art, but the color red always signified blood and black, death.

It took courage to write like this and so unexpected from a good Midwestern guy. In a program that deified realism and the art of the personal narrative, it would have been easy for him to buckle under social pressure and create a less challenging art form. But to know Adam is to know he favors the indirect route, for the direct route robs life of its mystery.

It is mystery and verbal gamesmanship that lie at the heart of his writer's project. Like an impish philosopher, he experiences the world as a language game. Sometimes a striking image takes center stage from which he constructs an entire narrative, where the destruction of the world he describes in color gradations. Once we were walking through an unfamiliar section of a new town and it yielded a story title, thus forming the centerpiece of a fictional universe. Many of the stories in this collection are like found poems, but unlike poetry's insistence on metaphor, his is a pared down style, stripped of tropes except for the occasional simile. He might use an adjective as a noun, or a noun as an adjective, creating a unique effect.

Throughout this collection, images rise up and sear themselves into the reader's brain: A dead boy becomes flowers. Take from these stories what you will. Do they point to a deeper reality or are they simply surface, the milky sheen on pond water? If the latter, does the pleasure in reading them dissolve? What they do is surprise, they shock, they ennoble, and the images he constructs return to you in your quiet moments and continue to fester. I am thinking of a village surrounded by a forest of thorns. In an early story, and allow me to paraphrase, he wrote of the berry picked by the picker's hands, retaining the essence of the picker's soul, transforming the juice within. These moments are like the joy one finds if a dragonfly has suddenly landed on one's shoulder—a moment that bewilders and delights simultaneously and one is afraid to move so as not to alter the feeling.

Here and there classical myths, Orpheus' trek into Hades, religious iconography, fairy tales, have dislodged from their meaning, morphing into baffling allegories where meaning is subsumed beneath the image or a setting. Or, he presents a wicked darkness, for darkness pervades these stories. He summons dystopia. Ruined landscapes serve as the backdrop of romanticized death, maudlin sex, broken relationships, fractured psyches, and a world whose end he never explains. If we stop and ponder why the world ended, I believe we lose the thrill of reading his stories. I believe this is philosophy yielding to art, a transition Adam needed to make to fully embrace fiction.

The effects of technological hubris, linguistic paranoia, the cessation of time and resulting mythmaking to account for change are just some subjects Adam explores. Some stories are as equally puzzling as they are lovely, blurring the distinction between horror, dystopian fiction, and noir. So blind men work at desks in underground caverns, writing the history of the world. This might be science fiction or like Borges' "Fantastical Fiction," or may mean nothing at all. So erosion is given a voice; color a character. These are impossible things made manifest by the author's vivid imagination and talent for telling details. Many of these stories scrape the mucky bottom of the psyche's basement, where the monsters of your childhood no longer hide beneath your bed or in closets, but have drifted into every corner of your life—family, love, knowledge, and work.

In short, all the bonds that hold us together he alters by the darkness, more creeping mist than static, negative substance like deep space. But dark matter still requires a point of contrast. So the points of light through the diseased world he conjures are stars that tremble and scream their light down upon us, if only to remind us that they are also the vestiges of an ancient death.

Literature, like life, raises important questions. Although we want our art to be nicely packaged and contained, compartmentalized into genre, neatly wrapped up (each question answered and each theme fully explicated), art deserves more than such imprisonment. Fiction of the kind Adam writes is open-ended. It also serves as a bridge over genres, a bridge crossing from light to dark and back again. I think Adam's work resists classification, so perhaps that is his motivation for self-publishing this collection. Even to call his writing fantastical or surreal steals its essence somehow. Can we not just read these for what they are? Highly stylized fiction.

"Every explorer names his island Formosa, beautiful" wrote Walker Percy, and he said that it is beautiful because it is first. The fact that this collection is the first of its kind as cross-genre, hybrid-surreal, pseudo-philosophical hyper-sensationalist-mind game, or what have you, marks it with a unique creation that could only originate from Adam's highly inventive mind. At the very least, his fiction forces us to vacate our comfort zones, travel the circuitous, sometimes nebulous, often depressing routes through his stories back to ourselves. By the end, we find ourselves altered and this experience makes us experience ourselves anew. I think Adam makes the darkness, the uncomfortable, and the nightmares of our subconscious visible in a way that mixes high-art with the banal, expressive language with slang, depth with surface, and light with dark.

It's been several years since we completed our graduate degrees. I published a novel titled *The Stove-Junker* and Adam returned to Kansas City to continue work on his short stories and novels in progress. Statistically speaking, the odds are against most MFA graduates from being full-fledged writers, but what do I mean by that? Publishing contracts, best sellers, accolades, and awards do not a writer make (though these are nice). What differentiates writers from non-writers is one thing: Writers write. They write every day. They write no matter if inspiration strikes or if their muse is off somewhere else. Writing *is* hard, something most non-writers don't or won't understand. But as someone once put it, *not* writing is harder. You write because you love it, hate it, because you have something to say.

That level of intimacy with self and dedication to sustain it day after day is one of the most difficult things in life, so it's no wonder so many quit. And it's no wonder that non-writers, many of who skim the surface of life, judge success by the amount of books sold, or by the relative fame and awards received. They will never know the fear, anxiety, depressive states, euphoria, and dangers writers face every day when faced with the dictatorship of a blank page, afraid of annihilation. Dedicated writers find the courage to do it and do it daily. You will find before you a collection that exemplifies that courage.

So, I invite you to immerse yourself in these stories, discover muted connections, or just read them for the pleasure of the experience. I invite you to discover the bridges (sometimes golden but often rusted) that unite the images to states of seeing, feeling, being, no matter how dark or unpleasant or confusing. In reading these stories you may feel uncomfortable, or not (for each reader has a different threshold for the weirdly dark). And I invite you to let go of your assumptions of what stories *should* be and lose yourself in these dark dystopian gems.

September 11, 2016

S.K. Kalsi

Author of **The Stove-Junker**

Headers, Margins, and Footnotes —
http://suryakalsi.blogspot.com/

In The Morgue...

…a white lily blooms up slowly from between the blue lips of a dead boy. It is fitting, perhaps, that this is how my tenure here ends, that my long career of deaths stacked upon each other ends on the final image of a blossoming flower whose roots, I imagine, spread out deep inside the cadaver on the table. For the briefest of moments, I allow myself to visualize the thin tendrils snaking down into the lungs to tickle the alveoli.

The boy is not quite a teenager. He is old enough to be in that awkward place where one finds themselves before ever truly finding themselves – that place where confidence wavers like long blades of summer grass – around others the same age. Minus the normal discoloration of a lifeless body, he is pale and seems to have spent little to no time out in the sun, which makes the lily's appearance all the more stark and shocking. Its pure white petals against his washed out dermis is a contrast I'm sure to never forget.

He is neither skinny nor muscular, but somewhere in between. I'm guessing he may play an indoor sport or simply has a high metabolism; his physique has tone, but not due to spending hours in a weight room. Appropriately manicured nails on both the toes and the fingers, no obvious injuries from childhood are apparent and no scars to speak of. He is sixty-five inches in length and weighs approximately one

In the Morgue…

hundred and thirteen pounds, give or take for swelling and decomposition.

I move my hands up his right calf and notice out of the corner of my eye another lily sprouting, oh so slow, from his left ear. This one is pale pink and it opens, timid, unfurling its petals as if to test the surrounding air first. It is a delicate and careful unwrapping of a strange gift from an even stranger place. This time, I imagine its tendril-like roots finding purchase around the tympanic membrane, but originating deep inside the snail-shaped cochlea. If the boy were alive, would he be able to describe the sound of blooming?

Another lily, of lightest blue, stems from his other ear. Two more erupt from the mouth and one from each nostril, all different hues. It is spring-time in fast forward, a nature movie splayed out on my table with each scene faster than the previous one. Tiny lily buds poke through his pores and fatten, spreading outward easily from the decay into beauty. He is no longer a cadaver; he is an ecosystem, a compost pile returning his skin to the earth that bore him. After several long minutes, it is not so much a body on my examining table as it is a mound of someone's perfect garden. The explosion of color erupting from him is astonishing, but that it is coming from within him forces me to sit, breathless at the wonder, and take stock of the moment.

In the Morgue…

I sit on the metal rolling chair, stunned. The lilies have made a grave of him, an altar of flora and fauna smothering him in color as if painted on and left to mummify below their stems and stamens. His is certainly not the first death I've seen that has evolved into a post-mortem surreality, but this is probably the most poetic I've ever witnessed. I feel like allowing myself, for the first time in forty-seven years, to sob uncontrollably at the majesty of this tiny living meadow on my examination table.

I almost want to leave him there in peace for the medical examiner replacing me as a matter of respect. I don't want to cut this boy open now. I want to leave him be. I want to leave him for the generation coming after me, I want them to see what death has become over the last decade. I want them to understand that death is not as easy as it used to be and that the living seem to understand this better now. I want my replacement to walk in and see this, to be as struck as I am by the profundity of the situation, to be as mind-boggled and awe-struck at the possibility of things they've never imagined before.

Each body comes in a little different these days, turned in ways that make anatomy books irrelevant, outdated, written by some subspecies of a culture long since moved on. Limbs twisted out into irregular shapes, orifices blown up and out, sprouting one tragic, sometimes grotesque, art project

In the Morgue…

after another. What was once a random occurrence is now the norm, if that is even the proper word. Man, woman, child, pet…they've all become the world's playthings. Toy vessels caught up in the maelstrom that rages around us now.

It's hard to pinpoint the first influx of oddities, but I remember one of the first very well. He had only been in office two years before coming into my examining room. I remember watching him on the television month after month, thinking he looked different each time, worse. Like something was physically eating away at him. This was no ordinary graying of the hair on the temples or wrinkling of the skin around the sleepless eyes, this was something else and I'm sure other people saw it as well. Until the Governor was released into my care, I had no idea how bad things had gotten or how bad they were going to get…

But that was the beginning. I have given up hope that we are nearing the end, but the end of what, I wonder? Is this a new step in an evolutionary staircase? If so, is the staircase leading up or down? Impossible to tell when an autopsy requires garden shears and leather gloves as opposed to latex and a scalpel.

I hear the quiet swish of the examination door behind me. My replacement has arrived. I have been trying to impart my years of knowledge upon him in the span of a few months, but even I am at a loss as to how to explain the body

In the Morgue…

bouquet before me. I close my eyes and inhale; the normal, white sterility of the room has been replaced by the aroma of a spring morning. Considering the source, it's oddly comforting.

"Morning, Doc," he says, oblivious to the meadow-covered cadaver.

I nod without turning. "Riley."

"Good weekend?"

"Quiet, but yes."

He hangs his coat on the wall and tosses his shoulder-bag next to the desk. I hear the buttons on the front of his lab jacket clasp together and soon he's standing next to me. His cologne is strong, but is soon overpowered by the body. "Wow…" he whispers. "Art project?"

"Body."

Disbelief. "No."

"Oh very much yes. He bloomed not five minutes before you walked in. Teenage boy. Damndest thing I've ever seen." Riley reached out to touch one of the lilies, but I swatted his hand away. "Gloves first. Always."

"Yes sir."

Once prepped, Riley stands on the other side of the body, eyes wide but observant. A smart kid, but with a tendency to be smart in the mouth sometimes. I have stopped trying to break him of this habit. With this being my

In the Morgue…

last day, I'm more concerned that he sticks to proper
procedure than proper social etiquette.

"How is this even possible, Doc?"

I shake my head. "I have a feeling you'll see more of
this kind of thing once I leave. Not necessarily this kind of
flowering specifically, but cadavers covered or filled with
substances and things our anatomy books and science
journals have never seen before. I don't understand what this
influx of strangeness portends, but it feels like it's happening
with more regularity. I would urge you, starting from this
moment, to be delicate and deliberate with your note-taking
on each body from here on out. You may find it of the
utmost urgency later."

We look up at each other over the floral mound.
Tufts of dark hair spill out from beneath his surgical cap. The
look in his eyes is one of a man who has just been dropped
off a bridge into raging waters.

"The important thing is to remain objective. No
matter how bizarre the cadaver or case may be, you *must* be
on top of your game, Riley. Too many people depend upon
the work done in this basement. Do you understand?"

He swallows. "I do, sir, yes."

"Good. We do this one together, but you're the lead.
Today, I am *your* assistant. Understand that since we are in
such unfamiliar territory here, I don't know that there is a

In the Morgue...

wrong way to approach this, but I will constantly ask why you are choosing to do something. I want to hear the logic behind your every movement. Now, what would you do first in this situation?"

Riley impresses me over the next hour. Before he touches any of the surgical tools, he examines the flowers, locates their exact phylum and genus, physically examines the human pores that have released them into our presence; he understands the origins of the flowers in the physical world so that he can better understand their strange existence here before us. With hands I once believed indelicate, he clips a single stem and blossom only to have it quickly replaced. The new bud slips up through the old stem and blossoms within seconds. We look up at each other, bemused.

"I'd like to try something," he says after a brief silence.

"What are you thinking?"

"Treat it like a weed. Or a virus. A cancer, even. Get at the root, expunge the entire source, perhaps prevent another from taking its place."

I nod, wishing I'd thought of it first. "I think that's a solid idea. Have at it."

He grips the base of the stem and begins to pull slowly. It doesn't budge at first, but then slowly gives way as slick white roots erupt out of the pore. He holds the blossom

In the Morgue...

in his hand and we wait, we watch. No replacement flower is forthcoming. Riley hoots in excitement and I clap once.

"Well done! Let's hope the idea sticks for all the others," I say.

We both begin to pluck the stems. Each one trails behind it a clumped network of the slick white tendrils. That so much non-human material is being pulled from the cadaver is as astounding as the initial visual it provided. Soon, we have one of the empty examination tables full of multi-hued flowers. It takes us close to an entire day, but by the end, the cadaver looks like a cadaver should, albeit with distended, inflamed pores across his entire body.

Riley exhales loud and slow as he removes his gloves and wipes his brow of pooled sweat. I pull one of the rolling chairs over to the table and slump down onto it easily, weary and glad that we could finally give the boy some small appearance of normalcy. I've explained this to Riley before, that though it is the mortician's job to make the body perfect again, there's nothing that says we can't try to keep it intact for whatever family may come down to our corner of the basement. It's a respect thing. I desperately hope he remembers long after I'm gone.

"What now?" I ask him across the table. He puts on a new pair of gloves and wheels the utensil table closer.

In the Morgue…

"Now…the incisions from both shoulders to the sternum and another incision from the sternum down to the pubic bone."

"For what purpose?"

"So that we can view the internal organs of the deceased. We do this to find any evidence not seen on the outside of the body. It also lets us look at any damage done to the organs that may or may not relate to the death of the deceased in some way."

"Good. Will you be making a 'Y' or 'T' cut?"

"A 'Y,' I think. I feel that it allows me more room to maneuver. Also, it may be an illusion, but I feel like I'm seeing more all at once with the 'Y' incision."

"That is my preference and thinking for it as well. Before we do that, however, make a hypothesis; considering we just spent the last seven hours removing budding flowers from this boy's entire epidermal area, what are we likely to see once we open him up? If the outside is so unusual, what kind of internal damage or mutation do you believe we'll find?"

Riley looks down at the body and strokes his chin. It is a good question and one I don't know that I'd be able to answer myself. The world has been knocked out of tilt; the things once thought unbelievable and impossible have become possible, have become truth. He and I could have two completely different guesses as to what the boy's insides

In the Morgue…

look like and it's possible we'll both be wrong. We've gotten used to being unsurprised by surprises.

Riley opens his mouth to speak, then closes it again as if unsure. He does this twice while staring up and down the length of the cadaver. He shuts his eyes and runs a newly gloved hand along the distended pores of the abdomen. "Considering the unnatural nature of the symptoms, I am hesitant to make a hypothesis. However, I think there is the strong possibility that many of the organs, while no longer working, are being utilized as fertilized bases in the same way as the epidermis."

"Meaning what, exactly?" I ask, genuinely curious.

"I think we may find another kind of floral ecosystem covering the organs. Perhaps not the same type as the outer layer of skin, but I think the possibility of something else entirely is not unlikely in this situation."

"Interesting. I'll take that idea a step further. I'll say that the organs have themselves turned into their own form of floral ecosystems, not that they are simply covered in flora."

Riley looked up. "You think his body has transformed into a kind of postmortem ecosystem? That his lungs have ceased to be lungs and have instead become one kind of vegetative host, his liver another, so on and so on? That he

In the Morgue…

has become, in effect, a host body containing a photosynthetic microcosm?"

"That I do. Loser buys the winner a nice bottle of single-malt?" I ask with a grin over the cadaver.

"You're on," he replies with a wink.

Riley grips the scalpel from the utensil tray and starts at the right shoulder, slicing through the dead skin slowly across the chest to the breastbone. A second cut from the left shoulder meets the first and then a slow downward stroke towards the pelvic area. Riley's hands shake imperceptibly as he pulls the skin flaps up and out delicately, exposing the inner workings of the deceased boy. As he peels back the third flap, we let out a collective gasp. We see everything; we understand nothing. My last night in the morgue will be one to remember and one I will recount over and over before my death. However, no one will believe me when I tell them.

"Riley?"

"Yeah, doc?" he whispers back.

"This would be a good time to start taking detailed notes. Very detailed notes."

"Yeah. Should I go get your single-malt now or should we wait?" he asks. We both succumb to nervous laughter as Riley grabs the camera and starts snapping detailed pictures.

In the Morgue…

I look up at the clock. I had planned on being home by now, sitting down to a celebratory dinner with my wife, but this was far too interesting to leave now. "Finish taking the pictures, then go and grab that bottle while I call my wife to let her know I'll be late."

Riley looks up in shock. "Are you messing with me? A test of sorts?"

I shake my head, smile. "Not at all. It appears that it will be a long night and this," I say, waving my hand over the body, "is far too interesting to leave alone tonight. Wouldn't you agree...Doc?"

In the Morgue...

Photo Finish

*"One Mary Eppstein, at 1530 Western
Drive, was found dead today in her home.
No foul play is suspected, but it took officers
several hours to remove her body from the
building due to what they would only call
'complications.' No one was allowed in to
survey the scene other than police officials
themselves. Chief Mallory said it was the
policy of the Oakdale Police Department not
to comment about ongoing investigations. She
is not believed to have been a member of any
anti-American skirmish organization."*

The coastal skirmishes raged on, but Mary still
looked forward to the arrival of her mail every day, as
she had done for the last 25 years. As a child she
remembered fondly joining her father on his daily
treks down the long gravel road of their farm to the
tiny silver mailbox at the end of the drive. She would
delight at the red arm sticking up, telling them that
some sweet paper or packaged surprise lay within.
Her father would reach in, sometimes simply pulling
the mail out, but other times pretended that some
unseen monster had grabbed his arm and was pulling
him farther inside the mailbox because he knew this
made her laugh.

There was no weather that prevented her
from joining her father on the walk every day after

Photo Finish

lunch. When she got older and had to go to school, he waited for her to come home, met her at the mailbox, and they walked back to the house together, his boots and her shoes crunching across the gravelly surface while he flipped through the mystery envelopes.

On occasion, a box would come, but never for her. Brown parcel paper packages were always for her mother or her brother, but never for her and rarely for her father. He never seemed to mind, but Mary hated that nothing ever came for her. The joy of walking the distance to the mailbox was an elation that never wavered even though she walked away from it disappointed every time. Her learning curve was nil. Soon, that joy was tempered; she enjoyed the walk more than the actual getting of mail.

Her father passed away. Her mother moved across the country after retiring from teaching. Her brother went off to school and then enlisted. She lived alone in the house she had grown up in, had emptied it of most of its memories, made the home her own. She repainted the walls, changed the locks, fixed faulty shingles in the roof, replaced aged doors that creaked with ones that swung on silent hinges.

But she left the mail box the same shiny silver, a tiny glimmery beacon out on the edge of the property.

And then, seemingly out of nowhere, a package came, mysterious and brown-parcel normal on a sunlit afternoon.

Mary had never expected a package, having never received one before, so when the mailbox was filled with the brown parcel paper, she gasped. It was a sound she'd rarely made and instantly she believed the package to be for someone other than her, for that's how it had always been. Perhaps the sender had not realized the other members of the family no longer lived here or no longer lived at all?

Her fingers slid beneath the parcel, pulled it out easily and scanned the ship-to label: "Mary Eppstein, 1530 Western Drive, Oakdale." No return address, no markings other than the sticker with her name and address on it. The package was, unbelievably, for her.

She ran her hands across the surface, felt the rough paper crinkle beneath her touch. Her fingers trembled and her breath caught in her throat. It was beautiful because it was for her, had her name writ across it intentionally in firm, thick pen strokes. The black ink was fluid and purposeful and held not a whit of hesitation. Someone had intentionally sent this to her and her alone and the thought was intoxicating. She held the package against her chest, feeling its hard corners dig into the folds of her arms and shoulders. Its flat bottom pressed against her bosom and she rested her chin on it, memorizing its shape before she held it out in front of her again.

The edges had been folded in and taped to the sides like triangles and a seam across the back showed the rough edges of a scissors' cut. She lifted it to her nose, sniffed the package, drank in its scent; paper, ink, woods, light glue, promise. So mesmerized by the package's smell, she hadn't realized that she had walked all the way back to her porch, smelling the thing the entire way back. She couldn't remember having even moved, couldn't remember even willing her legs to move, and yet…here she was, some fifty yards away from her mailbox and a foot away from stumbling into the lowest step of her porch.

Mary rushed inside the house, letting the storm door slam behind her, and had to stop herself from ripping the packaging to shreds so she could find out what mystery, what delightful gift, hid inside its paper folds. She sat on the couch and placed the package on her lap, ran her fingers around its

Photo Finish

circumference again, disbelieving. Finally, she allowed her slim finger to slide beneath the tape on the right side, loosened it from the parcel and let the fold fall out. She did the same to the left side and felt her breath quicken, excited.

She flipped the package over and unfolded both flaps, letting the paper tear along the backside to reveal a shoebox the same color as the paper surrounding it, its former brand name faded into inky gibberish on all four sides. The lid was taped on and quickly she ripped through the adhesive, folding the tape up under the lid. Once lifted, Mary sat in silence and stared into the tissue lined package, puzzled.

*   *   *

The next day, another package arrived. And the day after that and the day after that. Each new day brought another package, each addressed specifically to her with no return address, wrapped in the same parcel brown paper. There was never a note included, never a hint as to who had sent them, only what was written upon the objects inside.

The first box was full of pictures. Random pictures of people and places Mary had never known

Photo Finish

or visited, no scent of a memory on any of them. Each one had upon it one or two line notes attached that seemed unrelated to the images; daily devotionals from strangers with no return addresses and no explanation, but all were cryptic in their own strange unspoken way.

She remembered the first picture she pulled out. The picture itself was interesting enough: a pair of modestly skirted legs and old shoes standing out some where during some when. It reminded her of childhood and Saturday sun-tastings, an innocence, a piety she could no longer run to, but it was the words splayed across the image that made her brain itch in the most pleasing of ways. The simplicity of the message complicated the meaning infinitely.

Four words: *"You are completely remarkable."*

It could be read a thousand ways with a thousand more inflections possible, but it brought more questions than Mary could answer. Was this some strange lover's ode to her? Did she have a secret admirer out in the shadows of the world? She flipped through the other photos in the box, hoping to find some clue as to the sender.

Images and phrases she found:

Footprints on a beach.

Photo Finish

(You are missed.)

A sunspotted picnic with hard to see faces.
(I love that you love that I love you.)

A broken wall with graffiti across the bottom.
(Art will save us if we just let it touch our hurt.)

Skyscrapers that seemed to be touching the kingdom of
clouds.
(I wonder what mistakes I made to lead me to this
point?)

The rosy cheek of a baby (girl? boy?) and half of their
lips.
(Living without you is my biggest fear.)

A teenager standing happily against a first car.
(Even knowing the now, I'd still make the same
mistakes over again.)

Soda fountain store fronts with boarded up windows.
(My first job made me into the person I am today.)

A girl holding a flower in a meadow full of the same.

Photo Finish

(Five years ago today, I said goodbye to you.)

Several pairs of colored socks strewn across a floor.
(No amount of outfits will ever change the me that I
am.)

A tarnished trumpet lying in a drainage ditch.
(I gave up music to be with you; now I have nothing.)

A woman covered head-to-toe in mud, smiling.
Laughing.
(One breast gone, one life left to live.)

An ocean at dawn.
(I miss our secret talks.)

Rush-hour on a bridge.
(How much of my life am I wasting every day?)

Cars picked clean and rusted over in a full junkyard.
(I have been dry for 13 years, but still fight the urge to
drink every day.)

A woman crying into her hand while standing outside
a burned down church.

Photo Finish

(I am faith. I am love. I am invincible through Him.)

A sleeping infant on a sleeping man's chest.
(I love you bigger than the sky, deeper than the lowest
sadness.)

A woman in tawdry fishnets sitting on a dirty Santa's
lap.
(Remember when you gave me what I asked for?)

A boy in an astronaut's helmet, staring up into the
dusky night sky.
(I wish I could remember all my dreams. They
disappear by morning…)

Lawn gnomes and pink flamingos, seemingly at war
with each other.
(At night, I pretend my lawn ornaments are the ones
making all the noise so I
don't have to believe it's my parents.)

A pile of spent shell casings next to a child's sandaled
foot.
(If we continue to fight around the children, the
children will think it's normal.)

Photo Finish

Two nuns on a park bench, laughing, their robes pulled up to their knees.

(Breaking convention can sometimes be all you need to get through the day.)

A broken doll, a dirty jump rope, an unmade bed wearing tattered sheets.

(I don't remember the first or second foster home, but I wish I could forget the last.)

Mary recognized no one in the pictures, recognized none of the locales, and yet still she felt herself splitting inside, cracking along each fissure, trembling both in delight and sadness as if she knew each of them personally. There was a truth to the photos and the words etched or written on them. It was as if someone had collected the hopes and dreams of a hundred people and sent them off to one (random?) person in the world to be shared.

She put the pictures back in the box and got up from the couch, clutching the box tightly as if it were a thing so fragile, so close to breaking.

Photo Finish

*　　*　　*

Each day another package arrived, full of new photos and new phrases. Mary spent entire afternoons looking at the photos, reading the script across them, sometimes weeping long into the night. Rather than being an annoyance, these parcels had become an object of anticipation and excitement in an otherwise uneventful day, so it was hard to simply shrug them off as simply a weird occurrence. The writing on the ship-to label was always different, so Mary didn't think it could've been the same person anyway, oddity that it seemed to be. It was always one package, never more, over-postaged with ten stamps in the upper right corner and a sticker of some sort along the back flap.

The packages were saved after the cards were removed and an entire room had been designed around the influx of one-liners; pictures now hung in perfect patterns on the wall within. Another couple of inches all around and the room would be covered. Most of the images were clear and concise, but others were blurry or confusing and blotted out, but the words were what made the walk to the mailbox worth it every day. The red flag would go down on the metal container and a spring would find itself in each footstep closer to home as her eyes scanned every daily bit of linguistic art sent from who knew where and for what purpose, but the end result was always the same; a calm smile before bed and after waking.

On the fifth day, Mary took the photos and spread them across her guest bedroom floor, admiring the imperfection of each image. They were washed out or developed poorly, angled strange or too close to recognize the objects in the frame. Some were flimsy, some firm, some rippled with water from basement floodings or tears, and still others gleamed like new while many reflected nothing but age and crease.

With care, Mary began taping each image up on to the undecorated wall beside the fold out bed. One box of photos covered up a good section of wall and she began with another box, then another, then another, and finally the fifth. Her fingers graced the edges of the photos, left partial finger prints that she covered with tape and stuck to the wall easily. Side by side, they became a menagerie of memories, a flipbook of unknown faces and places with sentiment attached. Her wall had become the singular diary of a nation of strangers' voices.

Photo Finish

She worked well into the morning. All five boxes had been affixed to the one wall with a few stragglers creeping over onto the adjoining one. She sat on the fold-out sofa and stared, letting her eyes rest on the arresting imagery, letting the words permeate her weary mind. The sun tinted the horizon beyond the window-shade, turned white into orange and she slipped into dreaming easily, falling asleep quick and quiet to a chorus of whispered voices she did not recognize.

After a full week of appearing parcels, she cleared out the garage and the guest bedroom. Once removed from the parcel, Mary taped each photo up on the wall of the guest room, none overlapping each other so that every bit of writing was visible. The first seven batches covered an entire wall. The empty boxes became a small stack in the garage.

This continued for a month. The empty boxes became a small wall of their own, stacked up against the garage wall neatly like soldiers. Mary found herself liking the new aesthetic; the brown boxes calmed her thoughts the way the pictures inside them churned her emotions. By now, the guest bedroom had become smothered in pictures. The original wallpaper covered over completely, masked by the frozen moments of other people's lives. Not even a tiny glimpse of the wall could be seen behind the random visuals that now spread across the ceiling like the creeping fingers of a virus.

She removed all the furniture, stacking it up in her own bedroom, cramping the space so that she had to crawl over dresser drawers and recliner arms just to get into her bed at night, if she even made it to her own bed. Many nights she passed out in the middle of the guest room floor, staring up at the ceiling, itself now covered in pictures and text, with the latest emptied parcel spread out across the floor around her. Her sleep came while surrounded by Polaroids of the past that wondered about the future.

*   *   *

Mary began having her groceries delivered to the house, leaving only to visit her mailbox. The packages kept arriving and she kept taping up image after image along her walls. The spare bedroom had shrunk; 144 square feet had become just a pathway into the middle of the room, a passage into an overload of sensory. It was just tall enough and just wide enough for her to step into sideways, but the images had spilled out and crawled along the hallway walls and ceiling like ivy. More pictures and furniture were removed, put into the master bedroom that had became a collection of personal belongings stacked up and nearly covering the bay window.

Her grocery deliveries shrunk; she was not eating. Mary spent all of her free time reading the cards over and over, shuffling through the house at one end and reading her way to the other, often never stopping to use the bathroom, itself covered in the word-scribbled images. Her once pink robe had turned a filthy pale and stunk of urine and glue. Her skin hung in limp folds beneath, gone grey from spending so much time in the darkness of burnt out light bulb hallways. She worried the heat from the bulbs would destroy the pictures she had come to need like the day's first meal, a drunk's first drink, or an after dinner cigarette followed by another and followed by another. The only light that came through the house found its way through the crevices of stacked furniture or tattered curtains. It shimmered and glinted off the surface of the pictures like dim starlight.

And still she simply accepted the packages, absorbed the photos and their sometimes poetically vague maxims, cocooned herself within their very personal meanings. Her walls had shrunk faster than she had, but even now, she found it difficult to walk through the hallways and rooms. The thick barriers made of glossy paper forced her to suck in her stomach, will herself into thinness.

Sometime later, when a thin divot of hallway remained, Mary got stuck trying to move from one end of the house to the next. The pictures had finally grown too thick off the walls, imprisoned her, kept her immobile. She could feel the images burning against her, through her robe and then soaked up in her skin. Her eyes would roll up and over every glossy surface, drinking them in as she stood, wedged between the collected and wall-pasted pictures. Her chest constricted and left her with shallow breaths. She could look up or down, but not to either side. Her shoulder had pinned her in on the right, but she could wiggle her left foot. Unimaginably stuck and with no way to get herself out of the position. Statuesque and strangely calm.

Five minutes, twenty. An hour, three. Mary's sense of time disappeared with the wallpaper. She would feel the pictures tickle against her, each single edge itching against the bare skin peeking out from

Photo Finish

the robe. During the longer moments of impassibility, she would take to peeling off a single photo and nibbling at its edge to pass the time. She would graze on these new walls like a goat hungry to taste everything it saw.

She could taste the chemicals in the processed image, imagined the flavor of reds and blues, wondered about the caloric intake of yellow and the health benefits of black. The paper, rough-edged and indigestible, felt like stiff rock as she swallowed, scraping the lining of her throat before struggling down into her stomach.

Mary became full and by the week's end, she stood wedged between her pictured walls unblinking and unmoving. Her throat had finally caught and prevented her from swallowing. She couldn't breathe and slowly, the lives that she had so decorously pasted up on her walls had taken hers from her.

Outside, the packages stopped arriving at the mailbox.

Photo Finish

Scaring the Stars into Submission

3:48am

Sleepless. Not just for a string of nights, but for several months. Is this what dying feels like? To be in a constant state of shuffling through the ether but going nowhere? Melodramatic, maybe, but there is something heavy pressing in around me. Katherine sleeps soundly on the other side of the bed, but I…I can't seem to force my pillow to make dreams. She sleeps on her side and I watch as her chest expands up and out with each rhythmic breath. If I catch her at the right moment, she will snore a little, but only enough to elicit a smile and never enough to keep me awake. She denies that she does this, but I hear it. I know it to be true.

The sheets are warm between us. Our collective body heat has sucked out the coolness found at the moment we slip beneath them. My pillows are the same, warm to the touch with no cool side to flip over and rest upon. I sit up against the headboard and stare out into the dark room. I know the furniture; I could walk this room blind and never touch a thing, but my eyes eventually adjust and I get up quietly so as not to wake her. I won't be returning to bed anytime soon. Once I'm up, I'm up for the entire measure of the day.

I head down the hall to the guest bathroom and take care of my morning business. In the kitchen, I slide open the window above the sink, turn on the exhaust fan over the stove, and light a cigarette. I exhale through the window, the smoke from the cigarette disappears up into the vent. The first smoke of the day always makes me woozy in a way that makes me feel I exist.

I don't know how to explain it better than that.

4:15am

Lift lid, add filter. Scoop three spoonfuls of coffee into filter. Fill pot with water, empty pot into reservoir. Turn on. Brew.

The smell of coffee fills the kitchen, mingles with the leftover tobacco. The paper has not arrived yet, so I'm alone with my thoughts. I rummage through the drawers, looking for nothing in particular. I open the linen drawer, lift each pot holder and hand towel, find a pair of orange-handled scissors. I place them on the kitchen table. In the living room, I come across some old magazines; pages of art and celebrities, political news and home furnishings. I take a stack of the periodicals and place them next to the scissors on the table.

Open cupboard, remove mug. Open fridge, remove creamer, fill mug a quarter of the way. Put creamer back into fridge. Pour coffee. Watch it swirl from black to vanilla brown.

The steam from the mug wafts up to my face, bathes me in smell. I sit at the table and flip open the first magazine, one filled with home improvement projects and how-to guides on making your home less cluttered. *These simple bookshelves can be run along the walls of any finished basement or unused room as storage*, a page reads. I wonder why someone wouldn't just toss the stuff out if it's clutter. I turn the page.

A wrap-around porch on a stout two-floor ranch home is spotlighted. The roof covers every foot of it and it seems obvious there is room for a dining set and a rolling barbecue grill beneath the eaves. *Perfect for hosting!*

Katherine and I wanted a house with a porch. We wanted one like in the magazine, big and comfortable in case the weather turned, but the houses themselves were either unaffordable or just too big. We settled on a place crammed next to others that looked the same, deep in wild suburbia where you could get lost in the maze of same-looking streets lined with same-looking families.

Wake up, go to work. Come home, have dinner, watch television. Lay in bed reading, fall asleep until whenever. We rarely talk anymore, Katherine and I.

Each day tastes the same flavor of beige. Even after the dawn started rising red.

Scaring the Stars into Submission

5:27am

But it's Saturday. Katherine will sleep in until I wake her with breakfast, something I have done every weekend since we married eleven years ago. Perhaps it has lost its sentimentality because she can count on it. Perhaps she still secretly loves that I do it, despite the quiet fracture that has come between us as of late. It's early yet and I won't start breakfast for another few hours.

I go outside, shut the front door behind me gently. The morning sky is cloudy and the alarming color of deep maroon. Even the grass seems to be dew-kissed with little, glistening droplets of blood. Unnerving at first, this change in the weather and morning routine, but we adapted. It's what we do, I suppose. Change our routine into something unexpected and we adjust to it accordingly. We thought the red skies would dissipate, that some scientific phenomenon had occurred, but they stuck around and we later heard they were man-made. The fear never really left, but it's abated, tamped down, simmering just below the surface and ready to come back out and play sometime. Maybe we've just adjusted to the fear, infused it to our daily living.

We've heard a thousand excuses for it all, never truly believing any of them. Solar flares, the earth moving closer to the sun (though we weren't getting hotter), airborne pollutants mixing with atmospheric molecules, so on. I don't claim to know much, but these all sounded like nonsense to me. One day the sky was perfect blue and the next? The next day looked like the world had been painted in blood by some new millennial angel of death. We felt like aliens on our own planet. Perhaps some still feel that way. It's understandable.

I walk around the perimeter of the house and pull random weeds from the dying flowerbed. Without proper sunlight, our lawns have withered, but we keep on trying to play house. What else are we to do? Nightly news is one-note and depressing, but there's always been work to be done around the house. We try to forget the red is what's killing the flowers and work at the garden anyway. Doing something helps in the forgetting, but we know it's a Sisyphean thing.

I often forget to put shoes on before coming out in the morning and today is no different. The grass feels lush between my bare toes. When this happens, I like to imagine I can feel the grass growing up and out, covering me like vines as it tickles its way across every inch of skin.

5:43 am

I carry the weeds to the garbage cans on the side of the house. From the corner of my eye, I see an object in our backyard. The sun peeks up over the horizon and blinds my line of sight, burns corona images onto the back of my eyelids. It's a large thing, squatting perfectly in the center of our backyard and rising several feet higher than the fence. I cannot remember it being there last night and I've heard no one make any noise near the house since waking. I place my hand over my eyes, try to block out the sun. No good.

I pass through the chain-link gate and shuffle through the grass. The dew feels especially nice, but my feet are covered in grass clippings now and start to itch. The object is massive. I walk around it twice, once clockwise and once counter-clockwise. I think I am just tired, just seeing things, perhaps hallucinating. It is a fluffed kind of round shape, but not perfectly so, and seems to hover just an inch or so above the lawn. I get down on my knees and press my face to the ground. I see right through to the back fence.

Cotton candy. The phrase screams in my head. *It is a giant ball of cotton candy.* Of course this can't be right, but the texture, the look…I imagine burying my face into its gossamer surface, biting into it, and swallowing the tendrils of whatever it is made of. I imagine it tasting oversweet as it melts on my tongue.

I lean in closer, inhale. It smells like sky and rain, snow and lightning. It smells like everything and nothing all at once. It is a singularly unique smell that I cannot definitively place or name, but it is calming and reminiscent of quiet autumn evenings. I rub my hand across its surface, feeling it give softly beneath my touch. Spongy, springy. It rebounds slow when I take my hand off. The texture is incredibly plush, pillowy, a softness that I don't believe man has ever achieved on his own.

6:01am

I could not be sure before, but I am now. It is a cloud, sitting fat and soft in my backyard. Tendrils of cloud fiber snake out into the morning air, lifted and moved by the first breezes of the day like medusa hair. I climb up the side of it, feeling my hands and bare feet dig into the spongy surface easily. I pull myself up over the edge. My first thought is that it is a large atmospheric cushion or pillow and I fall easily into slumber. The top layer gives beneath my weight, creating a large man-sized divot in its surface, and cocoons me in a *feathersoft* embrace.

8:45am

I awake to Katherine calling out to me, wondering where I'm at. She is on the ground below and, I'm sure, shocked at this new manifestation resting in our yard. I feel lighter, as if some unnamed burden has been lifted while I slept and my body tingles with a soft energy. I suppress a laugh; she won't have expected me to have climbed up and fallen asleep here. I lean over the edge and wave. *Hello, dear*, I say. She gasps and gives me an unsure smile, waves limply.

What are you…what is…Jesus. What's going on?

I shrug my shoulders. *Come join me.*

How?

Climb. I'll take your hands. I'll help you up.

She begins to climb and the oppressiveness of the morning seems to have gone away. I watch her struggle up the side of the cloud, tongue hanging out the left side of her mouth in concentration. She reaches up and our hands touch, clasp together, grip tight. Her face is lit up by the sun, seems to glow in a way I have not seen (*noticed?*) in years. I feel like I'm twelve years old and crushing again.

I don't know how to explain it better than that.

9:17am

We lay next to each other. My hand rests on hers which rests on my chest. I can feel my heart thump through her. Or maybe it is her heart I feel thumping through her hand and our arrhythmias match.

Her face is nuzzled into my neck, her leg draped over mine. This cloud mattress has done something to us, something wonderful that neither of us wants to question for fear of losing the moment. We drown ourselves in the feeling, let it wash over every pore and slip into every orifice, let it fill us to the brim before overflowing.

I feel her breath along my neckline. It is warm and sweet and I breathe it all in. For the briefest of moments, I'm reminded of our courtship, of days spent laid out on shoddy quilts and blankets at the park, swapping secrets in whispers and napping with each other beneath a yellow sun in a blue sky. The memories are *fuzzedwarm* and comfortable. I slip into them easily, but find my way out of them less so.

9:18am

What do you think it means? she whispers.
I've no idea, but I like it so far.

Scaring the Stars into Submission

You were up early again.

He nods. *Though, somehow I napped up here before you came out.*

It's like laying on a wish, she says, murmuring into his neck.

Do you remember the last time we did something like this? Just curled up together with no plans of doing anything?

Three years, two months, fifteen days, six hours, and twenty minutes ago. Far too long.

He runs his hand through her hair, feels her irregular scalp below, agrees. *Far too long.*

She opens her eyes and sees, across the red sky, bits of cloud breaking off, falling slow as if the entire city were caught in a molasses dream.

That one looks like an elephant, she says.

That one, an alligator with sunglasses.

A flower.

A bus full of children.

Popcorn.

A snow fort.

An ocean liner.

An angel.

A second chance.

They watch the tufts fall soundlessly from the sky, remaining wrapped up in each other on top of their own bit of grounded heaven. It is a strange storm falling in slow motion. The surfaces of buildings and cars become dusted with cumulus. Large chunks fall in backyards and intersections, parking lots and highway exit ramps, on playgrounds and sandboxes. The world stops and takes stock of itself for the first time in forever.

They lay next to each other. His hand rests on hers which rests on his chest. He can feel his heart thump through her. Or maybe it is her heart he feels thumping through her hand and their arrhythmias match.

10:01 am

Katherine vaguely remembers him waking that morning. His early risings had become small anomalies in her dream time, bumps in the road on the way to the subconscious. Her eyes would flutter open when he rose, but would calm again once he left the room.

His side. Her side. Wasn't the bed supposed to be *their* side? Why had it taken this strange bit of *skycandypillow* to get them to curl up into each other, to feel each other from the inside out? For the life of her, she couldn't remember what he sounded like when he slept beside her in the bed, but she knew she'd remember what it was like for them out here.

Scaring the Stars into Submission

She'd remember his breathing, the heat beneath his undershirt, the throbbing of his blood pumping out to every appendage, the un-showered smell of him, the feel of his fingers combing through her hair, the way her lips dry out against the skin of his neck, the *soundfeelingmovement* she feels through her skull when he swallows, the way she feels protected laying on top of him. Before she awoke in her (*their*) bed, she saw:

Confined in black. Not swimming, not moving, simply there. Feet planted in a nothing ground. From the black, a hand extends, gives her a bouquet of day-glo yellow daisies. The arm connected to the hand is sheathed in the same black and disappears off into nowhere. There is no face to the figure, no form. She presses her nose into the middle of the bouquet, feels the petals tickle her nose and cheeks, rubs them across her lips and feels their color melt on her face. Pollen colored lipstick drips down her chin. She looks up. The flowers are gone, the black nothing has been replaced. A once verdant valley stretches out for miles, now the color of brown burn and blackened char. She walks, feeling dead, flaky petals turn to ash beneath her arches, feeling the ash cake between her toes like thickening leather thongs. The ash becomes grey mud, sticks and dries to the top of her feet, hardens and cracks, becomes a thin layer of varying shades of blue scales that climb up her legs, her torso, her breasts, her neck, her face. She is a myriad blue, except for her lips, which remain yellow, though she doesn't know how she knows this. The ground beneath her opens up, sucks her down into the slickery ash-mud, begins to

pile itself on top of her, the sludge slipping into the
gaps between each blue tinted scale, covering her yellow
lips and filling her mouth, her throat, her lungs.

When she wakes, she sits upright, breathless, gasping, alone in her (*their*) bed. She remembers flecks of moments spread across her memory. She cannot remember it all, but she is distraught, heavy, weighed down by a something she cannot put a name to, cannot wrap her brain around tight enough to squeeze out meaning.

She doesn't know how to explain it better than that.

10:17am

Things that happened to others:

Herman Effen saw himself mirrored in the side of the cloud in his front yard. His reflection danced and laughed. He put two shotgun shells into the side of the fluffy interloper, but the reflection continued to dance.

Rita Jackson-Danforth was gardening when hers fell. It shamed and excited her, made her tingle beneath her sundress. She said it smelled like fresh laundry when she grinded her body against it like "a teenager again in the back of a car with some boy."

James Ritter and his friends climbed on top of the one that fell in the forest near his home, turned it into a club house, a meeting place for their neighborhood "gang." They imagined themselves as pirates and cutthroats before fighting and disbanding over ownership rights. James Ritter is, ultimately, brained with a rock by young Joel Martin from down the street.

Ethel Madison was crushed by one she could not escape from fast enough. It fell on her, around her, suffocated her within its ivory fluff. As she struggled to breathe, she felt the decades of dry twist in her bones dissipate.

Bethany Pilatas found herself unable to stop tearing off tufts of cloud and stuffing them down her mouth, not bothering to chew. She did this for an entire afternoon and swelled up, puffed out grotesquely. Her parents found her when they returned home from work, a fat, lifeless smile across her lips.

Roger Matthison cut large swathes of cloud off, replaced his mattress with the stuff. He fell asleep inhaling deeply the new smell the new surface. He woke up inhaling deeply the new surface. He spent a week doing nothing but inhaling deeply the new surface. He quickly withered into a shriveled version of himself and became folded deeply into the crevices of the new surface.

The residents of the Oak Valley apartment complex found themselves crushed beneath the weight of a hundred clouds, all bearing down on the roof, which came crashing down on upper floor apartments, which crashed down on mid-floor apartments, which crashed down onto those living in the basement.

3:28pm

We hear the noise of exploration across the city, Katherine and I. We hear the excited screams of children having preconceived notions shattered and parents turning into children themselves. We hear the thunder of clouds falling and resting upon buildings and people, jostling birds and scaring the stars into submission.

We take an entire day of watching the clouds dissolve like cotton being slowly pulled apart, wispy curls frayed and stretching out as if begging to be put back together. It is a cotton-candy bombardment against which we have no defense. Katherine is mesmerized and I hear her questions through a muffled haze, a buffer. Her words are warped by the atmospheric spell cast upon me.

I turn to smile at her, to acknowledge her even if I can't hear what she is saying. Her body is light, not weightless, but glowing faintly. Her veins are lit up with a pulsing white and her skin is translucent, melting into and becoming one with the cloud as I struggle to speak. Her face is wide with smile, her hair wafts below inside the clouded bed already. She is sinking into the ether of this thing and I am powerless to stop her descent.

I see it in her eyes; this is not bliss, but frightened improbability, impossibility. She fights the smile as I thrust my hand down into the cloud to scoop her out, to save her, to fly her back to the last few hours. My hand passes through her body as easily as it went through the cloud. She is ghostly now, pale and untouchable. Intangible and unreachable. Her hand reaches up and out, touches my chest.

My hand rests on hers. I can feel her terrified heartbeat thrumming through her. Or maybe it is my own terrified heart I feel thumping through her hand and our arrhythmias match.

A breeze wafts over me, blows unshowered hair across my face, and she is gone. There is no face, no body, inside the cloud below. She has disappeared.

I don't know how to explain it better than that.

Black Crush

I felt my breath mingle with that of the others. The basement was dank and humid, impervious to light of any sort, the color of pure pitch. We all struggled to stay silent in the dark, but the soft rustle of fabric on fabric, shoulder against shoulder, chest against back...these sounds felt magnified to us, like wild animals traipsing through a dead forest. A soft whimper came from a corner of the room, a sympathetic hushing from another.

This was our designated place to hide. Nada, the wife of our grocer, had some experience with these kinds of things and arranged it all. Having immigrated as a teenager from Abkhazia shortly after the conflict in 1998, she understood perfectly what self-preservation meant. When the separatists had begun their own form of ethnic cleansing, she and her brothers found themselves alone; her father had taken to the streets to fight back (and eventually died) while her mother had bled to death due to a stray bullet as they all tried to escape.

I remember the first time she told me what it was like to leave her mother lying there in the street as her brothers tugged her towards their escape. No burial, no ceremony, the matriarch left unceremoniously to the carrion birds. This was life for many outside America's borders and I realized then we had been sheltered. How could I respond to her tearless eyes and her quivering lips as she spoke? What experience did

Black Crush

I have that could have alleviated her pain? What would Aiden or Aria do in that same situation now? She was a tough woman and the only person I knew for sure down in this dank hole of a hiding place. But I trusted her, and I assumed everyone else down here did as well. Or, at least, she trusted them and that was enough.

The smell of soap mingled with ash and dirt. I held my nose and tried not to sneeze. Someone shuffled their feet, a teardrop splashed against the floor, a finger brushed an eyelash from a cheek, a quiet worried sigh. Silence could be deafening when it meant the difference between living and dying, when it meant keeping one's bloodline intact to perforate the width and breadth of history, if only in the tiniest of margins.

How long do you think we'll need to stay here? a voice whispered in my ear. I shrugged, briefly forgetting they couldn't see me. The voice was deep, a man's. I could smell the nicotine on his breath as it passed my face.

Shut. Up.

A woman's voice, a concerned hiss devoid of anger.

Aiden, my ten-year-old son, stood in front of me, my hands draped across his chest, his fingers clutching mine painfully tight. I could feel his heart thumping loud and hard beneath the skin. I ran a hand through his hair to calm him, to let him know he was safe. But he's a smart boy and his heart never wavered, never stopped beating strong despite my attempts to soothe him.

His mother and sister were elsewhere in a similar hidden situation. The *harpsound* rang across the city and she and I scattered to find the children after kissing each other for what, we hoped, was not the last time. We had talked long into the night after the kids had been put to bed about what we would have to do when the time came. We knew we couldn't let sentimentality take over when the *harpsound* came. Let other families be careless in their protection; I couldn't afford to put my emotions before the safety of my children. Jessica had allowed only a single tear loose before running off to find Aria while I ran to find Aiden.

We'd practiced it numerous times in the weeks building up to the occupation, first deciding on our proximity to the children, which became complicated as communication by phone or email had been deemed illegal for civilian use but legal for any member of the military or political leaders still left in charge. For simplicity's sake, we each chose a particular child as our own personal responsibility. We each were to know where they were at all times of the day, who they were with, what they were doing, where they would be going, so on. Once we had the children adhering to a particular schedule, Jessica and I were able to breathe a little easier. One problem of many solved to a certain degree.

Black Crush

Then we had to sit the children down and ingrain in them the idea of self-preservation. The children stared down at the floor or looked at each other, nervous and unsure, as we spoke, but we could tell by the downturned lips and furrowed brows that they were listening. And they were scared, but they seemed to understand what we asked of them but not why they had to know:

Don't go anywhere with anyone else.

Don't panic; we'll be there.

Don't be afraid if you hear loud sounds; fear leads to bad choices.

If you see a soldier before you see either of us, run. Your mother or I will meet you at the designated spots.

Do not get caught, do not stop running.

Some hard truths for children to hear, but we ran out of time to play it safe with the realities of the moment. I had Aiden here beside me, and that was good. I could only hope that Jessica had found Aria in time to get her hidden. I worried that Aria would be inconsolable, would unintentionally lead the soldiers to their hiding place. It's hard to get an emotional five-year old to stop crying in any situation, much less one that made silence a life or death situation.

A muffled cough from across the room, as if someone had buried their face in the fabric of their coat. A soft shuffling of feet. An exhalation of breath. Someone was whispering a prayer. I could smell sweat and fear, could feel them tickle my nose with their prickly, pungent odors. I felt Aiden's fingers clutch mine tighter, uncomfortably so. I leaned down and put my mouth to his ear.

Are you okay?

I could feel his hair against my lips as he nodded. I remembered a soft roll and an apple his mother had shoved into my pocket before we parted. I leaned down again, felt my lips against his ear.

Are you hungry?

He shook his head and I leaned back up, running my hand down the back of his neck. I wondered what he would remember of this time period when he got older. That he would get older was of no question to me (I refused to entertain the thought that he would not survive long enough to see adulthood), but the memory has a funny way of slanting the truth when the hair has gone gray and the bones a little more brittle. Recounting those stories over and over cements them into our consciousness in a way that the spoken word cannot do alone. With each recollection, the words may dissipate into the air with every breath, but the memory becomes a little clearer, a little more vivid for the telling though the memory may be incomplete.

Flashes of memory came back to me, my father standing behind me the way Aiden and I were now. Family photos, vacations, Sunday church services. The smell of his cologne barely masking the cigarette odor embedded in his clothing, yellowed fingers petting my hair. I wonder what my father would have done in this situation. Would he have taken these same measures that Jessica and I had? Would he have broken up his family this same way…?

A shuffling came from across the room, a whisper, a creak. The room fell silent again for a minute, then two. The sound of breathing through nostrils, the whistling wheeze of old age and bad habits. The air filled with guarded exhalations, aching from standing up and still for so long. It felt like the room was slowly sucking the life out of us and we were more than happy to let it. We knew that killing ourselves for a little while would allow us to truly taste the sweetness of life when we finally emerged from the dark. That first breath in daylight would be ambrosia.

*   *   *

In the middle of fear, you forget everything but self-preservation. You forget what music sounds like, you forget the names of friends, you forget love, you forget, for the briefest of moments, who you are beyond the immediate

Black Crush

reflex of needing to survive, but you remember that your life is worth holding on to for a little while longer no matter how black the world around you becomes.

You forget the minutiae, the mundane, the inconsequential. You become acutely aware of the internal workings of your body; blood pumps hard and fast through every vein, artery, and capillary, expanding them all and making its way through every appendage up into a heart that takes it all in before sending it right back out. Sweat beads up in places you never believed could sweat. Your shirt sticks to your body and for some strange moment, it is your armor against the naked. The more you wear, the safer you feel, guarded against some unknown and unforeseen danger. This is a lie of course, but this is what the irrational mind does when endorphins and the adrenaline take over.

Here in the dark, everyone a possible stranger, everyone a possible traitor, this fear amplified inside me. I couldn't tell you what the room looked like. I couldn't tell you the ratio of men to women, or adults to children, former rich to former poor, but I could tell you what they smelled like collectively. I could tell you how they breathed; I could differentiate between their respiratory tics, the length and breadth of their sighs, the smell of last meals on their breath. I could tell which individuals moved more and which side of the room was better at remaining still as stone. It seemed like hours that we stood there, huddled together, one small swath of citizens sizing each other up like the blind as we waited and hoped for a cavalry instead of a firing squad.

My muscles ached, my legs close to giving out. I couldn't remember what it was like to be ten again, but I imagined Aiden's tiny body was close to exhaustion if I was under this much duress. Had I the strength or had he been smaller, I simply would have picked him up and held him against my chest while he napped in the crook of my neck, but this was impossible. I had to be content with him pressed up against me, had to be content with every inch of arm covering him to remind him I was wholly and completely there.

He was an unplanned, but wonderful, surprise to us. I had just finished my doctoral work in gothic literature studies while Jessica was working at an investment firm not far from the campus. Neither of us had planned on marriage, content to simply live together as monogamous partners. We both felt a ceremony was for the guests more than for the guests of honor, but I proposed to her in the OBGYN's office when I saw Aiden's blurry form on the screen. I couldn't help myself; I had no ring and no speech formulated when I fell to my knee, but it all felt right. Thankfully, Jessica felt it too and said yes. Two of the greatest moments of my life experienced at the same time. It was unimaginably wonderful.

Black Crush

Four quick years later, Aria arrived. Jessica still worked at the same investment firm, earning the bulk of our income, while I stayed at home with the kids doing freelance writing and a little translation work here and there. University jobs were scarce as most classrooms had gone digital. A single professor could give several video lectures on one day to three thousand students across the globe and still get the same academic results. The universities made money, the students earned degrees, but the teachers fell slowly by the wayside unless one knew somebody or had been grandfathered in to the profession. An ugly kind of nepotism to be sure and I still refuse to believe the students are better for the changes.

Rather than bringing us closer together, as some genuinely believe, the digital age has reinforced a kind of human disconnect by allowing us to feel we're being brought closer together through the use of binary code and computer screens. The majority of the populace socializes through their phones or their computers, seemingly never leaving their homes except to go to work. We've turned our interactions into bite (byte?)-sized moments meant to make the most of a minute. Each second maximized to fit into our "busy" schedules rather than to make our schedules work for us. They can have it all; give me a book and a face to face conversation every time.

When Aria was five, foreign hackers found their way into the U.S. economy. Wall Street was crippled beyond anything we'd ever seen, even the derivatives fiasco of 2007. The three largest banks were digitally wiped clean, effectively eliminating every bank account across the country. Some blamed the North Koreans, others blamed the Chinese. I didn't put much stock in the former, but the latter made sense as we'd caught them several times over the years trying to hack their way in to our other systems.

Imagine the 1's and 0's that stream across stock tickers and bank accounts had all disappeared. Imagine your lifelong savings account completely drained and absolutely no one is able to recover it. Magnify that frustration by the nearly five-hundred million people living in this country. Now imagine everyone, from the most poverty-stricken all the way up to the wealthiest, finally and actually coming to the realization that money was the only thing separating us all. Imagine all those people, side by side awash in the same anger, consumed by the same level of rage against an unseen enemy.

It was emboldening to see all walks of life, all political stripes, banding together as an actual nation. It was also unimaginably depressing to see that these little pieces of green, numbered paper had kept us so distant from each other for so long. But once you unleash the hounds, it's hard to get them back in their cages if they haven't hunted down their prey. You cannot contain that level of rage with any number of rational arguments or the presence of police officers. Or so we thought as we watched unimpeded rioting and looting, the slow destruction of government buildings by tall flames of licking fire, the broadcast images of fists and objects slammed against bank windows until they spider-webbed and shattered. It is strange how quickly a revolution can turn the common man into history's remembered and revered revolutionary.

Welcome to the now.

*   *   *

A gentle rumble arrived, shook the walls of the complacent dust. We quietly shushed one other, each assuming someone else had made the noise before we heard the rumbling grow louder with every torturous second. More dust flew about in the dark, found its way into our shallow breaths, dared us not to sneeze or cough, dared us to not betray ourselves. I imagined all of our faces turned up to the ceiling as if hoping for some kind of heavenly reprieve as we tried to see through the floor above us. All eyes on God, all mouths stuck in silent prayer.

The rumbling became an angry growling, a metallic rhythm getting louder as it continued to vibrate the earth around us. I clutched Aiden harder, pressed him against my body as if to make him a part of me, as if to cocoon him completely from whatever was to happen. His heart pounded through his chest, his breathing quickened, his hands wrapped around mine, white-knuckled. What terror he must have been feeling that his body could barely contain it, standing here in the dark with other frightened adults. I could tell he was trying to be braver than his age should've allowed. The world was asking too much of him now.

The growl reached a feverish pitch, a thick and monstrous sound that split ear drums and wormed its way into our brains, intensifying the fear already nestled there. A repetitive *thump-duhduh-thump-duhduh-thump-duhduh-thump* added itself to the noise. My imagination reeled at the spectacle that must be, at this moment, filling our streets and boulevards. Oh but if it had remained imaginary.

I knew the sounds well, had seen firsthand the events that followed the arrival of the war machines and their army-fatigued escorts that marched on either side. I had seen the elderly crushed beneath the ever-moving track shoes, had seen their homes and businesses turned to smoke by the deafening turrets of the tanks.

The soldiers had pressed on in lockstep, faces calm and empty, as they stepped over the bodies left in the tank's wake. Armed automatons wearing our flag on their uniforms. I did not understand, would never understand, how they had turned against their own countrymen. Had none of them felt the same intense rage at the current state of affairs that affected not just a few, but *all* of us? Had none of them possessed the strength to refuse the orders handed down to them? Was there no soldier among them, raised to notice and fight injustice, who had the strength of character to remove him or herself from the frontline and place themselves squarely in front of the populace like armor? I worried that the time of that kind of man was over.

The minutes ticked off, slow as midnight's leaky faucet, as we all stood there, waiting, holding breath for fear the slightest sound would give us away over the din of a thousand boots thundering across the pavement. That a sneeze or a cough would give away our position was not a ridiculous idea and I'm sure it was the only one swirling around in everyone else's minds as well. The rumble came and came, an ocean of destruction washing over the top of us, drowning us in its unending sound. I tried to picture how many troops and tanks were moving past us and could not fathom the number, could not believe the amount of people it would take to fill our streets with that sound, that heavy and uneasy moving of earth and stone.

Aiden turned around in the dark, wrapping his arms around my body and pressing his head against my waist. His body shuddered against me and soon I could feel his tears soaking through my shirt. I leaned down to kiss his head and ran my hand through his hair. *We'll be fine*, I whispered into his ear, hoping he could hear me clearly over the noise. *So will your mother and Aria.* He nodded and wiped his eyes on my shirt and still I held him close, waiting.

I wanted to tell him that all this would pass, that all this was something he'd erase from his memory when he grew into adulthood. I wanted to make sure he understood that this wasn't normal, that normal was him running home in the streets with his sister after school. Not because they were being chased, but because some inner fire had been ignited inside them and came bursting out of their bodies in the form of innocent laughter. I wanted him to live in the blinding light of the sun rather than feel like he needed the protection of the hidden dark.

This is what I wanted to tell my son before the door was kicked in by armed men. This is what I wanted to tell my son before the silvery light of the cloudy day illuminated the basement. This is what I wanted to tell my son before the screaming started and we all pressed against each other in

Black Crush

terror, our faces finally known to each other moments before the terror came and swallowed us whole.

Saudades & Ossuaries

THEN

I remember my father, an avid ornithologist before the occupation, would randomly remember facts about his avian pursuits. *A group of finches is called a charm,* he muttered once at the dinner table. *If keeping them as a pet, they should always be caged in pairs and never with a parrot, which may injure the smaller bird.* I would pretend to keep eating the dinner I had no interest in, never engaging my father during these rambling reveries.

I could always tell when father was about to sink into the weird depths of his mind; his head would tilt down slightly to the right, his eyes would shift up to the left, as if the information could be found in the upper part of some unseen ethereal space, and he would drum his fingers three times. Table, thigh, bookshelf, glassware, whatever. Three times, silence, then the rambling.

Eventually, father's demeanor changed, became serious. His ramblings took on a fevered kind of urgency that spooked me. Older now, I could shake it off better, pretend it was the slow decay of a brilliant mind gone crusty with plaque. Dinner table conversations became awkward monologues of a man trying to navigate the right brain avenues but constantly getting lost. This was the status quo for many months. Our world was bathed in the daily chaos of our separate ideologies locking horns.

Then the fire of the occupation came. It lit cities and grassland up the same, swallowing everything in glorious orange and heat. Like most, I was afraid at first. Great walls of burn washing over concrete and metal and skin and hair; it was a majestic and beautiful violence I succumbed to quickly. I stayed up late, keeping sleep dreams at bay so I could watch the night sky dance an angry and fluid amber. I swooned at the curvature of her movements and fell deeply in love with her nightly performances.

Fire-gazing became my addiction while so many others preferred to dim their existence through the fuzzed out vibe of needles and snort. The decision to mentally clock out while surrounded by brilliance and violent interlopers never made much sense to me. It seemed too lazy. Too selfish.

Let's be clear: I didn't care for the violence or destruction the fire brought. I fell in love with its movement. I fell in love with its color, a shine that made me believe it had a soul drowning deep inside each licking flame that grew into spiraling towers up to heaven in the hopes of being saved.

As the armed violence and fire awoke something inside me, it awoke something in my father. It wasn't just the reddish-orange glow reflected back off his cornea, there was something deep behind the iris, something that had taken flight and illuminated his mind, allowed him safe passage through every nook and cranny and gave him access to everything again.

Months later, father volunteered with the rebel factions, offered up his limited expertise in military strategies, stories of the generals from history books, ideas that required splitting up the occupation battalions into smaller, more manageable targets. Through all this, I continued to go to school in one of many "safe zones" outside the city away from the skirmishes, hoping one day to rid myself of the crumbling city and its constant taste for death.

I continued to keep my head down and, without realizing it, learned the different sounds of the bombs and missiles used by the occupation. The MX-15 had a low pitched whistle to it as it descended. The Bunker Buster whooshed like a strong toilet before smashing into the ground. The L12 (nicknamed "the eel") came silent and flew through city streets like an angel of death on nightmare wings.

The flat faces of owls help funnel and magnify sound to the ears. Owls also have three eyelids: one for blinking, one for sleeping, and for keeping the eye clean and healthy.

Only years later did the occupation finally start to wind down. Father's ideas had fostered other ideas that had eventually pushed back the occupation to a tolerable level. They hadn't left completely; they were still a presence. But by then, I had made my way up through the ranks of the rebellion. I never had father's brain for strategy the way he never had my taste for the more physical aspects of the rebellion. When father learned of my acceptance, he cried a tear or two and patted me on the back. Not out of congratulations, but out of sorrow.

I was what they called a "legacy," since father had been so instrumental in the beginning. I guess they expected me to finish what he had helped start. I was smart with the weapons and picked up hand-to-hand combat techniques easily, but I only followed the plans. I never made them. I had also been put in charge of training all the new recruits in these aspects.

Late one night, after an attack had backfired, killing two of our top lieutenants and fifteen of our foot soldiers, we sat on the balcony of a bombed out condo and shared a cigarette.

It's not the dark you should be afraid of, he said. *The things that wait for you in the dark are what should scare you the most, the things that sit back and watch the world eat itself before swooping in to sweep up the crumbs of hope left to go stale on the floor.*

NOW

Outside: Bodies swung from lamp posts. Each one missing from the waist down, entrails dried up and hanging or completely ripped out and feasted on by packs of feral dogs. Several crows perched on the shoulders of one, an older man, and continued to peck out what was left of his eyes, his ears. I had seen this so often now that it was no longer revolting, it was simply the way things were.

I remember when the first body appeared outside the city library, a place the occupiers had originally holed up in and gotten organized. It was the governor's child, a message to those that even thought of fighting back, of trying to reclaim the (*our!*) city. Our elders, after shedding quiet tears for the girl, became emboldened. Arthritis and bulleted scar tissue could not stop their need for justice. Though from the outside, I can see why some might believe our atrocities to be revenge instead.

The war changed us; both sides fought to capture the enemy alive purely for the sake of hanging them on display. Two of their men here, three of ours there, four of theirs there, in fives and sixes and sevens (as many as tens and twenties at one point), men and women hung like slaughtered cattle, desecrated. Some of us wondered if maybe the dead hadn't gotten off easy; what had we allowed ourselves to become that this was our new normal? Man against man makes monsters of us all and there was no coming back.

And now? Now I stood outside our safe house (a misnomer; nowhere was safe) on the outskirts of the city. It was a bombed out shell of a bar whose name was forgotten years ago and whose signage hadn't glowed in even more years. I couldn't remember the last time candlelight wasn't both essential and an incredibly dangerous risk. I flicked my lighter, ran my hand through the open flame, closed the lighter. Opened it again, repeat. The smell of burnt hair tickled my nose as I stood in the doorway, taking in the city block. I saw no movement, felt no immediate danger.

Clouds the color of wilting vegetables gathered on the horizon. The sky lit up briefly with crisp, white lightning, followed long seconds later by a rumbling of the ground and the sound of the sky shredded violent by giant hammer and chisel. I wondered what kind of rain we'd get this time.

My father once spoke of a time when the rain was pure water, a crystalline bathing of the world that one could drink as it fell, bringing low the taste of clouds to those of us, mere mortals, stuck on the ground. Now, we cowered in doorways and buildings; never under tattered awnings or in the skeletons of cars left to rust on the streets.

The beauty of the strange and acidic rainfall is that the fighting stopped. No one knew what kind of damage it would bring or in what form, so the weather became a kind of forced truce between us all. The calming sound of weather replaces the sound of ricocheted bullets and buildings blown to smoldering piles of rock. But woe to the living man that finds himself out in it unexpectedly and without protection. Maybe this time, I thought, the rain would melt the bodies that still hung. Maybe we'd finally get to look at a sky unbroken by the reminder of our ongoing madness. Hope was such a dangerous thing to have anymore.

A group of rooks is called a building, which is apt as they are a more social kind of bird, living in large groups that can create an overwhelming feeling to other birds.

A hand tapped me on the shoulder as the rain fell in big gloopy drops over every surface. "He's here," Alexi whispered. I nodded and turned to follow him inside.

I looked around at the decrepit bar. The front windows were boarded up, the mirror behind the bar shattered, its shards littering the floor below. Lighting fixtures had been pulled from the ceiling and thrown to the corners, mangled and busted. Wallpaper curled and peeled from every wall, bits of ceiling had fallen inward and piled up on the concrete floor.

I stared across the broken booth. My father, a dark skinned man with wrinkles that cracked along his face, looked back with elbows rested on the table. His hands were clasped together in a fist that covered his mouth when he spoke. His eyes moved from left to right, scanning the darkened room around us. Two flickering candles lit the deserted bar and while we weren't in any danger of being overheard, he continued to peer into the darkness as he spoke, as if expecting the gloved hand of decades-old oppressors to reach out and strangle him again, to quiet his voice by crushing his spirit.

"You should be more careful, Ramon. You weren't there, but the days of hungry ears and money-slicked palms weren't so long ago. A man's greed can only amplify during the silence of war. He gets anxious and feels the need for movement in any direction that will let him move."

"We're fine here, father," I said, trying to hide my irritation. This wasn't the first time we'd had a conversation of this kind, this worry of disrespect and espionage. Now that I'd moved up in the ranks by default, he had taken to counseling me as often as possible. Though he was no longer as much a presence in the rebellion, he was still revered for his role during its early years, I just found him to be more paranoid in his old age. I once believed it to be the strain of growing older, but now that I was part and parcel of his (yes, *his*) rebellion, I knew if I lived to be his age, I'd end up in the same state. Maybe. "I'm your son, you don't have to do the cloak and dagger stuff with me."

He shook his head. "You weren't there. The songs you and your friends sing while huddled around the fire…they remind me of the friends I lost. Of the times I spent wondering who I could trust with my thoughts."

Alexi snorted behind me and I turned to glare. "Go watch the front door."

"But…"

"Go."

Alexi shook his head and moved to the bar's entrance, unhappily sweeping his gaze from left to right.

"Father…"

"Ramon, do you know how the male lark courts the female?"

I slammed my hand down on the table. "Dammit, *papa*, not this crap again!"

He grabbed my hand as quickly as it had fallen and looked around furtively while lifting his other hand high up above us.

"When the male lark courts the female, it ascends, it flies up into the sky several hundred feet." He tilted his upper hand, made it seem to fly before sending it slowly and shakily down towards the table. "As it circles downward, it emits a high-pitched, tinkling flight song. When it ends…" he began whistling through his teeth. "The lark, fast and dangerous as a bullet closes its wings and dive bombs the hell out of the

Saudades & Ossuaries

ground, allows itself close enough to suicide to taste the darkness before it pulls up and flies off." He let the palm of his hand glance the table top before pulling it back up into the air. "I used to call this kamikaze romance."

"What is the point of this, father? What are you trying to say?"

"What I'm saying is I don't trust this new girl you've been stepping out and about with and I want you in 'all eyes' mode around her. If you won't watch out, maybe Alexi will. I know you were never much for the planning of things, for looking at the world in five- or six-moves ahead as in chess, but you need to try. Think like your enemy and you will confound them and outsmart them every time. If you don't start, your generation will simply be the cannon fodder for the war my generation began. That cannot happen." He sighed, then fell silent.

I'll admit it; I hadn't expected that. He had winded me, surprised me. I figured it for another of his ramblings, the ones he had so easily shrugged off once he felt of some serious importance to the rebellion. He brought my hand, still clutched in his, up to his face and kissed the back of it.

"Just be careful."

And then he was gone, leaving me alone in the booth, stunned.

I turned toward the front door. Alexi still kept watch on the street out front. The rain had been brief, but efficient; the world looked bathed in a steaming, melty patina. No one would be fighting today even if it didn't rain another single burning drop. As such, it would take Alexi and I entirely too long to get back to the library through the mess. It would take another hour or so to clean the undercarriage of the truck to keep it from rusting and becoming unusable.

LATER

Her name was Keira. She wore her black hair in a short pixie-cut, though a thick tuft, dyed bright green, hung down low on the left side of her face. Her eyes were almond shaped, exotic, and her skin was a natural deep olive. She was a mutt of four continents and the last daughter of a hundred histories. I loved the way her name sounded when spoken aloud the way I loved the taste of her lips on mine.

Alexi had found her curled up among the rubble below a blown out section of highway underpass. Skeletons hung at intervals along the intact edge, twisting in the wind, bones knocking together like empty wind chimes. The remaining walls were covered in creeping vines and tall grass. Amateur graffiti, now quick on the fade, was slathered across the surface.

Rebelyon for Lyfe!

Your Mother is an Occupier

JFS + FHT encapsulated in an awkward and jagged heart.

It was a place we considered "home turf" to an extent. I remembered the place well, having thrown up my own tag back in father's early days with the rebellion.

The Face of the City Shines Bright Against Every Darkness

I don't know. It felt like it meant something when I was younger. Now it just seemed like unfortunate optimism. Alexi offered her his hand, and by extension, the rebellion's. Behind every good man is a woman there to unravel him at every turn, and oh how I had unraveled around her.

She took to the weapons quickly, showing a propensity for the more complicated guns and land mines. Alexi's brother Ivan (twin sons of Czech immigrants) caught her watching him make explosives for the next assault and, again, she took to it like a natural. Pretty soon, she was experimenting with different caps and varying designs for cars and doorways, the legs of already rickety structures…you get the idea. She was comfortable bringing down the fire, so really…how could I have kept myself from falling for her?

The eye of the ostrich is larger than its brain.

Not long after my meeting with father, I had taken her scouting. She was skittish about traveling through the city, but we'd made progress. I guess when you're used to living alone, moving from darkened doorway to darkened doorway, it can leave you a little broken. I know she felt she'd found a group of people in a place one could barely call "reliable." We were the closest thing she had to family or a home now, so I was patient with her, but she was getting better.

I took her through Old Suburbia, a place up in the hills of the city that had been home to the more extravagant, more well off people before the occupation. Doctors, lawyers, a few politicians – people that never had to fight in order to eat and who were, I think, the first to be hunted down and killed. Besides being a safer environment to train her in, there was a garden in the neighborhood that I wanted to show her. Maybe get lost inside with her. Maybe find myself splayed out, napping with her in the afternoon sun and leafy shadows.

The house was an old colonial thing; brick façade with four Grecian columns across the porch that reached up past the second and third floors to connect with the eave of the roof. The columns still stood, surprisingly, but many of the walls had been blackened, charred by fire, mortar rounds, or both. The house, looted. The driveway, pockmarked with ash and crumble. The entire grounds in ruin, but the surrounding nature had begun to creep back, began to climb up the outside walls as if starving for the nothing that lay inside.

We sat on the back patio staring out over the garden. Beyond the hills, we could see pockets of movement in the city, little specks of something scattered throughout the streets. I took bites from an apple; she nibbled on a loaf of week old bread. The day was cloudless and brightly lit. We said nothing but smiled when our eyes met, completely content in having removed ourselves from the struggle if only for a momentary bit of solitude.

"What did you do before?" she asked a while later. "Before the occupation, I mean." She had set to polishing her knife after finishing her bread. It was dangerously serrated, glinted bright in the afternoon light, scattered shining beacons across her cheek and neckline.

I finished the apple, threw the core deep into the garden somewhere, heard the rustle of it landing in thick vegetation. "Nothing. I was about to finish high school when my father joined up with the rebellion. Once they arrived, it was go out into the streets and fight or stay home and look after the family. Father did the former and I chose the latter. Now, oddly, the roles have reversed."

"Why oddly?"

I turned to her, grinned and ran my fingers across her cheek. "I wasn't any good at being smart like my father was. I was good at other things, but that, the inherent intelligence…I never had that. Always wanted it when I saw how people looked at him for having it, but could never…he should've stuck it out with us."

She began flipping the knife blade over hilt, hilt over blade, catching the flat end of the blade in her hand every time. "You could always bring him back in to things. He's something of a legend to the others from what everyone says."

I snorted. "No. He wants to die in peace, without a weapon in his hand. I think he enjoyed letting his mind wander around inside something bigger than him for once. If I know my father, I think he treated it all like one big puzzle or a game."

"Is that why he left?"

"Is what why he left?"

"Did he come to enjoy it too much? How easy it was to get wrapped up in the action while not getting caught in the middle of it?"

"Hm." I hadn't thought about that possibility. The years leading up to the conflict, I saw my father more withdrawn, like he was constantly looking inward for answers to unspoken questions. The conflict did, in fact, seem to inject him with some new kind of stoicism; you could see it in the way his skin didn't seem to sag anymore, like his face had been pulled back by a sense of purpose. I pulled out my lighter, clicked it open, ran my hand through the flame over and over.

"…mean to be rude."

I looked at Keira, confused.

"You went quiet. I thought maybe I'd been rude in asking the question."

"No no, it's a good question actually. One I'd never considered. Maybe? In a weird way, I can see how he might've enjoyed the violence too much. Wait, no. Not the violence. He enjoyed the winning and the strategy too much." I rested my free hand on her thigh absentmindedly, not meaning to hint at anything more than a lust-less need to feel something soft. I let the lighter fall to the ground.

Before I realized what I was doing, she put her hand on top of mine and leaned over to kiss me. I don't know how long we sat there, hands along shoulders and lean cheekbones, hair rustling against calloused knuckles, fingers feeling every inch of mudded denim and stained canvas.

When we realized there was a world around us and came up for air, the sun was on its way down, but still spilling golden beams across the property. She grabbed my hands and pulled me up off the patio. "Show me this garden before it disappears."

My finger clutched hers as we walked down the yard and through the tall hedges. She ran her free hand along the untrimmed vegetation. I did the same. A right turn, a left turn, and soon the hedges opened up into a quiet grassy area. Large cement fountains lay scattered across the lawn. With no water gushing forth, they had calcified over however many years the house had been vacant.

Her hand let go of mine and I felt like something had been taken away from me, like something had left me a little emptier than before. I watched her walk through the grass, running her hands over the broken fountains and the surrounding stalks of flowers long gone dead. Nothing bloomed here, and hadn't anywhere in some time, but the garden still held a beauty that was hard to explain. When I realized I couldn't hear anything except for the soft rustling of Keira's fingers on every surface, I knew it was the silence, the tranquility found here, that made it so perfect.

She stood there, unspeaking, staring into a sun that bathed her in deep orange light. She held out her hand, beckoned me, and it was all I could do not to run to her. I wanted the taste of her lips again, the taste of her cheek, the feel of her hair finding its way between my lips as she exhaled against my ear.

The sooty tern, a tropical seabird, remains flying aloft from three to ten years before returning to land to breed. It eats, drinks, and even sleeps while flying, never landing until it's time to populate.

We fell to the ground and undressed clumsily, my hands on her clothes, her hands on mine. I felt my heart pounding against my ribcage hard enough to break free from my chest. My body slid against hers, into hers, hands coiled within hands, the full length of my leg taking in the full length of hers.

Saudades & Ossuaries

We explored each other for what felt like a minute that felt like an hour that felt like a lifetime. When we finished, breathless and skin all glistened in pre-dusk, we lay there and said nothing. I was content. I had found a small measure of calm where I thought none existed or would ever exist again. She rubbed her hand along my chest, slid it down across my stomach and then tickled my inner thigh. Over and over she did this, calming me. She whispered an old story about the stars back from the days of our grandfathers and lulled me into a slumber I welcomed.

How much time had passed, I didn't know. But I shivered as I came to. Still naked, I reached out for Keira. I heard the cocking of guns and opened my eyes. Alexi and Ivan stood above me, pointing their weapons down at my face. A fully dressed Keira stood at my feet, looking down at me, a weird smile playing across her face.

The mockingbird has been known to acquire and utilize the sounds and songs of other birds. Until its death, the mockingbird will continue to add to its vocal repertoire.

No explanation needed; I had been careless with my lust and it had swallowed me whole. The immensity of the moment, how serious a thing it was, washed over me. If Alexi and Ivan, two of my closest, my most experienced, had been turned (or who had played us all from the beginning), who else had been slowly cannibalizing the rebellion from the inside?

I sighed, expecting the guns to sing out in the early evening sun, scattering flocks of birds from the surrounding trees as the bullets opened up the back of my skull, staining the barren earth below. Instead, Alexi and Ivan flipped me over onto my chest and pinned my arms back behind me.

I knew fighting back would be trouble. Alexi and Ivan were both twice my size and could handle themselves with a surprising agility. Keira…that one hurt. If I even had the chance to stop her, could I actually do it?

"Well. My father was right," I muttered into the ground. "What you all could possibly want is beyond me, though. You know I know nothing of use and you know they won't trade anything for my return."

I could smell Keira as she bent down. Her lips tickled my ear, which both angered and aroused me. "You know enough," she whispered before knocking me out with the butt of her gun.

Like I said, hope is a dangerous thing to have these days.

Firebug for Hire

In an abandoned office building across the street from a café, a man sits patiently at a window, waiting. The room is devoid of furniture, but walls shellacked with weeks-old bullet holes surround him. The building is a skeletal carcass of the skirmishes that have grown in number over the past months.

No one has come to clean the building, nor will they ever. The smart and the fearful have already fled the city. The dumb and the fearless remain, sometimes at odds with each other, sometimes hand in hand. Avarice, vice, persistence, and sometimes the rare bit of true altruism…these are what run the city now. These are what have caused the gaping chasms across the neighborhoods.

Singed papers lay strewn about, tinged with black and faded map-orange along their edges. Light fixtures hang like dead limbs from the ceiling, creaking in the breeze from open windows elsewhere in the shattered office. The smell of concrete and copper permeates the room, but the man doesn't care. He's been around more blood than has pooled up and dried on these carpeted floors.

The blinds of the window are pock-marked with holes as well, but still allow a veil of secrecy. A telescope, with microphone attachment, stands pointed down at the café through one of the largest gaps in the abused slats. Wires from the microphone dish spill out onto the floor, coil up and then snake over to a makeshift table where they insert themselves into a lightweight, but expensive, recording device. The man travels light. At the first sign of a problem, all but the digital camera in his hand and the recorder can be left behind. Take what's important, leave what's irrelevant. A thing is a thing and most often replaced, but information is invaluable.

He checks his watch; the client won't arrive for another half hour, so he gets up and moves around. A chair in the corner lies on its back with cushion stuffing spilling out from the seat. It's hard to see the dried blood on the seatback against the deep mahogany color, but it's there in a brownish puddle stain. Cloudy daylight spills across the surfaces of broken doors hanging on a single hinge.

On the back wall, a hole slightly larger than his head. It is ringed by paint melt and sludge singe, an imperfect circle that shows him the hallway, the office beyond, and another hallway beyond that. The wall there is blackened and soot-tarnished and he imagines he can smell the screams of whatever rocketed through the clutter.

In the next room over, a corner office missing two walls. There is no sign of any carpet having been here other than the dirt and dust that spirals around in tiny wind devils.

This destruction is the new reality. This is how one comes full circle as long as you can stomach it.

Firebug for Hire

He sits back down near the window and waits.

*　　*　　*

She used to say that revolution could come from birdsong in the morning, that it could be done through propaganda. She said revolution, more often than not, came from pulling a single metal pin and setting the world on fire for an evening. "Imagine the Earth," she'd say in that far off voice, as if she were imagining it herself. "Now think about flames licking their way up from the southern hemisphere. Forget how much heat it would actually take to set the South Pole on fire and just picture it burning the world like an old map from the bottom up. Fire brings death, death brings life, and hopefully we get it right the next time around."

*　　*　　*

Like most mornings in the city, the day was mausoleum quiet. The random sound of thunder across town never portended rain (which hadn't come in months), but instead warned of another skirmish somewhere nearby. A car exploding, a firecracker distraction, a gas station imploding from below, a building finally giving way beneath a throttled foundation. Today, however, only the sound of my dress shoes clip-clopping across debris-littered sidewalks and crumbling parkways echoed up and out against the buildings still left standing like half-burned cigarettes. The echo came back sideways and off, sounding strange and screechy against my ears. The sound unnerved me, made my spine tingle improperly and my palms moistened. Just being out in the open made me skittish. Why in the world had I decided to wear a suit today?

Habit, of course. I'm from the old guard. Up until the world had capsized and decided to feed on itself, I remained persistent in being well-groomed and well-dressed. The generations that followed after me had lost that sense of style, that sense of class that men were supposed to carry on their shoulders once they were done making the mistakes of being uneducated adolescents. So much so that even when I had a housekeeper, I would starch and iron my own dress shirts, buff my own shoes at the end of every day, and lint-rolled each suit by hand.

Order. Routine. These things that I depended on became obsolete once the populace revolted against the faceless machine of the city, a machine that I had become a part of over the years. I hadn't worked so hard for decades only to watch it disintegrate before my eyes, no. Who were they to say that I had been wrong in building up my small empire just because they were incapable of doing the same? Were they lazy? Unintelligent? I don't know and never truly speculated that deeply on the matter, but I stayed when everyone else left, when they jumped off the sinking ship of commerce and let it rot at the bottom of this concrete ocean I walk across now.

I had a towncar once. And a driver. These were niceties I could afford and I enjoyed them both. I remember when you could actually drive down these streets, when they were clear of stonework and chaos but full of the dirty and unclean, always with their hands out as if I had the power to save them all. By that time, money was irrelevant and people dealt in drugs, death, or information. If you didn't have one of those, you either left the city or you died beneath its crumbling edifices. I don't know that I'd ever want to know the true number of the dead hidden under so much rubbled concrete.

I turned a corner and saw the café several blocks down. The wrought-iron furniture out front seemed out of place, cozy and casual, against the backdrop of the crumbling edifices surrounding the shop. I ducked into a darkened doorway and waited, watched, slowed my breathing down to nothing and chameleoned myself against the rough brick wall in the dark. If I had learned one thing over the years, it was that playing the slow game was always the smart bet.

Always.

*　　*　　*

She slalomed the bike quickly through an alleyway, riding away from the explosion behind her. Molls had set the timer wrong, had gotten too antsy to watch something burn as if they'd never have another chance to make that happen. Had she not had her bike, she would have been so much blood and skin pollacked on the wall just like Molls. Stupid, stupid Molls.

The problem with true revolt is that it, too, can be infiltrated by the wrong people. People so hell-bent on ideology that they never see the moment as part of a larger history or take the time to weed out the misinformation from the truth.

This is why she had moved up in the ranks of the faux army; she understood both concepts better than most of the older folks who had been fighting longer, the ones who had lost more than she had ever conceived of losing in her lifetime. While they sat around makeshift barrel fires swapping origin stories and overly biased opinions, she had kept her history quiet. An interloper by their standards, there was no way she would ever earn their respect if they had known about her upbringing, so she remained quiet and loyal. Diligent. Always the first to volunteer as a new angel of death.

They gave her missions, she came back victorious.

They gave her a gun, she came back with an arsenal.

They gave her explosives, she made them bigger and louder.

The thick clinking of metal in her shoulder-bag reminded her to slow down. Full of tweaked grenades acquired in a previous skirmish, it was good that Moll had passed the bag onto her before setting the charge. They were too valuable to have been lost in such a shoddily completed mission. A weapons cache was a hard thing to build up, much less stumble across these days. One only needed to look at the city to see that so many had already been used. How much could be left now?

She had become their scythe-wielder, their black-veiled goddess of the night, their hell on wheels.

She turned down an alleyway and saw part of the café. She stood her bike up next to a demolished trash bin and walked the rest of the way, always looking up and around for trouble as she kicked the rubble out of her path absent-mindedly.

*   *   *

She said she felt dirty here and still did on occasion. "I got used to the money just always being there, being around me. After awhile, even the trees smelled like greed and I had to go. That was when I realized I wanted to do something more than consume for selfish reasons. I want to conceive for selfless reasons now."

"You just want to watch the world on fire."

"No," she said. "I want to watch it grow back into something real. I want to take from those that don't deserve it and put it in the hands of those that do. We stand in the middle of the era of inevitability. This is how things end. This is how it's supposed to be. This is how things will continue to be until we've turned the tide of unreason back into something that works for everyone."

"And what of the people? You can't eliminate them all in the name of some abstract cause. You aren't the only ones with answers."

"No, but we lack complacency."

*   *   *

Down at the café, the client arrives and sits at the agreed upon table. It is not so much a café as it is an old bookstore with wrought-iron tables and chairs out front and a barely working coffee machine inside. A meeting place for the wary and the suspicious out in the open, right in the middle of madness. The man sits up, adjusts the microphone and begins snapping pictures. The client wears a suit and nice shoes. A ridiculous outfit considering the setting. He will most likely find himself buried in it, but only because he will most likely die in it.

The girl approaches on a bike from the west. She rides close to the walls in the few shadows that splotch the street. She is smarter than the client in this way. She is dressed to move and ready to move quickly. Even the bike shows better planning than the client's own desire to walk here on his own.

The man snaps pictures of the girl. He snaps pictures of the client. He puts the digital camera down and takes a bite of the warm sandwich on his lap. A breeze wails through broken windows and fractured blinds, the haunted moan of a dead city and a dying populace.

The girl sits across from the client. A younger man brings them both coffee and scurries back inside the bookstore, shutting the door behind him. They drink. She smiles. The client does not.

*   *   *

The patchy shadows of clouds above the café patio washed her face – first in dark, then in light. It was hard to tell what she was thinking as her smile seemed to change with the elements. She sipped her espresso. I made fun of her for the pinky she always extended when drinking. "An old habit

Firebug for Hire

from my younger years," she'd say, as if protesters and firebugs had no place growing up in the upper echelons of society.

I could feel the coffee thickening against my teeth and immediately wished for a toothbrush. "So what's in this for you?" I asked quietly.

She set her cup down on the saucer, a sound like heavy coins falling into a glass jar. "I get the notoriety I need, you get an automatic way to make a change. My people will believe they're making a difference and you get a second chance. It's a win-win for everyone as long as there's no one inside when we make our move." She stared at me, waiting for my eyes to give her the go ahead.

"Will you need my assistance if anything goes awry?"

She shook her head and grinned. "We've gotten pretty good at making our own exits. Plus, we don't want there to be any ties linking us together. A clean break makes for fewer places for them to explore," she said getting up and grabbing her satchel. "You remember how to leave me the message?" she asked.

I nodded as a camera click-click-clicked from the building across the street. My own quiet insurance plan in case anything happened. I am a businessman after all.

"Until then, I suppose," she sighed. "Bye, Dad."

You Are the Key Witness to the End of the World

*You are the key witness to the end of the world.
Bloodied bricks have been picked up and piled on
street corners, leaving cleared paths for the men in
white chasing down the Angel of Death and trying to
fight her off with syringe and sirens. There is the taste
of plague in rainfall now; acrid anger that tickles the
roof of the mouth, driving the tongue crazy. The
morning shuffle sounds have been traded in for
overhead propellers and the echoes of the sparse dog
bark through empty streets of exploded fruit carts and
buildings turned into larger than life windows,
exposing pipes and rickety stairwells.*

In a room, deep beneath the earth, deep beneath the cogs of broken commerce and movement, twelve blind men sit at desks and scribe the history of the now. Pencils worn down to nothing scratch against parchment until the lead is no more, their sound that of old tree limbs rubbing against window panes. On the right side of every desk, a wide, circular holder contains a hundred new pencils, sharpened and ready to record the world's memory as it happens; on the left side, wiry, tireless hands lay the dead nubbins where they are removed by a child and put away as refuse with past nubs. The men do not rest, do not eat. Until the earth stops on its axis or ceases to exhale new moments, their hands fly across the page and record each firing synapse of its thought.

The child, Caspar, has filled more boxes with used wood and lead than he can remember; time seems to cling to the precipice of its last moment here, waiting for the blind men to catch up. Not yet a teenager, he feels ancient, ageless, one of the last holding on to the filament of unraveling earth – an unraveling earth that sometimes shakes around them. Imperceptible to him, but the blind men feel it. All twelve men look up towards the epicenter at the same time, stopping their writing long enough to let silence drown the room. When the rumbling passes, the writing continues.

No clocks and no windows. No real lights, but twelve candles, which Caspar keeps lit, understands they are only for his benefit and no one else's. On the right side of each desk sits a stack of empty books, pages thirsty for words and documentation. On the left a stack of finished volumes, satiated and pregnant and waiting to be shelved with their brethren. While the men start new compendiums or continue on in others, Caspar finds the spaces in the vast library shelves and slides the finished volumes in, imagining each as another key in the great tumbler lock of their prison of paper and binding.

He has felt their collective weary, the men. Once, and only once, they had all completed their books at the same time. The room fell silent so quickly that Caspar believed the earth had rumbled, that he simply hadn't felt it again. But the closing of cover on parchment echoed across the room, a heavy thud that reverberated soundly. All twelve men put pencils down, rubbed their tired hands together, and then placed each finished volume on the floor to their left. Caspar watched as they seemed to work in unison, reaching down to the right for an empty volume, spreading open its pages, grabbing a new pencil and beginning again without so much as a smile or sigh. Caspar didn't think he'd ever get to see that moment replayed again, regardless of how funny time seemed to be down here.

Caspar often wondered how old he actually was now. No birthday had been celebrated as long as he could remember and there was a sadness that came with each new birth recorded. Each of the twelve men had a tic, a tell, that let him know when this happened. The eruption of a wailing infant into the living world brought different reactions.

Blind man number six (for none of them had names that he was aware of) releases the tiniest of sighs, a soft exhalation that wanted to praise life ongoing, but was tempered by the knowledge that the child would most likely not survive its first year in the world above.

Blind man number ten cocks his head to the left briefly as if trying to wrap his head around a particular mathematical problem, but returns to writing as normal.

Blind man number one lets his pencil stop for several long seconds, drinks in the knowledge that new life has just been created. He twists the pencil around to its eraser-capped end as if knowing the life would be a short one, inconsequential to history, but flips it back and continues on with his scratching of lead on parchment.

Number seven snorts, shakes his head mirthlessly, holds back a joyless cackle at the futility of it.

Number two shuts his eyes, giving a moment of silence through milky cataracts and the thin skin of eyelid.

Number eleven taps his pencil twice on the desk and his gnaws at his inner cheek.

Number eight lets go a soft, mourning whistle through aged lips and teeth.

Number five stops writing, returns to the sentence, and strikes a single line through the name of the child.

Number three cackles loudly on behalf of seven. It is a dry sound that cracks and splits the room for a fraction of a minute.

Number twelve releases a single tear, leaves a wet spot near the name as monument, as memorial.

Number nine keeps a separate running total of names on long paper that spills over the desk and into an overflowing box.

Number four dog-ears the page, folds its corner, and draws a star at the top of the text.

He wondered once which of them recorded his own birth however long ago; did he arrive on the wings of a cackle or had he arrived with his name tear-stained and bleeding? Was he just another name in a box overflowing with others or was he the product of a near silent sigh, an exhausted exhalation? Mayhap it didn't matter. Mayhap it never would.

Caspar looks on; the men continue their studious scribing, fingers scribbling across pages with little hesitation, white eyes looking up toward the front of the room. Their pencils will last for awhile, as will all their current books. He grabs a hand-truck, loads up the finished tomes on each left side and heads deep into the library to shelve them.

*   *   *

The room is cavernous, stretching down a long hallway for miles and miles, dimly lit by electric light between each shelf standing just above twelve feet tall. The tomes are all the same size (a foot tall, a foot wide, four inches thick) and fit perfectly onto each shelf with enough space at the top to remove them, though no one has done so since Caspar has been here, he thinks. The spines of each book are a deep blood red with three gold rings splayed across; one at the top, one in the middle, one at the bottom. Until they are placed on the shelves, the spines remain unmarked. Once removed from the room of blind historians, their volume and location numbers swim to the surface, deep black lettering in roman numerals and dead Latin phrasing telling Caspar where to catalog them.

Each bookshelf contains twelve single shelves – one for each historian – but each bookshelf is separated into categories unknown to Caspar. Some remain empty, waiting to be filled with future words while others stand firm and full like walls of the world's gray matter.

Caspar doesn't care which books contain what information, only that they go where they should. There is an imperative buried deep within him that forces his work to be perfect. There is a knowledge locked away in the crevices of his brain that tells him these must be shelved right else things go awry topside. The thought has crossed his mind that the one before him (or before them…or before them, even) shelved some of the books incorrectly. Why else would there be such a pall hanging about the room now? He knew there was some terror happening up above; he could see it on the faces of the historians when the earth rumbled around them. Someone before him had been a terrible caretaker and Caspar hadn't found the time to right the wrong, to fix whatever mistake had led them to these darkened days.

He shelves the books quickly, making sure their new homes correspond to the now visible ink on their spines. All in all, twenty-seven books are shelved into the historical record, sat amongst their brothers in weaving the world's fairy tale gone wrong. How long has he been gone? An hour? Half that? Surely no longer than an hour and a quarter. But again, he can't be sure and heads back to the scribing room, wheeling the hand-truck behind him.

A rumble. A shake. Books nearby jump slightly out of place as if to leap off the shelves with covers spread, a suicide of words and deeds splayed out on the floor. Down the hall, he sees the fluttering of leather and pages, flames licking the edges of the bookshelves on either side of the hallway. The fire moves steadily closer, burning each tome from who knows how many long years, and the hall slowly fills with smoke.

They will all be trapped if he doesn't think of something. The men will continue writing even while choking on smoke and flame unless he corrals them all to the surface. He races back to the scribing room, letting the hand-truck fall with an echoing clang to the marble floor. He must not only provide the blind men their tools, he must also be their shield, their protector.

You are Charon, but finding no silver in the eyes of the dead. Your hands are useless here and Cerberus has left his post, knowing the lifeless will arrive en masse. The men in white will eventually turn syringe on self, never catching up to the Angel of Death, but hoping to numb down the silence; a pin prick to join them on their throne of blown-up brick. Birds no longer congregate at the statue in the square and the few that visit do so silently, a quiet squawk to mourn the morning. The sun explodes so bright and violent upon rising, the few survivors left recoil, assuming another attack is quick on the heels of dawn.

From **Volume MDCCCXII**

Vicis Incendia, Vicis Attero

(The Time of Fire, The Time of Waste)

Pages 237-238

…and buildings fell.

~~Elizabeth Anne Thersat is born.~~

Joseph Malle, age 33, employed by Unity Heart Hospital, hides in the doorway of a crumbling church. He opens his work bag, removes a hypodermic needle and fills it with morphine from a small glass jar. He ties off a tourniquet around his upper arm and injects the medicine into the prominent vein. His ambulance is parked around the corner. It is nearly out of gas, but debris blocks it from three sides.

Esther Salazar, age 68, retired, checks the locks on her windows and doors. There is no electricity in her apartment, so she knits in the dark room, making outfits and scarves for no one. She no longer cries; she is waiting for God to remove her from this station.

~~James Chance Fitzgerald is born.~~

Demarkus Hosen, age 27, revolutionary, is chased by a group of teenagers. He wears a black windbreaker and sunglasses. The teens chase him into an alley where he is beaten until unconscious and then beaten some more. The teens walk away. No one is around to see the act.

Demarkus Hosen dies.

Calvin Friedreich, age 23, pilot, flies circles around the city. He scans for survivors of the last bombing. He sees a group of teenagers walking down the street, sends the plane downward, and strafes them with bullets before returning to the sky. He calls in the kill count to his superiors, who give him another destination to "clean."

Johnny "John-boy" Gonzales, age 18, dies.

Shepard "Shep" Youst, age 20, dies.

Mary Fitzsimmons, age 19, dies.

Jacob "Jake" Hostler, age 19, dies.

~~Christopher Lewis Gough is born.~~

You Are the Key Witness to the End of the World

Francis "Frank" Hedgman dies.

The TransNational Building crumbles, its last pillars folding beneath the weight of ten floors. There is no one inside, but the dust billows out from the bottom and spreads out across the vacant city.

Jessica Anne Ellsworth, age 42, unemployed, lies on a blanket in the empty vault of the bank across the street. The empty foyer fills up with smoke, ash, and dirt. She breathes in and out repeatedly, inhales the airborne motes. They cling to her lungs as she pushes a final time, feels her body clench and release.

> ~~Amanda Jane Ellsworth is born.~~
> ~~Allison Jennette Ellsworth is born.~~
> ~~Arthur John Ellsworth is born.~~

A breeze blows through a splintered window and across the face of an exhausted family. Frank DiGrossi, age 35, father, Elanore DiGrossi, age 33, mother, Vincent DiGrossi, age 6, Benicio DiGrossi, age 8, and Isabella DiGrossi, age 12, stir, but do not wake. It is the first time they have slept in a week.

Jessica Anne Ellsworth, age 42, dies.

Henry Rockler, age 53, ex-marathon runner, sprints across cracked and broken pavement. He is chased by three men (Javier Martinez, age 27, revolutionary, William "Will" Cartwright, age 32, revolutionary, and Vanessa Hilldebrandt, age 29, revolutionary), all wearing black jackets and bright green bandanas covering their faces. He ignores the stitch in his side and continues to run in long, even strides. He empties his mind and forgets they are there and utilizes the adrenaline efficiently.

~~Unnamed is born.~~

Javier Martinez, age 27, William "Will" Cartwright, age 32, and Vanessa Hilldebrandt, age 29, stop as the runner turns the next corner. A shot echoes from off the buildings around the corner.

Henry Rockler, age 53, dies.

Marla Hemming, age 47, thief, and Robert Hemming, age 49, thief, force their way into an empty penthouse apartment. The furniture is ripped apart. Scattered bits of stuffing lay across the floor. None of the windows are broken; the air is still and quiet in the apartment. Upon exploring the rest of the level, they find the previous owner. He hangs from the ceiling, a leather belt tight around his neck.

Amanda Jane Ellsworth, newborn, dies.

Allison Jennette Ellsworth, newborn, dies.

Arthur John Ellsworth, newborn, dies.

Keira Spinoza, age 22, unemployed, leaves her dying father and heads to the underground library below the center of the city. She navigates the hidden path through the rubble and trash (made to look random) and heads deep into the underground parking garage. She plays the future in her head, over and over again, wondering what it will feel like to be blown apart.

Jeremiah Clinton, age 12, boy, Yusef Mondavi, age 14, boy, and Hazel Etting, age 13, girl, corner a wounded dog in an alley. The dog is backed against a fence, shivering and whimpering. The children take turns shooting at the dog with Jeremiah's father's stolen pistol. They laugh with each ricochet as the dog whimpers and barely howls. Hazel Etting finally shoots the dog, laughs, and the children run out of the alley. They leave the dog to die in its own blood.

You haven't slept in weeks. A quick nap in a dark corner, hoping the black shields you from the bombs and bullets, but then awakened by the earth moving and shaking and soon you're on the run again in search of sanctuary. You are a nomad in a city you've lived all your life, a gypsy of the refugee marketplace. The cloying smell of smoke and retribution clings to clothing, unwashed for days. You are the key witness to the end of the world.

Keira plays the future in her head, over and over again, wondering what it will feel like to be blown apart. She is not afraid of the force with which her fingers will come off her hands, or her hands from her wrists, or her arms from the rest of her – she is excited by the prospect. She will touch them all, will stain each of them with a wall of blood, thousands of single drops will anoint every forehead and each fluttering bit of parchment. She wonders if it is natural to be this calm in the face of a death chosen rather than that of a death imposed.

The so-called historians would wake the next morning, shaken, and in the changing of clothes they would spy the crimson along the shirt collar or the seam of canvas pants. Tiny, almost missed. But it would remind them of her and soon the ringing echo of compressed thunder would return to them. They would remember.

You Are the Key Witness to the End of the World

Her father said the blast would expand upward and out, so her decapitation would be quick; she wouldn't even feel the rest of her body scatter across the library. *They will wear your memory like weighted reap charms hung tight around their necks,*' he said, his fingers deftly fiddling with the final touches of the device. *'If they continue to live after, they will remember this day as the blackest one. It will poison every other thought they have and you will be the epicenter. You will have left your mark on their books in ways previously unimagined. I will always have you here,*' he said, pointing to his heart, *'but* they *will always have you here.'* He pointed to his head and smiled.

And now? Now she holds the device close to her chest, like a secret bundle of wires and fluid and a strange kind of hope. Her father had wrapped it up like the swaddling of a toy doll, but she can feel its rough edges scraping against the callused flesh of her palms through the makeshift blanket, young hands so used to the gravity of reclaiming a world.

'Soft work begets soft people,' he always said, and oh how she had worked. When the fire came, when it turned the sky a permanent blood-orange, she tried to keep the home clean. Rubble littered their lawn. Chunks of concrete had landed on their roof, tore holes in the shingles and sat in the attic until she moved each piece from attic to living room to yard. Some were the size of her head while others required her father's help in getting them outside. For months they toiled, trying to

keep the inside cleared of any reminder of the atrocities raging outside. Always in silence, always at night and never with so much as a match to see by.

A thick layer of dust coated every surface in the house. They tried early on to feather-dust often, but it became overbearing, took up too much time of days already too short for living. Her father told her to stop, said *'It's too much, Keira. We do not live to clean, we live to live.'* And so she had stopped the dusting, but not the clearing of rocks and small boulders which now covered the lawn in intentionally random ways to mislead those that might walk by. Drawing attention to oneself was the fastest and easiest way to meet death.

As the violence moved closer to them, the neighborhood emptied. Whole families picked up, moved on, left behind pictures and remnants of lives they would never return to, lives they would reminisce about until their final hollow gasp. At night, Keira and her father would sneak out and pilfer what they needed from the empty homes. Jugs of boiled water, canned goods, weapons, batteries. Scraps of clothing, jackets, belts, tools. Dead animals, skinned and roasted, when rations ran low and hard to find, though they did this reluctantly.

'They won't return,' he told her with a solemnity she didn't understand at the time. *'None of them will come back. What*

was theirs is now ours.' She thought him cold then, unfeeling. She knew now he had been sad in his pragmatism, that he hated how easily the words came tumbling out of his mouth. *'History and her keepers have turned their backs on us when we needed them most. It's time we made them listen again. It's time we let them know they're no longer needed. The recording of time has become irrelevant. No one will look back to the past and wonder what happened to us, they will always look forward. Yesterday is frivolous, tomorrow is survival.'*

And so she walks, making sure to keep her footsteps light on the fractured concrete of the parking garage. Ten levels down until the stairwell appears; she bounds down each flight of stairs, red security lights flooding every floor as if someone has already bathed themselves in blast here. She is bolstered by the illusion. It is a sign that what she is doing is right, is necessary. A joyless smiles plays across her lips as she comes to the final floor.

The heavy metal door creaks open, long gone without grease or oil to still its voice. *'Once you're down there, don't worry about making noise,'* her father said. *'It will just be you and them. If you've made it to the bottom of the stairwell, and I have no doubt you will, the rest is easy.'* He had kissed her forehead, cried and smiled, then released her into the world, hopeful.

The hallway is empty, dark. One long hallway stretching down for what seemed like miles. It is dimly lit by electric light between each of the shelves which stand just above twelve feet tall. The tomes are all the same size (a foot tall, a foot wide, four inches thick) and fit perfectly onto each shelf with enough space at the top to remove them. She wonders how many of them have actually been read.

The spines of each book are a deep blood red with three gold rings splayed across; one at the top, one in the middle, one at the bottom. They are covered in the deep black lettering of roman numerals and dead Latin phrasing, words and numbers she does not understand, has never seen before.

She walks, lets her fingers run along the spines on her right. She sniffs the air and smiles; dry, brown, brittle. Perfect for the fire that is sure to consume. She wonders how quickly the leather will burn. The pages will erupt quickly, charring between the covers and spreading fast down each wall. Her father had said as much and she believes him now.

After a half-hour of walking, she comes to a meeting of hallways. All four directions are covered in books and shelves. The ends of each direction cannot be seen, they all end in fuzzy darkness. Keira stands in the middle, confused. Which way is she supposed to go now?

'Let me be clear,' her father said. *'Don't worry about the men. I've been told the place is a maze, so it will be up to you at that point as to where to give your sendoff. This is why it's important that*

your mind be free of any distractions while you're down there. If you do this right, you will have wiped out the unredeemable past completely. If there is to be a future for our people, we must wipe the record of our deeds clean. Start over anew. Springtime for the world.'

A maze. It was hard to tell how the walls moved down here, even though they'd all been straight up to this moment. Was the stairwell the only way out? She looks back the way she came, to the left, to the right, then forward. Four paths, all covered in paper and leather, aching to be burned. She imagines the pages inside begging to be put asunder, wanting to blacken.

She unwraps the device, lets the blanket fall to the floor, plugs in the final coiled wire. *'I love you, daddy,'* she says and flips the switch.

Keira Spinoza, 22, dies.

Marina, Patina, Corona

A shellacked cathedral sits on a cliff overlooking a dirty ocean. A single bell tower juts up into the midnight sky, an admonishing finger to the heavens that have let this house of God come under such disrepair. A lone figure in tattered, dirty robes roams about, sweeping and polishing, praying and keeping the grounds to the best of his ability while keeping counsel with himself. No one visits anymore; no one comes to pay their respects. The world no longer bows to any deity. It is nearly time for the midnight tolling. He climbs the dirty stairwell, a broom slung over his shoulder, to keep the tradition of the midnight chime.

"Kiss the ruin. Taste the brimstone of the soul's exodus from the stem. Leave a carcass of legacy. If the bad memory comes, talk it down, crush it, tamp it out. A soul cleansed is a soul saved. Only He that is shall ever be."

He only exists in your mind. He never was.

"Bah!"

Each robed leg swish-swishes up the concrete stairs that spiral upwards toward the belfry. Dirt and rubble lay strewn about the stairwell and his sandals, beat and torn as they are, kick the detritus around, settle it elsewhere. The soles crunch on pebbles blown off and in from the buttresses above. The wind continues to erode loose rock from the holes left by mortar rounds and grazing bullets, so the broom became his *aide-de-camp* each night. Slow motions from left to right, right to left, all the way down from the pinnacle of the tower, cleaning each step.

There are twenty ogee-style arches along the stairwell, each opening up onto the watery vista. Tiny portals that let the ocean air, once fresh and crisp, permeate the stairwell. He stops halfway up to look out onto the placid water. During the day it is a murky reddish-orange, but tonight it is as black as the world surrounding the moon's ghostly aura, itself reflected in the dark below like a molding fruit.

"Take apart the man and his world goes brittle. We are all slivered shards, glinting in the devil's eye, wanting to be put whole again. Take apart the world…"

You're talking rubbish again.

"Cry foul!

Another brick has fallen from the wall, whether by wind or by gravity's silent hand. He bends over slowly, feeling the ache at the base of his spine shoot up to his neck, and moves the weather-worn material out of his way. When the first few bricks had fallen, he had moved them to the inside, fashioning a kind of blockade against the open shaft, but when one fell and nearly struck him dead months ago, he spent an entire day shoving them all against the wall. It left precious little room for his feet as the tower continued to crumble, but at least he wouldn't get brained by one now.

Marina, Patina, Corona

"Death comes not on the cawing of crows, but on the breath of the sparrow. Its feathers carry souls forever and beyond. That is the wind of the eternal liar in your hair, on your lips, whispering in your ears. It is not the voice you seek."

Your mind is a terrible thing to taste. It leaves a tongue wilted and sour.

He shakes his head as if to expunge the voice like water from a drowned ear. Another row of steps and the Godbell will be in reach. Another precious few moments (his skin tingles at the prospect, limbs quivering with every step) and he will hold the fat rope between his hands, feel its weight against his palms. He burns for the burn the twine will give his fingers by the twelfth ring as it sounds off across the cityscape and out across the choppy ocean water.

Another labored step up, then another until he steps up into midnight. The dais directly below the bell is windy from the openings on every side. His robe whips around his legs, tangling around his knees like a sea of fabric. The wind dies down briefly and he hears (imagines?) a knocking from deep below the stairwell. A muffled voice echoes up the tower chamber, but he cannot hear what it says.

It's just me.

"No. It is the haunt of humanity come to repent, come to save its already lost soul."

Marina, Patina, Corona

It is your doubt come to collect; your fragile disbelief has found you hidden away in a house you've hidden for too long.

"Let the shadows come, then. I have not hidden; I taste no fear of my end."

You are imagining the things you desire. You are frail, an old man whose body and mind are slowly being erased, deleted from...

"Enough! Decorum and tradition beckon."

His gnarled hands grip the thick, fraying rope. His palms are calloused from years of this duty, pulling down the great weight of the Godbell as it swings back and forth, a pendulum of sound that echoes out across the water and toward a city full of dead parishioners. He does not care how loud the bell rings, only that it does and continues while it's in his power to do so. The ringing is long and sonorous. It reverberates across the fractured cityscape, through broken windows and boarded up doors, across rubble-littered fields and around blackened cars with no wheels. If there are still people walking those nightmare avenues, he has never seen them. They never came to ask where God went when their worlds fell into decay.

*   *   *

The shivers overtake Joseph Malle. This close to the ocean, his skin prickles in need of warmth and cover from the wind, but he's not sure if it's the wind or the ache (the absolute *need*) for another poke that makes his body tremble incessantly. He can feel the bile puckering up the back of his throat like a thirst. His fingers seem to have disconnected from his brain; they do a dance beyond his hands' controls. He is the addiction marionette's puppet now. He is scatter-shot, limbs and desires push-pulled into fifty different directions that feel wrong. *This is what they warned us about,* he thinks. *This is why they were so adamant about us understanding the sickness that follows.*

He stumbles down the street, right hand against the rough brick façade beside him. His paramedic's uniform is filthy; frayed cuffs on each pant leg from the dogs he barely outran; other grime caked along his back and chest from landing on the other side of the high wire fence that was his escape; the white is brownish-grey now. The smell of his exertion surrounds him like filthy aura, pickles his nose.

The streets have been quiet for too long, eerie in their unwillingness to elicit anything other than silence. Sounds that used to echo seem to die against the walls that still stand erect up into the evening sky. Why he'd even bothered becoming a paramedic is a mystery; he knew there'd be no need when the world started to sour, but still he'd learned the ways. What else was there to do when the rest of the population ran away from the city? When those that remained were too infirm to leave or too young to care about the penalties for looting and murdering.

He turns his head and retches against the wall, sick spraying against the bottom of his pant legs. The warmth of it covers his ankle and slides down into his shoe. *So…this is what the bottom feels like.*

He continues on, skirting the walls as he makes his way to the church. Through the silence, the bells had always rang out, had always given their siren song to the dying city with a regularity that felt off in a place where the new normal was without boundaries, without anything to hold on to for balance.

Only a few more blocks, he thinks, the phrase even seeming breathless in his mind. *If only mother could see me now, I bet she would laugh and say, "What did I tell you? If only you'd listened." Typical.*

Mother had been one of the last to leave, unwilling to part with the home she'd grown up in, unwilling to part with the home in which she'd raised her own family. As the riots started, he was the one that left the barricaded house to find food and supplies, bringing them back with an extra bruise or extra cuts along bare skin, the mark of ash or dust across his face. She refused to leave, even so she could live, so he had gone in her place.

He turns to retch again. There is nothing left in his stomach but hot bile and it comes out hesitantly, never giving the pleasure of full release. Over and over again, little driblets coming out in spurts before he wipes his mouth and moves on.

The one day, that final day, he'd come back from a supply run to find the house concave, blown in, blackened with scorch marks and small flames licking the shutters like living decoration. He had been gone too long; she had been taken or crushed by the weight of the roof. Either way, he would never find her again. He walked by the house as if it weren't his own, scanning the street for movement before slipping into one that had been abandoned months previous. What was a home anyway other than a place to sleep and eat?

That night, he lay awake, unable to stop wondering where she had gone or if she had died. The question hung above his makeshift bed on the couch and kept him from slipping into dreams. He got up; the moon outside was high and the church had rung its bells an hour or so previous. One in the morning. Hopefully those left pillaging the city fell under sleep's charm too.

He scurried down the street, keeping to the shadows of the darkened houses. The char of his own filled his nose as he got closer. The roof had fallen in, but the front door hung aslant; the living room seemed relatively untouched, all things

Marina, Patina, Corona

considered. His black paramedic bag remained beneath the end-table.

Another retch at the memory of the smell. Another retch at finding his mother crushed beneath the dining room chandelier, covered in fragments of ceiling and broken picture frames, curled wall-paper and splintered furniture.

He had grabbed the bag, held it close to his chest. He held it close enough to feel the stiff glass bottles and tools beneath its leathery surface and ran back to the place where he now stayed.

And now? Now he wishes he'd never gone back into that blown out bit of home. Now he wishes he'd never opened the bag. Now he wishes there is actually someone up there ringing the bell twice a day, for he has finally made it to the church and slumps against its heavy oaken door, banging and screaming for help like he is at the gates of heaven themselves demanding entry and forgiveness as the bells ring out across the vacant city.

*   *   *

His robes swish around his legs as he walks down the spiral staircase, using the broom as a makeshift walking stick for support. *Thunk, swish, step, step. Thunk, swish, step, step.* This is the sound of movement in the belfry, the sound of finished work, the ritual leading up to the resting of head on pillow, of body on firm and unblanketed cot. Like other nights, he will shiver himself to sleep, believing it to be a penance, and wake up body-weary and sore, but forced to rise and move. The soreness is expected, is relished the way only blessed pain can be by those that seek the true word. The knocking comes again, louder, reverberating through the sanctuary, echoing deep against the stone walls that remain intact.

Hear that, friar? Your deliverance at the door. The horseman for your head!

"Silence! You are but a figment, a wisp, a dream gone sour and blackened."

Another knock, an echo.

(*an echo, an echo*)

He stops, believing he imagines the knock-knock-knocking at the door to be of his own delusion. The knocking does not come again and silence fills the giant halls of the cathedral. Ocean wind and moonlight spill through the cracks and crevices of the rooftop and the shellacked walls outside. A softened black permeates, cocoons the God-fearing caretaker in strange ways that he has become accustomed to despite the voices.

What…you think you are safe here? That this is sanctuary because you believe it to be so?

Marina, Patina, Corona

"Faith makes it sanctuary. Belief is caked in the brick and stone and mortar that surround, that create the frame."

You are a fool. Your holy house is ruined and keeps out nothing.

He brushes the voices away, swats at the air and shuffles forth through the darkness, knowing these halls intimately, knowing he could wander them blind and find his way without fail. A tiny smile plays across his face as he realizes this is the perfect metaphor for his faith, for what he has devoted his life to. For *who* he has devoted his life to.

He looks up and sees the great stars twinkle through the roof. The constellations had long gone askew, changed their shape and the midnight sky, their forms and names no longer important or relevant. Everything had changed so quickly and with so much violence. Man had set out to conquer the world and the universe had fought back. He doubted there was anyone left who could actually read the stars anyway.

You were all fools.

"Not I," the friar says to the empty cathedral, his voice bouncing off the walls. "I could see their wrong, I could see the endgame from my belfry and wanted nothing of it."

Do nothing, do everything. The damage done remains the same either way.

Marina, Patina, Corona

"The children of chaos begat the children of ruin begat the children of the days where the morning begins with the sound of whoremoan and the rush of dead souls creeping on the wind, aching to leave but unable. Hell is not nearly half-full and yet the souls continue swarming in by the thousands."

The voice he has become so familiar with does not reply, has no barbed and pointed response to give the friar in the dark. He shuffles through the dark to his room where he lays down on the bare mattress and shivers himself to sleep.

*

Morning comes. The friar rises and makes a meager meal of hardboiled egg and rotting toast, washes both down with weak coffee that tastes bitter and foul. The water supply has started to foul up now too and he simply accepts it to be the truth.

He sweeps the great cathedral hall, taking his time to get every corner. But why? When nature pours through every crevice in the building and coats the floor again, why does he stay firm in his ritual?

Because ritual is what one does. Ritual is truth and conviction.

Marina, Patina, Corona

Sunlight breaks, appears scattershot upon the great stone walls, reflected down in color from the remaining stained-glass images perched in lofty stalls that ring the entire cathedral hall. Bright shards of biblical scenes light up the stone in ways that make him smile.

A gust of wind rushes through the cathedral, whips his robe against his legs.

The great door of the cathedral creaks open slowly, a heavy weight slumped against it slides down and onto the vestibule's stone floor. The briny ocean air is sucked into the room and masks the smell coming off of the stranger, but the friar knows all the signs of fever and sickness and death. He knows what smells to expect from the dying body. They all smelled the same anymore, each one riding the needle off into the sunset as if the poke were some great savior from the madness that was the now, each one wearing the diseased track marks in the crooks of their arms like some angered proof of their existence.

He is awash with guilt and sadness, now knowing that last night's knocking was not, as he believed, a figment of his imagination, but the last act of a dying man in need of help. Whether the friar could have given him what he needed is a point not worth mulling over. Now, however…it was his duty to give last rites, to send this man's soul on to wherever it was destined.

Marina, Patina, Corona

There's nothing you can do for him now. You let him die on your god's doorstep. You are a nothing veiled in falsity.

The friar drags the man's body into the cavernous room and struggles to shut the large cathedral door against the morning, its angry reddish glare penetrating the pockmarked walls of the cathedral, muted red dots spread across the inner sanctum like a celestial rash.

He shuffles over to an old finery closet, rummages through it with shaking hands, and finds brittle, holey robes eaten by moths and time. They will suffice. Within the bundle he buries rosewater and incense, ready to pray across the man's body. He carries the bundle back to the body and dumps it all to the floor, unraveling it and spreading the cloth out.

Falling to his knees, older and arthritic now, he rolls the young man's body over onto the cloth and begins wrapping the corpse in the sheeting, neatly folding and tightening the fabric around his feet, then his legs, and finally around his chest. There is no reason for him to leave the young man's face exposed, but he does so anyway.

More will come to die on your doorstep.

The friar swats the words away as he dusts the covered body with incense.

More will come to take your time, to take your patience.

Marina, Patina, Corona

The friar ignores the words as he flicks rosewater up and down the length of the corpse, the smell mingling with that of the incense and bringing a new, fresh aroma to the vestibule. It will not completely cover the decay sure to arise later, but it will help.

More will come, they always do.

The friar sighs and leans back on his knees, benedictioning himself before speaking. "If desire is the knife upon which the heavy heart sits precarious, then the heart that sits atop it is scarred indeed. May you travel onward without desire and a heart made light by the Lord."

The voice laughs in his ears, a hoarse, raspy sound that seems to have no beginning or end. The friar presses on, reciting the burial rites as it echoes inside his mind.

"Almighty God, who hast knit together thine elect in one communion and fellowship, in the mystical body of thy Son Christ our Lord: Grant, we beseech thee, to thy whole Church in paradise and on earth, thy light and thy peace. Amen.

"Grant that all who have been baptized into Christ's death and resurrection may die to sin and rise to newness of life, and that through the grave and gate of death we may pass with Him to our joyful resurrection. Amen."

Ah, yes, men. What joy they've reaped upon the world you see with your own eyes.

Marina, Patina, Corona

The friar kisses his balled fist and benedictions the body, opens his hand and runs it down the stilled features of the man's face as if to calm him for the long celestial journey ahead, one the friar hopes to make himself once his earthly duties have been deemed complete.

He stands, kisses his fist again, and shuffles off to retrieve the rolling cart from the antechamber beyond. He pushes it into the vestibule, its old wheels clicking and clacking across the stone floor, echoing up and out into the rest of the cathedral and drowning out the voice humming just below the surface.

With great effort, he maneuvers the body up onto the cart and pushes it slowly through the maze-like halls of the cathedral, each one darker than the one before the deeper he goes, the lights having long ago been snuffed out. But he knows the way, has made this trip too many times over the years, has done this chore too often.

Soon, a light appears at the end of the final turn in the halls. The cart squeaks and thunks as he pushes on and out into the glaring red light of the day. The hallway spills out onto a well-worn path in the grass that leads up to the edge of the cliffs overlooking the tumultuous sea below. With great effort, he pushes the body-laden cart up to the edge and stops.

Marina, Patina, Corona

The raging waters far below bubble up and crash against the rock face, sending spray towards him, splatter his robes. He says another prayer, sings a burial song for the fallen, and tilts the cart onto its side. The stranger's linen-wrapped body falls over the edge, disappears into the surf and, the friar hopes, is taken far out with the tide to be buried with the army of others he's had to dump out into the deep since the world turned rotten. The ocean as cemetery, the ocean a disguise to hide the sins of the souls left to rot at its bottom.

Why do you even bother? Why do you stay? Why do you not let them pile up at the doorstep of 'His' house?

Because ritual is what one does. Ritual is truth and conviction, the friar thinks as he pushes the cart back toward the cathedral.

Marina, Patina, Corona

Only So Far

This was when
the world was burning…

First came color. Mighty, multi-hued oaks grew
overnight. The scattered shard of stained-glass window had
turned to drip in the bake of over-violet sun, melting and
melding into the thirsting, bony-fingered roots of struggling
saplings. The liquified remains of Christs and Marys and
saints and sinners all pooled up on dying fields, becoming
one and the same, swirled into each other above loamy
topsoil, a vision of pooled vertigo.

Amaranthine red, carmine pink, the deep blue of
midnight's silence, emerald, mint, ochre, and onyx filled the
brittle bark veins that snaked up weak limbs held out as if
asking for rain that hadn't come in months.

Soon after, the fragile limbs fell to earth and spilled
their *colorsapblood* like secrets across cracked pavement and
brown grass. Rotting fruit remained hanging, calcified and
petrified, split open upon striking ground. Each broken piece
contained abalone swirl, each section a stone whirlwind of
shine and gleam. The pericarp, the septum, the loculus pulp
all glimmer and shine in the overbearing daylight. Incredible,
inedible. A feast for eyes, but not for belly.

The oceans receded slowly at first, relieving
themselves of dying fish on sandy beaches at low tide. Lakes

dried up, withered like aged skin, left carcasses of once moaning frogs and the silent shells of tortoise. Yellow heat had touched the world with sickness, had parched its skin and kept on, burning out the retinas of the few who'd tired of dying slow and ached for natural wither. The freedom in death was stronger than the prison of living.

This was when
the red fire of the east coast
danced a cross-continental lambada
with the yellowed smoke of the West Coast...

Televisions sang lullabies of black static and white noise. No reports, no warnings, no sirens, just the hum of *harpsong* through speakers set up hastily on street corners and meeting places, on street lamps and roving garbage trucks. The pluck of harp strings was quiet in the beginning – soft, soothing – but had come to scratch like nails along the metal of our ears.

The harp sounded, another block destroyed.

The harp sounded, another hundred people missing.

The harp sounded, but only after the explosions.

The harp sounded, and sounded, and sounded...

Until it became a thing to drown out, to ignore. No longer a symbol of calm, the harp came to be its own angel of death, waging war on senses and gonging long into the night like a death knell on repeat.

We could hear it reverberate through our teeth and in our dreams as we wept over oceans we could see, but could not reach. The ringing caused waves to swell and strike beaches cluttered with cans and plastic, sloughed skin and dying birds, eyeless heads of fish and kelp the color of melt. Each ring of strings sent us into convulsions, made our insides shake, liquified our cellular structures and controlled us from the inside.

Sunsets ceased to be, never came, never left. Perpetual bright on every horizon; dull red to the west, gaseous yellow to the east. We wondered if we were the orange middle of everything. We wondered if everyone else heard harps before dying too. We wondered if, once planted in the earth, we would still hear them long after death. Would our ears cake up with dirt and earthworm and maggot and rot and harp?

Strangers came from both sides, holed up in empty houses, made homes of hollow, nests of leftovers, wanting to live in our orange. The orange was getting smaller, crushed in from outside. Strangers slept atop us, piled up in rooms one on top of one on top of another like human bunk-beds. Soon no one could sleep through the always *harpsong*.

This was when
the screams of Boston
sounded like the screams of Atlanta
sounded like the screams of Houston
sounded like the screams of Seattle
and everyone burned the same...

Twelve hours, fourteen hours, seventeen hours a day; the sun kept constant vigil over the earth's browning surface. Ground split, cracked, dried up like skin set to be leathered.

The thirsty sucked final drops from spigots and wells, lay beneath open taps with dried and wishing mouths open, sucked dry every bottle at every gas station and grocery store before they ever had time to store them up in bunkers. The hot came too fast and within a week had allowed only a single hour of moonlight every day. For twenty-three hours, the world baked without reprieve. No way to turn off the oven, no way to keep cool.

Basements became as hot as lawns, but there was warm shade. Whole families curled up in dark corners, like vampires hiding from the yellowed-world. They slept fitfully, sweating together against the walls that seemed to bow inward from the heat, the home in slickery melt around them. Brother smelled like sister smelled like father smelled like mother, their tears becoming sweat, their sweat becoming sticky.

The metal of the family car crinkled, smooshed, pancaked into a goopy driveway mess of paint, rust, and rubber. Oil snaked out from the puddle and into the street, a black slither that stunk up the neighborhood and fouled the air with putrefaction. This was the new pollution, the earth was all heat-melt.

The house sank. Soil crawled through brittle foundation, buried some alive, still curled up in their corners hiding from the daylight. Earthworms slinked across cobwebbed basements in search of moisture, found none, dried up like twigs along windowsills and doorways.

This was when
skin boiled, flaked, and flew into the skies
mixed with the ash and sparse rain
that never seemed to be enough...

If left out in the sun too long, a person's skin sloughed off, fell to the ground, lay puddled up and stinking in the lawn like old deli meat. There was no burn, only melt and puddle. Like a pile of human there in the grass, folded in upon itself and melting together as if under heat lamps.

Rain showed its wet face again. Brief and taunting, a quick minute of downpour surprised us over and over again. We sat in darkened doorways, staring up at skies that promised only ashen snowfall. We emaciated, dry, stick figures stood in silence, mouths upturned, drinking past the ash that collected on lips and tongues, stuck to lips like lover's kisses we no longer wanted. The ash was briny, bitter to the taste, a sour death upon the palate. It was the taste of neighbors, their children, the taste of strangers sun-baked and withered and picked up by uncaring gusts of wind and dust and carried up into what atmosphere remained.

We could taste their religion and their fear.

We could taste their passion and their dreams.

We could taste their silence and their screams.

We tasted air and death, waited for the sky to open up and fill our bellies with drink, soak our faces and bodies in wet. Green clouds turned brown, swirled menacing but still the sun penetrated. And still we stood in doorways and watched our arms and legs drift off in pieces of tallow skin, never to be seen again until landing on another's tongue across the city.

Would that they could taste my religion and my fear.

Would that they could taste my passion, my dreams.

Would that they could taste my silence since I refuse to scream.

This was when
the sun's settings and risings
were at their most vibrant,
but no one had the time to stop and watch;
they feared being gobbled up
by its clumsy, earthly protégés...

Some learned to speak the language of fire, spoke in
tongues of flame, tasted heat and ate in hellish burn. Their
voices were ash and soot, their eyes betraying *hyperviolence*,
their fingers twitching and in need of heat. Nimble with wires
and timers, hands flew across containers and tape and bits of
nail and screw, ball bearings and hurt compacted into hand-
sized packages. Some learned to harness anger and madness
in the time of anger and madness.

The silence before the booms made tension, crackled
up spines, up into craniums, tickled nervous systems in
awkward ways. Little spurts of voltage climbing up backs and
muscle. The sound of nothing echoed off long-empty
basketball courts and cul-de-sacs, vacant apartment buildings
and businesses already half-blown to char. The air was fat
with possibility; death hung like fog across neighborhoods.

Uncle got caught in the beginning. No one could tell
amongst all the rubble, but he stepped wrong on a trashcan
lid, became supernova there in the middle of the street. He
became starlight, orange and white, smoke and flame, alpha
and omega all in an instant. We never knew who left that one

for him to find, but it didn't matter. Soon, everyone was a firebug. Everyone had a missing limb, a missing friend or relative, a missing pet; all blown skyward and scattered across a dying city, little clouds of flesh and red. We were all part-phantom.

Mother became martyr. Weary of hiding, we strapped flame to her body, hid it beneath fabric finery, robes, a t-shirt from my childhood. She called out to them, they came, surrounded her, smelled her as victim as she feigned fear. They circled, grinned. Saliva dripped from snarling lips, blackened fingers reached out to grab her.

She did not scream. She did not flinch. In the moment before loudest silence, they saw the fire in her eye, turned to run, felt the ground shake beneath them as she unleashed her own Prometheus valentine upon them. The streets are quieter now. The city naps longer and so do we.

*This was when
everyone's lips cracked,
when sleeping in a full bathtub
seemed logical...*

When the constellations reappeared, they were askew. None were recognizable anymore though no one could remember their original positions. We just knew. Ursa major was a cluster of gleam, Cassandra shined black - obsidian. Libra leaned heavy to one side, Taurus became a mewling calf.

We drank soured milk, thirsted for the clump, became ravenous for *greenmoldbread*. Pus dripped from sores at the corners of our mouths and rot replaced enamel. The skin hung from our bones, oozed and peeled and left in heavy footprints behind us. We were walking dead, too weak to run from the fire that was surely on its way to consume us. We could see its phosphorescent glow beyond the mountains on either side.

Our ribs were song-less xylophones, our fingers frail tools corroding, breaking down into slender maim. We never felt the blood dribble out and off the fingertips. Never felt our hands go numb from loss. Our lungs sang in whistles and breathlessness. When the fire came, we could only stand and watch.

The porcelain protected. Too slow to get out of the way, we turned our makeshift houses into battlements; metal sheeting around the sides, slathered in creams and frozen. We hid in bathtubs, their slickery white an armor against the laughing, dancing flames that rose up over mountain ranges and sprinted across *deadgrassfields*, hungry just to burn.

Thin and frail, we all fit in the tub together, me and son and daughter. Like sardines, staring up through holes in the roof at cloudless sky. The fire ate around us, over us, singed bits of hair and parts of diseased skin. I wondered why the moon smiled down at us. I wondered when we last smiled. The fire passed, turned brown fields to black, left in smoking ruin. Still the moon smiled.

This was when
everyone ran
towards the middle of the country,
clamored over mountains and
fought over soon-to-be dry rivers…

I awoke from a dead dream, full of nothing white and soft ringing. Hands reached out to me from the ether, tugged, pulled, pushed, waved off. They laid their hands on, cupped my face and twirled my hair, ran fingers over my eyes and touched gray matter through the crevices. The voice of rotting angels made love to my ears, filled me with cold and want, pimpled the skin on my arms, whispered that it wasn't my time, that I was time, that time was all I had left. It was the most touch I had felt since ever. I wanted to stay. I wanted to remain in someone else's cold grasp.

I awoke in a field, a bed of burned grass beneath me, stiff stems of char my pillow. Ashen scars covered exposed skin like I was sacrifice. The sun's corona bled through the black clouds above, burned its image against my eyelids, kept shining when eyes closed. I saw the earth in circles, each object magnified by this new corona-sight. Everything was rounded, shaped, curved into itself over and over again, never breaking the rim. The oily clouds above parted, spilled red light onto the surface, covered us all in hot, broiled the ground. Some died of heat-stroke. Others wished they had.

I awoke sheathed in metal, hot from the sun and smoke clamoring towards the mountainside. The ranges were visible; snow-capped pyramids in the distance. I wondered if I could remember ever seeing snow. It was so white. I could only remember red and yellow, orange, black, gray, dust, char. White was a nothing color, snow was a nothing thing. I could see it, so I could touch it and if I could touch it, then I could taste it. The metal got heavy and I moved again, plodded towards the mountains.

I awoke in melt, snow dripping down my scarred skin. I had packed myself away in ice, hoped to avoid the mob racing to the top of the screaming mountain. I had covered myself in snow-crystal, waited, watched through the magnification and replication of molecules, like spider's eyes, as their heavy feet thudded over me like thunder. I was thirsty, drank from the walls of my hiding place, remembered the names of my children as the fluid coated my throat, wept at how things had become and drank those tears as well.

Only So Far

I awoke in bombed-out shed. A concrete structure bathed in graffiti and old lives I could smell as if they were standing right beneath my nose. Rubble coated the floor, dust and mud covered the shattered windows that remained. In the moment, I felt new and clean. No one else had found it yet and I claimed it as mine. Snow-chill wafted through crevices, crept up legs, tickled hair and skin, reminded me of its constancy. They had not come yet, but someone would come across my place (*my* place!) at some point. Would that I could fight to keep it. Would that I could fight to stand any longer. Would that someone would simply end me and let me pass on.

This was when
an untouched field of wheat
was a danger instead of a way to feed...

We awoke in drown, lungs full of flood. Restless, placental. We floated in the home, watched our life swim by and sink below us. Fractured picture frames, unpaid bills, the family pet, good china, building blocks, a dimly lit lamp still plugged into the rotting wall, glowing beneath the surface. The brick house eroded from the inside, the insulation tearing like dead tissue.

Our bodies filled, bloated, dead whitened. Fingers plumped like sausage, broke wedding rings. Shirts stretched, tore, ripped with the sound of soft breath and broken lover's hearts. On the wall: the children's heights, marked in pencil and pen, slowly being erased. I screamed at the vanish, inhaled more water, forgot the names of my children.

The wall clock cracked under pressure. The big hand between twelve and one, the little hand hung limp in the current, swinging between five and seven. We could hear the chimes faintly through the water, fighting tide and flow.

Water filled my orifices; clogged my nose, my ears, found ways past my eyes and filled my skull. I could feel me bubble up from inside, liquid fill rising. I heard the waves crash against the arterial walls inside me, collapsing against bloodlines and pumping organs. Water mixed with blood mixed with water mixed with blood.

The phone floated by. I put it to my ear, heard sea-sirens on the other end scream-whispering as if a universe away.

You have our deepest sympathies.
Our condolences.
You have such a lovely home.
The picture is heartbreaking.
Your clock is broken.
You are drowning.

The water kept me, floated me, bumped me into the ceiling and the chandelier and other furniture. I let the phone sink to the floor, watched its hypnotic drowning, a spiraling downward. My wife was sending the children up the chimney, motioned for me to join. I wouldn't fit and she knew it. Our eyes locked, our fishy lips locked, held each other until the bloat made that impossible and soon she was gone. I floated there in the quiet roar, watched our things float and sink, move and sway, before sitting in the chair still by the fireplace. I waited for the return I knew wasn't coming.

My skin began to prune, spoil, suck in on itself.

Only So Far

I waited.

This was when
the roads clogged with automobiles
full of gasoline, dormant and laying like a wet wick
across the world
ready to be lit by
the fires on either end...

The sign is portal, remnant history, memory leavings. Sun-faded red and black paint, the words indecipherable now. But we know the gist, we know the slant. The signs are nothing marks, near-prehistoric scribbles made by ancestors recently dead, paid for by ancestors recently dead, followed by ancestors recently dead.

Chunks of concrete where the road used to be. Chunks of buildings where our cities used to be. Chunks of bite where our skin used to be. The world halved, cleaved in two, the pieces falling into smoke and ruin. Char-rusted cars became playgrounds as we make-believed our way from the flood of flame behind us, crawled and jumped on exoskeletons made of Chrysler and Ford, Volkswagen and Audi, Honda and Fiat. What was left almost made us laugh in its obviousness; the world was here on the road, dead or dying. No country had escaped the burn; we all burned the same.

This was when
the explosions, like firecrackers,
started in Santa Barbara and Miami
and didn't sleep until
the last car had been
kissed with flame in Topeka weeks later...

Crushed by the waiting. No news came from anywhere, silence from the television, the radio. Papers had been hoarded, turned into a million wicks, gave us inky snow. Words curled in the air like frost breath:

> *Another fi*
> *highway shut-do*
> *ies on the brin*
> *no answers fr*
> *engulfe*
> *nic ensu*
> *e missi*
> *mass graves*

Someone had set the earth in revolt, tilted its axis askew, found the chip in its shoulder and dug fingers deep inside the undulating wound and kept digging until they finally scraped its heart raw. I hope they burned themselves in the process, lost hands to magma rising, core melt, lost self within the shifting plates because our hearts are made of dust now.

Only So Far

Dried out, crumbled, held in place by the fear that cocoons us. No one touches anymore. We hug for protection, not for affection. Held hands means helping someone run from the noise. Kisses are meant for the dead and the dying. Tradition, decorum, history…these are nothing words now.

Everywhere looks the same. Ash coats the air depressing gray. Our clouds are anemic, in need of sun and fresh air.

The world is arid and the sky thirsts the way we do.

This is when
we could see
flaming highways
from the heavens…

A postcard, still (unbelievably) stuck to a kitchen wall:

"Be glad you weren't here."

This was when
hiding out in open fields
made of burn and fallout
was our best solution...

A rabbit stared at us from its one remaining eye, as if to blame us for the one that dangled low from socket. Optic nerves kept it in hang, coated in blood-dried maroon and crust. No movement from his furred face or ears; whiskers limp and twitchless, one foot mangled from some other nameless terror. He hid beneath the porch, became family, eulogized with us but broke none of the bread we left out as apology.

It was the first animal we'd seen in forever. Pets had disappeared or died in waves; cats and dogs became vanish, song-less birds flew far out of eyesight, we were lucky to hear crickets over the destruction. Rivers and lakes were coated in dead fish, rot-float, glimmerless scales and scum. We took to eating root and plant, nut and berry where they hadn't mutated into things inedible. Our mouths tasted like earth, gaps in teeth filled with topsoil, blackened at the gums, ached for something juicy.

Our lips wetted over the rabbit. We hungered for a single leg of deer or frog. A sparrow would be feast in this moment, red breasted and roasted over ruby fire. Old meat in the pantry, spoiled and brown-rotted, but we ate it anyway.

Got sick on ourselves, sat around in wallow and filth. Felt the sick inside us, gnawing away at our insides and withering our bones to brittle.

I wondered if there would be future generations to excavate our bones and what they would think when they dug us up, great holes blown out of our skulls, our cheeks, our femurs and ribs. What will they think when our brittle bones dig up black instead of off-white? What will they think when they see whole families buried together, bones clung together as if to shield from blast? What kind of history will they put together from the stories that our bones tell them? Will they even care?

The rabbit moved from beneath the porch. We all gave chase.

This was when
we understood real fear
and ran away together...

They had warped. Neighbors had become fun-house mirrored versions of themselves, morphed into flat-faced reflections with no mouths and no noses. Their rheumy eyes stared out from skin web-cracked like divorce china or newly split earth. A small army stood at the foot of the porch, itself warped and cracked from rumblings deep beneath the foundation.

The stars fell to whisper. The neighbors breathed as one, rapid wheezy whistles, and stared. It was no use for us to hide behind tattered drapes; they smelled us inside, aware that we were whole and unmarred. They could smell our completeness, could hear our blood running quick beneath bruised and yellowed skin, pumped through better veins and aortas and arteries. Our living was loud, our lives were grate against whatever they had become.

Daughter clung to teddy behind the couch, crouched as if waiting for explosion. Son stood, shaking with eyes closed, on the other side of the window. Mother had passed already, falling into sickness before trying to claw her way through the walls in search of death's chariot.

The divots of her nails left tracks along the wall, the only physical proof of her travels, maps of her descent into

the virus. Bits of blood still splattered the once beige walls.
Bits of hair and nail, tears and dust, remained along the
floorboards.

Son stopped shaking. Daughter whimpered. Son
looked out the window, sighed and gripped the rebar tight,
white-knuckled around the rusted brown. Strength blazed
somewhere deep behind his pupils; something inside him had
caught fire and burned hot. We waited for them to
come…and then they did.

Trauerspielen (Mourning Plays)

He walks along the crater's edge, can feel its former heat glowing and filling him, penetrating and permeating his skin. The crater itself is deep and dark, a reminder of the concavity of man, the emptiness that comes and replaces selflessness so quickly and without apology. His ratty shoes, pockmarked with holes and crusted mud, skirt the talus-covered ground and send little rumblings of scree down the crater's slope. He watches the pebbles tumble down, each one racing after the others until finally they stop several hundred feet below, but nowhere near the center.

He lets his gaze wander; from the walls down to the epicenter, from the epicenter up to the far (much farther) crater's edge and up to the gray-black horizon. A small red dot, a dying sun, pierces through the haze as if to keep itself relevant to those that would search it out and ask it for answers. The man turns, takes in the wasteland around him slowly, without judgment, and sits. His legs dangle over the edge, heels against the rock face. As he watches the pinhole of sunlight sink and disappear, he thinks and dreams.

*   *   *

Scribbled on the concrete wall in neon yellow paint: "This is where you became something else."

Below that: "This is where we tried to stop you."

Trauerspielen (Mourning Plays)

Below that: A place for flowers and candles, notes of grieving and want. Images of the past, cut and pasted to the wall, are faded and torn by the elements. Beads hung draped over tarnished candelabras and framed pictures. Tokens of remembrance, unread letters filled with rage and questions.

On the ground: the place where tears fell and dried.

*   *   *

The child floated out to sea like some kind of Moses, some kind of Perseus, a sacrificial lamb given up to malevolent gods. The nubile skin drank of the sun, felt its warmth soaking every pore deeply, riding along his tiny veins and heating up the arterial passages far below the surface. What malevolence these gods had for men was for them alone; the child's skin remained a crisp, cool tone. Rosy blossoms of color sprouted on his cheeks, but only when he squinted up during the midday and cried with enough force to silence the gulls gliding by.

When night came, swallowed up the day, the infant's peals fell silent. The stars were lullaby, the moon a light to keep full darkness at bay. The soft lapping of waves below and around rocked the child into rhythmic slumber and gave way to dreams of unknown things with unknown names, all towering over the child like giants.

Trauerspielen (Mourning Plays)

*　　*　　*

A woman with wings and old, leathery skin whispers to him in the dark. Her breath, hot like ash, tickles the lobe and courses through his body like quickly moving fog. "This is how the world began," she says. "One breath spread across a nothing landscape, rolling up and over itself, curdling and giving life at the same time. Do you think it will end the same?"

He stands, unable to move, as if planted firmly in stiff molasses. He can hear the woman's lips at his ears, moist and dangerous; her breath even and measured. "You walk into the world alone, but leave carrying the ghosts of those who've already gone. How many more will you carry before the weight finally presses your face into the dead earth? You are no Charon."

She steps in front of him, looks him up and down before placing a gnarled finger against his chest. She pushes, he falls back into the smothering dark. Her voice, a whisper, fills his mind:

"Unburden yourself. Give up the ghosts."

Elsewhere, the world glistened tundra.

*　　*　　*

Trauerspielen (Mourning Plays)

She is motionless and underwater. The seaweed swirls around her with its tendril arms, wraps around her ankles and moves up, tightens around her thighs. Lilies blossom up from the tips, tickle her bare stomach and chest before opening up completely near her mouth. The petals quiver and slide against her lips; the stamen tickle her tongue. In the moment, she feels as if she is kissing the soul of her reflection. Petals are lips, lips are petals. Flower is woman, woman is flower. Still the sea rages on as the seaweed dances with her in the depths of the dark.

The embrace ends, the kelpy grasp loosens and leaves her to sink to the bottom. Her feet slip easily into the silt below, feels the grit and grime slide beneath toenails. She is breathing water, she finds this natural and not at all strange. Above, the waters rage beneath a blackened sky filled with electricity and thunder. She cannot hear the sky crack and rumble, but the ocean lights up briefly with each fractured branch of light that follows. It is then she realizes there are no fish. None. The seaweed fingers do not come back to dance with her.

*   *   *

Trauerspielen (Mourning Plays)

The teenager's eyes are broken, covered in a milky film since birth. He has wandered into a vacant building he has visited over and over since gaining the confidence to explore the world on his own. He has run his frail fingers over the edge of nearly every surface, felt each crack and crumble, felt each new coat of graffiti, every bit of exposed and rusted rebar jutting out into the unseen air. The silent walls seem to breathe for him and him alone because he pays attention. He and the concrete make a connection the way the seeing can never know. His fingerprints know the taste of rust and ruin.

The gentle curves of his palms pass across rough cement, dried paper paste, faded and curled posters. He mistakes the craters of bullet holes for decay until he feels the crumpled metal of bullets crushed within the wall. The paper paste becomes dried blood, the life of someone passed rests upon his fingertips. He is reading obituaries in the foundation, speaking private eulogies in silence for the unknown victims. A family of birds nested in the upper crevice of broken ceiling squawks before falling silent. A stranger he does not hear arrive stands behind a support column and waits, watches. The teenager will not leave the building today. He will become another death certificate painted on the wall.

Trauerspielen (Mourning Plays)

*　　*　　*

I am the rock face, the culmination of the world's age, the sediment of eons pressed together by time, movement, and gravity. I am that which breaks the skin and scrapes the bones. I have tasted generations of blood, kept the remnants in pockets of amber and solitude. I have seen the sweeping away of civilizations, the propagation of new ones, themselves swept away and replaced a hundred times over. The lessons never change; the people never learn.

I am the erosion, the unseen forces of wind and water nibbling away at the edges. I am the drown and the suffocation, the choke and the asphyxiation. I am the weightlessness of tides; I am the unstoppable force of displacement. I am the pebble moved from great heights, I am the divot carved in earthstone. I am the scree and detritus blown across hardpan, I am the whisper you never truly see, never truly hear.

I am the song, the spirit, and the silence. I am that which moves between worlds effortlessly – the first breath of life and the final exhalation in death. I am the music of the newly birthed child's scream, the proclamation of life's arrival. I am the notion, the idea, the halo and the horns. I am the sound of leaves on limbs in the wind. I am the sound of clouds passing overhead. I am the tune the sun hums as it

Trauerspielen (Mourning Plays)

sinks below the horizon. I am the cacophony of starlight, the chaos of a silent winter day. I am the wisp of snowflake falling onto tongue, I am the discordant tune of thaw in the spring; I am melt.

*   *   *

I could feel the cold muzzle against my head, could feel it leaving its round cylinder mark, a divot, in my skin. They asked, and I could not answer. They asked again and I still could not answer. They kicked my legs out from beneath me and I fell to the floor, knees knocking against the concrete.

  I could not remember my father's name.
    The memory was a faded yellow photograph.

  I could not remember the color of his eyes.
    The memory was fuzz, a circle out of focus.

  I could not remember his brand of cigarettes.
    The memory smelled of shoe leather and cancer.

  I could not remember how he smelled.
    The memory tickled my nose, but no more.

  I could not remember how he held me as a child.
    The memory was placental and ancient.

  I could not remember his teachings.
    The words were garble, encoded and unbreakable.

Trauerspielen (Mourning Plays)

I could not remember.
bang.

           *   *   *

I woke up covered in lichen, smothered in moss, my limbs rusted metallic and stiff. Through the copse of tree boughs above, I could see unnamable, unplaceable constellations that made no sense, had no memory. Like movement, the sky was revisionist history to be relearned. A murder of crows sat perched on the lowest limbs, tilted their heads at me, pretended to be vulture. What skin lay bare to the night air prickled and shivered.

I could see a splotchy moon to my left, bright like a dying bulb, through the leaves. I never saw it smile the way others claimed. From the leaves fell a torrent of insects; the husks of ladybugs, cicadas, crickets, and moths no longer fluttering. Death pitter-pattered all around me, covered my limbs and found its way to choke me. I felt the hard scrabble of tiny legs and antennae against the walls of my throat, imagined sacs of unborn laid into my stomach wall.

I fell into shock, felt my body turn in on itself. My eyelids became movie screens, flashing nebulas of knotted, angry veins against a field of embryonic skin. I latched onto dendrite, gripped axon, rode synapse to the always watchful

Trauerspielen (Mourning Plays)

self below the surface that spoke only in sleep. I cannot remember what we spoke about.

*   *   *

You found yourself wandering through the tunnels of an old train station. The tracks had been corroded brown and dying blades of grass grew along the rails. Ahead, you could see a platform bathed in the greenish sunrise filtered through the broken brick and missing mortar of the opposite wall. The chunks of cement glowed like neon, like heavy emeralds, in the warmth. They seemed to keep your path well-lit, though you knew this was false in every way.

You walked on, followed the tracks to the end of the platform and jumped up, and took the long upward-sloping path out. You could not hear the voices of the dead, but you imagined them echoing off the walls as if they'd just exited the trains. You could smell coffee and urine, could hear the jingle-jangle of money and guitar strings, could see the swarming mass of heavy coats and umbrellas moving up and down this corridor.

The green sunrise had turned orange up at the exit, turned bright. You turned your head away, back towards the platform behind you and saw a dual-headed deer, the antlers of both heads intertwined together so that the two faces

Trauerspielen (Mourning Plays)

worked in tandem. Both mouths chewed silently and stared at you.

*   *   *

The quivering sigh of a napping infant; the soft rustling of fingers through hair; the vibration of the hummingbird; the gentle shifting of leaf-heavy tree limbs; the slow ripple of water against submerged boulder; the light kiss planted on sleeping lover's shoulder; the lifting of gulls in mid-glide; the scattering of dandelion seeds across a meadow; the sound of bloom as petals unfurled; the sound of fallout happening three counties over.

*   *   *

The grandmother lit candles in the windows to keep the memories at bay. She kept the fire stoked in the hearth to keep the ghosts from leaving. She set the kitchen sink on fire, kept it roaring while she slept, for fear the nightmares would creep up from the darkness through the pipes and finally steal her away. She soaked the door jambs and hinges with gasoline, lighter fluid, grain alcohol, gun powder. She singed the hems of all her dresses as they hung in the closet, hoped the char and ash would make her a protection charm against

Trauerspielen (Mourning Plays)

the things she could not see, but hovered around her every hour of the day.

The electric blankets were turned up high, mottled and blistered her skin as she slept, but she would wake in the morning and that was proof that it was right. She would sleep in fire, she would dream of fire, she would walk, awake, with thoughts of fire and smoke and feel her lungs close up in fear of the things the fire kept away.

She made necklaces of matches, earrings from the flammable tips. She hung wind-chimes made of old grenade pins and hung them around the porch to ward off the beasts she saw in dreams. She made lamps of propane tanks and welding equipment, took baths in paint thinner and sulfur.

*   *   *

The man came to on the peak of a rumbling mountain he did not remember climbing. Carrion birds circled overhead, silent and waiting. He felt the breeze of high altitude pass through him, but did not feel its chill; his limbs had become ice, his fingers stiff and crystalline. He ran his awkward hand along thigh, felt it slick and stick against the frost of his new form. He gleamed in the sun, a reflective beacon for anyone paying attention. He was glimmer, he was shine. His breath froze on the air before him, cracked, tinkled to the ground like a dying song. He tried to speak, wanted to hear what broken silence sounded like, and only heard the slide of ice against ice erupt from his throat.

*   *   *

She gnaws on her fingertips, aching to taste the lives she's touched. Her tongue runs along the whorls on her skin, the ridges and valleys that make up her identity. She can taste the decay clinging to the print, can taste the ruin caked up beneath the nails. She chews each nail off, spits it to the ground, lets her fingers bleed thick and goopy to the ground. The blood pools around her like a protective barrier. She can feel it against her toes, her soles; she will leave footprints wherever she goes. She will leave a bloody trail behind her, each toe and heel marked bright against the blackened ground.

*   *   *

On the long desk, beakers and tubes bubbled and frothed in a menagerie of shadowy, murky color. Tiny flames danced below the glass, turned on high and made to look like they alone held the equipment aloft. On the countertop below, a flurry of papers, documents, covered in scribbles,

Trauerspielen (Mourning Plays)

notations, and equations; the work of a sleepless mind and restless hands. On the shelves lining the room, tall glassware filled with formaldehyde and failed experiments stood watch:

Contents of the jars:

- One rubber ball, colorless and rotting from the inside out, bits of particulate floating near the top. The water is a greenish yellow.

- The heads of two dolls, an image of unthinking, unblinking mermaids drowned in the deep. The water is the color of bruise.

- A hand missing the thumb and pinky. The water is a bright, unnatural blue.

- Unknown. The water is thick and gray like ashen snowfall.

- The ears and snouts of pigs, wrinkled and tough. The water is the color of oxygenated blood or lust.

- A silver ribbon, lilting, beautiful, and frayed. This water is clear like the glass it floats inside.

Trauerspielen (Mourning Plays)

New Hire Video

[*Video starts. The images are fuzzed out, much like an old VHS tape. A middle-aged Asian man in a suit sits comfortably on a large desk, his left leg barely touching the ground while his right hangs limp off the edge. His smile feels forced and false. It sparkles unnaturally through the grainy nature of the tape.*]

"Hey there, I'm Alan Cho, Vice President of Production and Assembly here at the G. Petto Corporation! If you're watching this, it means you've been one of the lucky few selected to join the G. Petto family of companion model manufacturing. And you're in for a treat!"

[*He stands, extending his hands out and then clasping them together again throughout his monologue, obviously speaking from cue cards somewhere beyond the eye of the lens.*]

"You're about to embark upon a journey like no other in the history of mankind. We at the G. Petto Corporation, all of us (including you now), have made it our lifelong goal to seek out, find, and replicate that ever elusive and distinct 'human experience' for our customers."

[*Alan Cho leaves the frame. The shot changes to a view of the hallway. Alan Cho exits a room, presumably the same office, and begins walking towards the camera, itself moving backwards down a hall lined with glass-walled offices. You can see people on phones scribbling notes, meetings of two or three*]

New Hire Video

*people that (conveniently) end in laughter and
handshakes across desks. One office is even staged,
audaciously, with an employee and a nude companion
model engaged in activity together.]*

"For the last thirty-seven years, we've been searching
for the thing that makes us uniquely us; looking for the spark
that keeps the fire of humanity burning hot throughout the
millennia. We may never reach true perfection without the
standard ovum penetrated by spermatozoa, but we've come
pretty close and, with your help, we're only going to get
closer. Let me show you; hear what some of the top members
in our facilities have to say about the different factories you
could find yourself working in! See the passion they have for
the work that they do here!"

*[Alan Cho disappears to the left of the frame. The
scene fizzles out, fades into the image of a square-
shaped, non-descript building made of randomly sorted
red and brown brick. The sky is a nearly neon blue,
bright and painful to look at as a new voice, full of
gruff and years of swallowing rocks, comes through the
speakers. No face is attached; the image of the
building remains. There are no windows.]*

"I'm John, I've been with the G. Petto Corporation
for about twenty years now. Hired right out of graduate
school. I oversee the daily activities of each factory, often
going between them all several times in a day to make sure

our production line is running smoothly. I start from the final step and work my way back. I think it's more interesting that way, personally. Plus, it also helps to find the origins of any issues we come across in the companion model production line by working backwards from the problem, thus saving time and money in the long run."

"Eight factories exist, each with their own sub-wings based on physiology. This final one, the eighth, creates not only toes, but fingers, noses, ears, thick muscled tongues, strips of eyebrow and scalps of hair (or non-hair), eyelids, and the complex eyeball (made by the eldest and most experienced of craftsmen). These are the final touches, the accoutrements that turn the G. Petto Corporation's fully fleshed ideas into partial-flesh realities.

"Factory 8 is the last in a long line of factories built to create each separate body part. To give you an idea, each individual toe is made of discarded ligament, "bone" made of firm but pliable rubber, skin made of skin donated from those no longer living, topped with toenails made of blended shale (for strength) and abalone (for shine). To the layman, this sounds, admittedly, strange, but this final product is the culmination of years and years of prototypes and brainstorming and experimenting.

"In the early days of the G. Petto Corporation's companion model production, we allegedly used products and chemicals that were unsafe for the environment and for the workers in each factory. While this wasn't true, we've made every effort to be aboveboard and transparent in the materials we use that aren't protected by various patent laws. Your immediate supervisor will be more than happy to show you a list of the hazard-free, non-toxic materials approved by the Environmental Protection Agency and Occupation Safety and Health Administration that you may be dealing with on your first day of employment."

[Factory 8 fades out and is replaced by a building with a shimmery, white dome and gray columns reminiscent of the Grecian times. People are shown in lab coats out on the front and side lawns, discussing god-knows-what nonsense for the camera's benefit. The lawn is lush and green with sidewalks snaking through it in curving lengths. There are no windows on this facility. A woman speaks over the image.]

"Hi there! I'm Jennifer Fasbender. I've been an employee here at G. Petto for a little over 8 years. I work in the Efficiency & Design department. We take the information from the Analytics department about each model design that's released and tweak different aspects until we feel we've got a better product than the one before. For instance, our first line of models had issues with blood flow, so we had to go back and rethink how we manufactured the veins and arteries, making them of thinner, more pliable materials that allowed for a larger interior space."

> [*The video leads the viewer through the front door of the domed building into an expansive courtyard lit by sunlight filtering through curved skylights. A large oak tree stands in the middle of the room. Several employees in lab coats sit on benches placed throughout. One can almost smell the nature that must surely permeate the space. It is calming.*]

"Here at Factory 7, workers create the outer skin and hair follicles of what we call the neo-dermis. The neo-dermis is produced first in large vats, and then rolled out into seven distinct layers which are then pressed together through a high heat process. We jokingly refer to this facility and its work as "the wrap phase" since the neo-dermis is literally wrapped and stretched around the muscle structures that arrive from Factory 6. We offer four styles of hair follicle: blonde, brown, black, and silver with red having been largely panned by early focus groups.

"I never thought my education in design would bring me to work on such a fascinating project. I just assumed I'd be stuck in some cramped office drawing up images for companies that really had no idea what they wanted in regards to their own rebranding. But I've been given a really fantastic opportunity here. The people I work with are great and everyone truly wants to make the best model possible. Some days I have so much fun working that I completely forget to go home until well after ten in the evening.

"Since I'm a salaried employee, I'm allowed to stay as long as needed after the federally mandated work-hour limits, but the G. Petto Corporation works hard to make sure you don't have to. More information on federal work rules in regards to benefits, wages, and daily work duration can be found on page 37 of your employee handbook."

[The video fades into an image of Factory 6, a short, but long, black building made of marble or glossy stone. There are, again, no windows allowing the casual passerby a glance at what goes on inside. Here, workers wear doctor's scrubs, mob caps, and surgical masks.]

"Welcome to the G. Petto family! I'm Reginald Locroft, a Design Implementation Specialist, which is just a fancy way of saying I take ideas and make them a reality. My work here consists of trying to create each companion model efficiently while preserving the quality of the end product. I'm sure you'll agree that there's nothing worse than a companion model that doesn't live up to expectations.

"I've been working here almost since the beginning of the company, so I'm thankful to have had a hand in the

New Hire Video

design of nearly every companion model that's been produced. With every flawed design comes a puzzle for us to solve, a way for us to make the next companion model better than its contemporaries. I can genuinely say that it's a pleasure to come to work every day."

> *[The image of the building seems to be pulled back into the black before being swept off to the right of the screen. Another image sweeps in from the left and fills the space. Long, metal tables in a cavernous room are lined with stretches of bundled tubing colored red and blue. Workers sit on either side of the tables, hands deftly, but slowly, braiding the muscle and ligament that dispense from long tubes hanging down from the ceiling. Not seen: the production room on the floor above that creates and disperses this material]*

"Factory 6 creates the muscle and ligament, intertwining and weaving each set of tissue with the veins and arteries laid out cleanly (and with painstaking care before being cryo-frozen for safe transport) in Factory 5. Factories 5 and 6 are filled with predominately female workers, an intentional decision made by G. Petto Corporation's board of directors after numerous studies concluded women to be more careful and precise when the work called for it. It should be noted here, however, that G. Petto makes every effort to be an equal opportunity employer that doesn't discriminate based on race, creed, religion, sexuality, political beliefs, dietary restrictions, past addictions to substances or past addictions to certain companion model features."

[The image of female workers braiding muscle together within and around skeletal structures shimmers and shakes, becomes another image of a nearly identical black building attached to what looks like a power plant behind it. The hum of large generators fills the speakers, then diminishes as a new voice takes over.]

"Hello, I'm Karen Cristoffer, Lead Productivity Engineer here in Factory 5."

[The image changes to another room full of long tables and women slowly piecing together organic material. Factory 5 is full of wispy fibers of discarded vein and nervous system hanging from dispensing tubes hung from the ceiling, each snip of length followed by the silent knitting of nerve clusters that lead from the brain stem down and out into the mostly skeletal structure where organs sit, ripe and shiny, unused and waiting to be connected to the rest of the body.]

"You'll notice that the setup for Factory 5 is nearly identical to the setup for Factory 6; this is by design. The outer building materials help in keeping the organic material from deteriorating under the harmful nature of the sun's ultra-violet light. Both buildings are kept at cool temperatures

New Hire Video

as an extra measure of keeping the cellular structure and the inner organs strong and healthy for longer.

"Both production areas reside on the topmost floors of the buildings and feed the organic material down to the workers on the production floor. Through a lot of long nights wondering why earlier models decayed from the inside so quickly and lost strength, we realized that keeping the vein and artery materials on spools actually served to weaken their cellular structures. The same thing can be said for the muscle and sinew.

"The nervous system is a slow crocheting; one mistake may lead to several others and the model may take to spastic motions which throw the entirety of the inner fleshy sanctum out of sync. Once the skeletal system has been pieced together according to strict company guidelines, the nerved skeleton is placed in a cryo-freeze before it (and many others) are transported to Factory 6.

Previous lawsuits against the G. Petto Corporation have heightened the quality control in all stages of the piecing together of models. This step in the companion model building process takes the longest and we do not have production quotas here for this reason; quality work suffers at the hands of quick work."

*[A tinkle of bells comes from the speakers. The image
starts to flip end over end before slowing and changing
into the image of a new building, one that looks like
an actual science lab. Large green windows span the
entire length and height of the building and show a
flurry of activity going on inside. Conference rooms are
full of men in suits and women in skirts all paying
attention to speakers utilizing white boards and digital
displays of brain information. Workers in lab coats
can be seen slicing brain material to be tested over and
over with complex machines.]*

"I'm Dr. Stephen Collins, and I'm a neuroscientist
and biologist focusing more on the physiology of the brain
rather than the psychology of the brain. We call it Factory 4,
but it's really more of a lab as opposed to a production line. I
work with a massive staff of other doctors specializing in a
host of gray matter issues. We currently work towards
creating not only the physical shell of the companion model
mind, but the mental shell as well. We work in tandem with
the skeletal professionals in the basement to ensure that every
brain is a perfect fit to every skull. Once fit, the skulls are
attached to the rest of the skeletal system and sent off to
Factory 5 where the work of piecing together the entire
nervous begins."

*[The video fades to a lab inside the building where
individual brains sit floating in large glass beakers.
Wires and electrodes are hooked up to each,*

New Hire Video

*information traveling to machines that print out brain
wave data. Some are poked in various spots to test for
electrical activity coursing through the corpus collosum,
the medulla, the cerebellum.]*

"The brain is a wonderfully, and frustratingly,
complex system. Grown in much the same way the rest of the
organs are, it comes with ever more problems during the
gestation period. Like anything in life, too much of a good
thing or too much of a bad thing can skew to the side of
deficiencies elsewhere.

"In humans, the formation of too many of the folds
in the brain (called 'gyria') before birth leads to a
neurologically debilitating disease called 'polymicrogyria.' This
disease can cause epilepsy and other system-wide anomalies
like muscle weakness, problems with speech or swallowing,
and severe intellectual disability. We have found the same
issues during our own companion model growing process."

*[The image changes to a close-up image of the brain,
going deep inside the folds where computer images of
electrical activity between the cranial areas occur.
Flashes of light and subtle movements along
neurological pathways sparkle and dance across the
screen.]*

"Too few of these gyria can also lead to epilepsy and mental retardation. Again, these problems have occurred in some of our previous companion model prototypes, and we've gotten better at finding that solid, healthy middle ground, but it's been tough. We're creating minds! Real, thinking minds from the cloning of tissue samples. It's a very exciting time to be in this field right now. We are learning so much so quickly and working here has given us the opportunities and the financial backing to keep digging into the mysteries of the human mind."

"Factory 4 is also where the memory comes to be implemented upon the companion model brain. But that's a process that's highly secretive due to patent rights and legal standings. Many of our processes are guarded by strict and long-term non-compete clauses coupled with gag orders should an employee decide to work elsewhere. We take our work here very seriously and so should you. Be sure to read through the entire employee handbook thoroughly. This information is vital."

[The inner workings of the brain fade to black as a low trumpet sounds. The image of a new building, this one a skyscraper with an uncountable amount of floors that seems to reach up to the clouds and through them. The building is beige and tapers off, becomes round, at its apex.]

New Hire Video

"My name is Helen Ackerman. I'm the Lead Line Supervisor here at Factory 3 where we produce the sex organs of the companion models. Thanks to great leaps in the sex toy industry during the early 21st century, we've been able to really streamline the realistic nature of copulation with almost endless amounts of funding and research.

"While we've made realism our top priority with this factory, we've yet to be able to replicate the reproductive nature of the ovum or the spermatozoa. We hope to one day make that happen, but for now, each companion model is outfitted to engage in the most basic of primal needs. Each set of sex organs is pre-designed to, hopefully, allow for companion model births in the future, but for now...well. We have to settle for the pleasure aspect alone, which we've had wonderful responses to."

[The video of the building fuzzes out and becomes a top-down view of one of the production floors. Veiny v-shaped structures move quickly across conveyor belts, too quickly to tell if one is looking at the inner ovarian structure or the inner testicular structure.]

"In the beginning, we had the basic "Adam" and "Eve" models. They all looked the same and acted the same, all had the same features and body sizes. Throughout the

New Hire Video

different evolutions of the companion model lifespan, we've been able to 'customize' each companion model's sexuality for the customer. Tightness, thickness, roundness, length…these modifications are all done here to specifications included in the orders.

"Before we began offering these customizations, we had issues within our own employee pool. We thought women would be best at creating the male organs and men the best at creating the female organs. Both groups ended up, intentionally or unintentionally, making outrageous modifications to the original models that were simply unrealistic in almost every way.

"While we in upper management take pride in the fact that we listen to the comments and concerns of our employees, there are certainly rules that must be strictly adhered to. Before trying to alter any part of the companion model physiology you end up working on, ask your supervisor if it's okay. Some aspects are more malleable than others and can be played with unendingly. Others remain very much tried and true based on past research and experimentation."

[The image of the v-shaped organs continues moving along the conveyor belt, slowly fading out and becoming the up and down motions of the rubber accordion tubes in ventilators. The ventilators are connected to new

New Hire Video

lungs encased in glass. One can see the bronchioles pushing out and forcing the costal surface to expand and contract, expand and contract, expand and contract. It is a nearly hypnotizing display.]

"My name is Ashwar Parvanee and I'm a Thoracic Consultant here in Factory 2. Like much of the other organic material cloned and cultivated for the companion models, these organs are manufactured from cellular splicings of human individuals, many of whom are living donors who have purchased companion models as a life-saving technique for organ donation later in life.

"As you can see, these cloned cultures grow into fully developed organs that we're able to implement into the companion models with relative ease. With blood donations from the original donors flowing through them, these organs remain pure until insertion or eventual removal from companion model systems.

"Here in Factory 2, we cultivate all of what we call the life organs: the heart, liver, spleen, lungs, appendix, intestines, stomach, kidneys, so on. This is less a lab and more of an assembly line approach as most of the organs are simply created and placed upon a sliding metal body slab, sewn together, and then frozen. The frozen batch of organs, specific to each particular companion model chosen, are then shipped to Factory 5 where they become one with the muscle, ligament, and the rest of the nervous system, which is an arduous process, but a gratifying one when you see the finished product.

"And really, that's one of the many joys of working here. When I come across a companion model in public and see them standing in front of me, acting so much like a real human, I'm always astounded. Then I realize – I had a hand in making that a reality. It's a feeling that just cannot be described in any measurable way."

[The camera zooms close in on the ventilators, then pulls out to reveal large steel presses that move down, click, move up, release steam. The camera pans out to show the empty cast of a skeletal structure fill up with a yellow liquid. The press drops, clicks, rises, releases steam, and a fully formed skeletal structure is quickly moved out from under the press and off to the side where it continues on its journey through the factory.]

"I'm Jamie Sommers, the Bone Density Mixologist for the skeletal models here in Factory 1. My team and I are always trying to find new ways to create a skeletal structure that mimics the growth and strength of bone material. On the one hand, we're trying to make the most realistic companion models possible, even when you can't see all the moving parts. On the other, we're also trying to find real-world solutions that can be implemented to solve human problems.

New Hire Video

"With calcium deficiencies at astronomical highs all across the globe, it's imperative that we at the G. Petto Corporation actively try to fight back against as many of the deficiencies as we can as quickly as we can in ways that are both long-term and completely affordable for those that need them.

"Here in Factory 1, we also create the memories that are directly implemented into the brains in Factory 4. I wish I could explain that entire process to you, but even I don't know what all it entails and I've been in this particular factory for over a decade now. Very hush hush.

"But as I know how our department's work affects the physical limitations of the human body, theirs is actively working against the mental diseases and deficiencies that tend to plague us in our later years.

[The video changes to a family surrounding a grandfather in a wheelchair. They are all smiling and waving at the camera. The image changes to a father on his knees, his son (you assume) wrapped in loving arms. A grandmother and a granddaughter walk hand in hand through a field, both holding flowers in their free hands.]

"This isn't just a job for most of us. Sure we're creating a product, but we're also a research company, a health company, a wellness company. Always actively trying

New Hire Video

to rekindle the things that make being human a great thing. We focus on the things that are hard to talk about, hard to think about, so that you don't have to. That's what G. Petto is all about and has been for close to forty years."

[Video fades to black and then back to Alan Cho in his office assuming the same original stance; sitting comfortably on a large desk, his left leg barely touching the ground while his right hangs limp off the edge. He is wearing a different outfit and a crooked smile that unsettles. When he finally speaks, it is a stilted speech.]

"Thank you to for enjoying this presentation. We hope you to enjoy working here at G. Petto Co-operation. Your hard work and smarts will be to benefitting we and the world. How could one not want work here?"

[He raises his arm in a stiff motion, makes to wave. The real Alan Cho steps into frame beside, what you now realize is, the companion model version of himself. His smile is wide and toothy as he waves as well.]

New Hire Video

Sugarhouse

The Man (Morning)

Sometimes I wake up in the middle of the night; two, three o'clock and it's pitch black. I sit straight up in bed and my eyes see the room laid out before me, the furniture shadowed into unrecognizable entities surrounding my bed. It's as if I've come to on a life raft stranded at sea and I'm filled with such dread, such abject terror, that I almost can't take it. It's like the weight of the room is crushing in on me from all sides and it's all I can do just to sit there and wait until it's finished. In those strange partially-awake moments, I get confused as to how I find myself in this position, I get despondent and self-loathing in those long drawn out seconds of the dusk, but then I lay back down and in the briefest of moments, the morning arrives and the fear subsides until the next night when it happens all over again.

If nothing else, I can count on sitting up, wide awake, in bed at some point before truly waking up.

I can count on these feelings arriving and destroying whatever dreams had gotten me to the waking point.

I can count on sleepless nights and shortness of breath upon waking.

I can count on nightmares and confusion during the day.

Sugarhouse

I can count on not remembering any of this when the morning comes.

I can count on nothing.

*   *   *

I awake. I'm awake. I don't remember this place at all.

It's noon. A large bay window to my right lets a warm breeze into the room. A bird chirps, a cricket rubs its legs together timidly. Sunlight spills across the floor. The taste of foul morning coats my tongue and I instinctively reach for the water to my left. How did I know that was there? The glass shakes in my hand as I sip.

The sheets have been kicked unceremoniously to the end of the bed and lay draped over the edge like a cephalopod climbing down to the floor. I am clammy all over. My boxers, the only clothing on me, stick to my body. A nightmare. Daymare? A terror.

I scan the room; an ornate armoire against the wall straight ahead. By the open window, a slim stand holds a rotary phone. No pictures hang on the wall, no bric-a-brac clutters the corners. It feels sterile. To the left, an open closet and in the far corner, a door. Shut.

Sugarhouse

Like a dam collapsing, I am suddenly surrounded by pressure, a feeling of steady force closing in around me. A claustrophobic feeling making me incapable of doing anything but allowing it purchase on every inch of dermis. My skin prickles and rivulets of sweat drip from underneath my arms before rolling down my sides. I have no concept of what day it is or, truly, what time it is. Minute-wise or year-wise. I don't know that this matters much, however. It doesn't feel like it does.

I hear the light jingle of keys on the other side of the door. The knob moves slowly before the door inches open. A woman walks in quietly, as if not to disturb me, then realizes that I'm awake and staring at her. She comes to the foot of the bed and lifts the crumpled sheets on to the mattress. I take another sip of water, not wanting to be the first to say anything. I don't know this woman. I don't recognize her at all.

She is pretty; shoulder length chestnut hair, thin face, little to no makeup. Her eyes are big and brown – true doe eyes – and seem to smile at me before she does. "Good morning, Martin."

She called me Martin. I roll the name across my lips and nothing…this doesn't feel wrong, but it doesn't feel right either. If she had simply called me "man," it would have felt

Sugarhouse

truer. I am Martin. "Good morning," I croak. My voice sounds strange, not my own. Though I cannot remember what my voice is supposed to sound like. I suddenly find myself embarrassed and awkward, sprawled out on the bed in nothing but my undershorts. I pull the sheets up and over my legs as she turns to the armoire. She opens the door and after a few clicks and crackles, the sound of music on vinyl fills the room quietly. Loud enough to be pleasant, but low enough for conversation.

"Do you remember this song?" she asks as she turns to face me. "We used to listen to this album on Sunday afternoons."

I shake my head and think Martin, Martin, Martin, Martin. I am living in someone else's skin, wearing someone else's face, but thinking my own thoughts. A look of slight disappointment crosses her face. Her lips tighten and her gaze falls to the floor.

"Do you remember me?" she asks, looking up.

I take another sip of water and shake my head. Her bottom lip quivers, but just barely. Perhaps she was someone close to me. A sister? A wife? Was I married? I look down at my left hand – no ring, but there is a noticeable stripe of skin not touched by sunlight. Could be something, could be nothing. Inconclusive.

Sugarhouse

The song on the record ends. A pop and a crackle play through the speaker as the needle finds its way to the center groove, a note-less track on black. The rhythm of the needle jumping in and out of its path thumps in the air between us. A pair of birds chirp outside.

"Are you hungry?" she asks. "I could make you a sandwich or some soup. Anything, really. Are you hungry? Would you like another water?"

I realize the glass in my hand is empty. No use stalling; I have to engage her now. "Yes, thank you. Water sounds good. So does food."

She nods and smiles before turning to flip the record over in the armoire. I watch as she opens a drawer and removes folding clothing, placing it on the foot of the bed. "These are some of your clothes. The doctor said you probably wouldn't remember where they were or that they were even yours, so…the shower is down the hall. Your toothbrush is the blue one by the sink. Clean towels are on the racks. Would you like me to draw you a bath?"

I shake my head. "I think I can manage, thank you."

She gives a small bow and leaves the room as quietly as she entered, shutting the door behind her. I get out of bed and stretch. My back cracks as do my toes and ankles. I walk across the cool wood floor and open the bedroom door

Sugarhouse

slowly. A long hallway stretches out in front of me; there are no pictures or wall hangings of any sort on either side. Several other doorways loom at the end of the hall, past a wide staircase that leads down.

I find the bathroom and bathe. The shampoo and soap are immediately known things; I have used them before and somehow I know this. So why can't I remember other, more important things? Like my name. Or where I am. Hell, where I've been, even. The steam fills up the room as I force myself to push deeper in the recesses of my memory. Nothing but black and I am growing increasingly frustrated.

I finish up in the shower and step out to a mirror, fogged over and blurry, and almost laugh as I can see my outline, but nothing else. No particulars stand out – I am simply a form without a face.

The Woman

[The book is leather bound with yellow, rough-cut blank pages. On the front, the print of an aged map that extends out past the edges of the book and no longer holds any truth. The names of places have changed, the preconceived notions of those unseen places squashed through centuries of explorers and travelers. The image is supposed to evoke in the journal's author a feeling that anything is possible, that worlds are left to explore. Instead, it makes her wish for a different life, one that exists beyond the edges of the book, one that is painless and page-less, where her pen writes on the backs of postcards to friends back home instead of scribing every fear, every thought that keeps her chained to the husband that does not remember who she is and cannot remember more than a day's worth of information before his brain loses it while he sleeps. Not quite an infant, not quite a man.]

Day 3
05/15/93
6:14am

He's been home for two days now, and I'm finally beginning to understand what Dr. Sullivan meant. He is not the same person; he is, in fact, not a person at all, but a shell just going through the motions. I have done so much grieving at his bedside in the hospital. The tears fell so long and hard that I feared I would dry up and wither like a dying vine.

I lost him. In my mind, he was gone despite his body lying in the hospital bed with my

Sugarhouse

hands clasping his. I had resigned myself to the possibility that he would not return, but now that he has, I wonder if would've been better for him to pass. I hate myself for even writing that down, much less thinking it. What kind of wife wishes for the death of her husband? It's a shameful realization to come to. When he begins to remember who he is, I will burn this book. I'll let the fire eat these words in the hopes that they never get read by anyone ever again.

I haven't slept since he's been home. Cat naps here and there, but nothing substantial. He sleeps a lot, which I hope will help in the healing. I worry that his subconscious isn't working hard enough to bubble him back up to the surface of whatever haze he is drowning in. He is restless at night; I hear him through the closed door as I sit on a wooden chair in the hallway ready to play nursemaid since playing the role of wife is not an option yet.

I thought about reading a book while standing guard at his door, but if I get wrapped up in a fiction of someone else's design, I may forget the reality of my own. So instead, I sit in silence, sometimes counting down the minutes in my head until the sun comes up or the seconds between each sound that he makes. For now, this is as close as I'll get to making new memories that include him. I'm doing double-duty for the both of us, though he may never understand that.

Sugarhouse

Sometimes the chair gets too uncomfortable and I'll kneel down on the floor to put my ear up to the door. The majority of the time, I hear white noise, a nothing, but my heart aches when I hear him cough or mumble through feverish dreams. The mother in me wants to cradle him in my arms and coo him back to health, to fill him with a warmth so comforting that it breaks this amnesia into a million tiny shards that can never be put back together again.

But I can't. And I wait. And I listen. And I wait.

The Man (Night)

I awake. I'm awake. I remember this place.

The room is black; night has settled outside and it takes my eyes forever to adjust to the lack of light in the room. I feel the evening breeze pass through the room; I shiver briefly. I clutch the sheets tighter around my legs and realize that I have not forgotten the day's events. The images my mind is able to conjure up don't feel hazy or fuzzy; each moment is a tangible thing I feel my brain wrapping around and holding onto tightly.

If the woman, my supposed wife, is right…then this is progress. I am making progress. I am forming memories, thoughts that can be recalled, I am repopulating the crevices of my gray matter. I am elated by this realization until I am struck by a fit of coughing, which halts my inner celebration.

I reach for the glass of water, full again, on the nightstand to my left. I gulp from the glass thirstily. The woman from earlier said my name was Martin and that she was my wife, but these concepts are still unsure to me. They feel like the wrong mathematical answers on a chalkboard problem. Erasable, but not quite right.

I put the glass down and lean back against the headboard. At the bay window to my right, a small girl stands perfectly still while staring out into the yard below. I think back to the day, but don't remember seeing her before. She has dark blonde hair that cascades down to the middle of her back, a porcelain face sprinkled with freckles, and a light green dress that falls just below her knees. She wears no shoes.

"Hello, honey," I whisper. "What's your name?"

The girl turns and smiles, says nothing. She comes to the bed in silence and takes my hand, turns it over to look at the top and then the palm, runs a finger across the creases of the soft skin there. She turns my hand again, looking at the top and then the palm. She looks up at me, smiles, and leaves the room without saying a word.

I am strangely comforted by her silence and quickly fall back to sleep.

Sugarhouse

The Woman

[The house accumulated a particular grime during the man's lengthy hospitalization. The event happened so quickly and without warning that dishes were left out on the dinner table and in the sink. Bath tubs collected dust, as did most of the other surfaces. Beds were left unmade; sheets unwashed. Wet towels that hung on shower rods had dried up and smelled of mildew. The smell of the last meal together permeated the dining room and spread out to other parts of the house slowly. Mice found their way into the shelves and pantry, ate themselves to death and lay, unmoving, next to boxes of stale crackers and condensed soup. Half-dead flies seizured on the window sills or remained carcassed and wrapped up in recent cobwebs in the corners of rooms. Everything was in decay; decay was in everything.]

Day 7
05/19/93
10:34pm

Today I tackled the living room. I didn't realize how badly things had gotten while Martin was in his coma. I opened the curtains to let the sun in, but when I patted the couch cushions, dust mites flew up and glistened in the daylight. Not just a little, but an embarrassingly large amount. I kept fighting the urge to clean anything other than the kitchen; I had to prepare food for Martin first and foremost. Then I cleaned his bathroom so he could bathe. These were the essentials and I kept them spotless from the day I heard he was coming home.

Sugarhouse

Our room, the master, was the hardest. I slept long and often and my will to keep order all but disappeared. The room was in complete disarray; worn clothing mixed with clean clothing in piles on the floor. Since the kitchen had fallen into such a putrid state, I'd taken to eating, alone, in my room, so there were a few dishes scattered beneath the bed as well. Disgusting really, looking back on it, but I was not myself. I was grieving. And I had no one's shoulder to lean on.

When I heard that he was coming back to me, knowing who he was or not, there wasn't any question that I needed to fix things, to right the wrongs that had taken place in his absence. The doctor impressed upon me the importance of routines of the past while building new ones as well, and a dirty house simply wasn't routine for us.

The doctor said that pictures of us might jog his memory back into place faster, but I had taken them all down and stored them away long ago. Some memories aren't worth framing, much less keeping around and I want us to build new ones – together. If that means it takes twice as long, then so be it. At least he's awake.

My god, he's finally awake! I hear him breathe at night and I see his eyes in the morning. He moves of his own volition and we converse. The conversations aren't much to speak of though; he's still a stranger and I struggle with

Sugarhouse

that idea. But he is mine and he is home and we are together.

Tomorrow I may clean the den. He used to love sitting in there after dinner. Perhaps putting him in front of his work will give his mind a good cleansing.

I am more hopeful than I have been in months.

The Man (Morning)

I awake. I'm awake. I don't remember this place at all.

It's noon. A large bay window to my right lets a cool breeze into the room. A bird chirps, a cricket rubs its legs together timidly. Clouded sunlight spots the floor. The taste of foul morning coats my tongue and I instinctively reach for the water to my left. How did I know that was there? The glass shakes in my hand as I sip.

The sheets have been kicked unceremoniously to the end of the bed and lay draped over the edge like a cephalopod climbing down to the floor. I am clammy all over. My boxers, the only clothing on me, stick to my body. A nightmare. Daymare? A terror.

I scan the room; an ornate armoire against the wall straight ahead. By the open window, a slim stand holds a rotary phone. No pictures hang on the wall, no bric-a-brac clutters the corners. It feels sterile. To the left, an open closet and in the far corner, a door. Shut.

Like a dam collapsing, I am suddenly surrounded by pressure, a feeling of steady force closing in around me. A claustrophobic feeling making me incapable of doing anything but allowing it purchase on every inch of dermis. My skin prickles and rivulets of sweat drip from underneath my

Sugarhouse

arms before rolling down my sides. I have no concept of what day it is or, truly, what time it is. Minute-wise or year-wise. I don't know that this matters much, however. It doesn't feel like it does.

I empty the glass and rise from the bed, an incredibly comfortable place with an intricate, wrought-iron headboard. Matching dressers sit on either side and hold aloft two old-school hurricane lamps turned into electric ones. I turn one on and light spills out from beneath the lampshade and fills that corner of the room. Inside the base of the lamp, however, a soft orange glow bobs and weaves as if being tossed about by a violent storm. The effect is strangely calming.

I leave the room, wondering if there is anyone else around. The house has been silent. I've heard no rustling or moving about. The hallway is well lit from a skylight at the end. I can see that it's cloudy outside, but not enough to stop the sun completely. Six doors line the walkway, all open, all curious.

I pass the first and look in. A child's bedroom, but larger. Toys and stuffed animals populate the tiny book cases and shelf space throughout. The tiny bed is empty and made; ruffled pink pillows and sheets cover it. A stack of quilts sits on the edge. An unsmiling stuffed monkey leans against the pillows as if standing guard for the child so that no one intrudes upon her slumbering place. A ceiling fan hangs, unmoving, in the middle of the room. The only window is on the back wall. From the doorway, I can see a vast expanse of green – sparsely forested areas surrounding tiny glens – and further out, a pond.

I move to the next door and find a bathroom. There is no window, so I flick on the light switch. It is half the size of the child's room, but feels larger than normal, though I cannot explain why. On the right, fresh towels hang from the towel racks on the wall. A see-through shower curtain hangs on a gently curved metal rod. On the left, dual, marbled sinks followed by a folded wash rag on the middle of the closed toilet seat. Little bottles, lined up like soldiers, stand between both sinks. I lean down to look: soap, shampoo, conditioner, face wash. I wonder if this is an invitation to bathe. The folded rag, the dryer-fresh linens, the toiletries.

Before I over-think it, I turn to shut and lock the door. I lift the rag from the toilet and toss it onto the sink. I urinate, wash my hands. I grab the bottles, peel back the shower curtain, and start the water. I put the bottles on the rim of the tub and undress, now realizing that a shower sounds like a phenomenal idea. When I'm done, I step out to a mirror, fogged over and blurry, and almost laugh as I can

Sugarhouse

see my outline, but nothing else. No particulars stand out – I
am simply a form without a face.

*   *   *   *   *

My bed has been made and the window has been
shut, though the shade has been lifted further to let in more
of the dim light. A pair of jeans, a shirt, socks and shoes have
all been laid out on the comforter. I assume they're for me
and, once dressed, I put the towel back in the bathroom and
continue down the hallway. Three doors lead to empty
rooms. Wooden floors, bare walls, nothing save for a curtain-
less window in the exact middle of each back wall.

The final door at the end of the hallway is ajar. I can
see bookshelves, a file cabinet, a couch – a reading room
perched at the top of the stairs. A woman sits on the couch,
flipping through a photo album. I don't know this woman. I
don't recognize her at all. Her face shows no emotion, but
she is pretty; shoulder length chestnut hair, thin face, little to
no makeup. I push the door open wider and it creaks. She
looks up from the couch, startled. Her eyes are big and
brown – true doe eyes – and seem to smile at me before she
does. "Good morning, Martin."

Sugarhouse

She called me Martin. I roll the name across my lips and nothing. This doesn't feel wrong, but it doesn't feel right either. If she had simply called me "man," it would have felt truer. I am Martin. "Good morning," I croak. My voice sounds strange, not my own. Though I cannot remember what my voice is supposed to sound like.

She pats the seat next to her and smiles wide. "Come. I want to show you some pictures, if that's alright?"

I shrug. What do I care about this woman's pictures? Then again, what else do I have to do at the moment? I can't even remember who I am, so the least I can do is look at some pictures. Oh, wait...

"Any of me in there?" I ask skeptically. She nods and again beckons me to join her on the couch.

I sit next to her. The couch is comfortable, plush. Fat cushions envelop me as I sink into the padding. She leans over and places the photo album on my lap. The pictures aren't old, but they aren't brand new either. More dingy than yellowed. Some are water-stained and others torn. "The basement flooded last year and ruined most of our pictures. I was able to save most of these, thankfully. I even kept the really bad ones if they were important."

She runs a finger across one of us with a Dalmatian. "Do you remember this day?" she asks.

Sugarhouse

I shake my head and stare at the photo. She is younger in the photo by many years. Thinner. Her smile is brighter. The me of then appears noticeably younger as well. It is obviously me, but I can't place the moment. I purse my lips as I claw at the inside of my head, searching and hunting, for something that reminds me of the day. Nothing. Not a tingle, no grasping of the tiniest of threads to help me unravel.

She sees me chewing the information slowly, struggling, and smiles. "That's okay," she says, flipping the page. "Dr. Sullivan said it may take you awhile to get back to normal. Don't worry." She rubbed my shoulder as I stared down at the pictures; on the left, the two of us standing in front of a large house. I appear to be overjoyed. She has both hands wrapped around my waist, her head against my chest, and looks up at me from an awkward position. I see love there, but can't remember it.

I feel her hand move down from my shoulder and across my back. She rubs the entire length of my back absent-mindedly and then runs her hand up the nape of my neck and toys with my hair. It is distracting, but also…so *very* relaxing.

The other page contains a picture of a distended belly. No faces are present. A hand rests on the upper curve of the pregnant woman, upon which the woman's hand rests as well. Their fingers are interlaced. The belly is smooth. The picture is black and white.

The Woman

[The house has a history, the man and woman have a history. The walls of the house have a deep and stain-like memory the way the woman finds herself constantly thinking of the past, wishing for things to be different, hoping that the man will somehow pull himself up out of his ailment of broken brain and remember her, dammit, if only for an hour or two. She tries to hold on to those memories tightly, unsure of whether new ones will be forthcoming. The man just wants a memory to hold onto by the time the sun sets, one that will return when he awakes. His tragedy is also his blessing; he cannot remember the important things, but if he could, they might break him down into pieces that could not be put together again.]

Day 22
06/03/93
1:03am

Stupid. Stupid. Stupid. Stupid.

I couldn't help it. I kissed him tonight because
it had been so long since I last tasted his lips
or felt the heat of his face against mine and I
knew that it wasn't really him I was kissing,
but I had to do it. I had to feel something
other than this waste that sits inside me and
god how I've missed the feel of him, the taste
of him. Everything. I miss *him*.

I had taken him down to the den (finally
clean!) and put him in his chair, a leather
burgundy wingback that he used to fall asleep

in after too-long nights of reading and
conversing with himself. I spread his favorite
blanket across his lap and opened the blinds
so he could look out over the front of the
property. I put his hot tea on the table usually
reserved for chess games that no one ever
came to play anymore.

I didn't move a thing in his den. Unlike the
bedroom, the pictures all remain. The
bedroom, "our" space, required his
permission to move or change anything, but
this room was all his and he can do whatever
he wishes to it when he finally remembers.

The old banker's desk, a heavy thing I wanted
him to sell, finally found itself a home here.
Against the back wall stands a bookshelf that
reaches to the ceiling and is as wide as it is tall.
He'd always wanted a room like this.
Something regal and academic. He used to say
it was a place for his body to work, but a
playground for his mind.

When I had gotten him all settled into the
chair, he looked up at me. I can't explain the
look. It was almost as if there were some
small part of him that seemed to remember
me – a glint, a glimmer – and before I could
stop myself, I was moving in as natural as can
be. The moment just felt right, like the last
year had never happened and we were alone
together at his desk again with him typing
away furiously at some unknown piece of
writing and me sitting on the arm of the chair,

Sugarhouse

watching and waiting to see what gifts spilled out of him onto the page.

His lips were dry, his skin flush with warmth. He did not taste the same, but he is still my Martin. I should have left my eyes open and stared into his, a slate blue I fell in love with the moment I met him, but instead I closed them and held onto the chair to keep myself steady. The leather of the chair felt warmer than the physical connection between us.

His breathing changed and his body stiffened up against mine. As soon as it happened, I knew it was wrong, but I kept my lips to his and tried to relish every second of it; the smell of him, the bland taste of his lips, the rigidness of his entire being. Is that selfish of me? To have briefly made him my plaything? What's worse is that I knew (I knew!) that he wouldn't remember the incident the next day. I used him.

Martin didn't kiss back. In fact, I think he tried to pull away as much as one can while held captive in a chair. He said nothing, not a word, but his expression was enough; I had crossed a line. I had offended this Martin imposter, a stranger in my house.

If I thought it would bring him back, I would sacrifice anything and everything to make it happen. My husband continues to stare at me as if I'm some kind of lunatic. I'm beginning to wonder if perhaps he sees me as I am. Maybe I'm the one with the real problems.

Sugarhouse

The Man (Night)

I awake. I'm awake. I remember this place.

The room is black; night has settled outside and it takes my eyes forever to adjust to the lack of light in the room. I feel the evening breeze pass through the room; I shiver briefly. I clutch the sheets tighter around my legs and realize that I have not forgotten the day's events. The images my mind is able to conjure up don't feel hazy or fuzzy; each moment is a tangible thing I feel my brain wrapping around and holding onto tightly. They are little life rafts floating along in my own mental sea of black.

If the woman, my supposed wife, is right…then this is progress. I am making progress. I am forming memories, thoughts that can be recalled, I am repopulating the crevices of my gray matter. I am elated by this realization until I am struck by a fit of coughing, which halts my inner celebration. I am still confused by her kiss. It was soft and warm and stirred something inside me I cannot recall ever feeling, but despite her protestations, I do not know the woman. I do not remember her, anyway. I don't know if I want her to kiss me again or if I want her to keep her distance. My thoughts are a mess.

Sugarhouse

I reach for the glass of water, full again, on the nightstand to my left. I gulp from the glass thirstily. The woman from earlier said my name was Martin and that she was my wife, but these concepts are still unsure to me. They feel like the wrong mathematical answers on a chalkboard problem. Erasable, changeable, but not quite right.

I put the glass down and lean back against the headboard. A small girl stands perfectly still at the foot of the bed. I think back to the day, but don't remember seeing her before. She has dark blonde hair that cascades down to the middle of her back, a porcelain face sprinkled with freckles, and a light green dress that falls just below her knees. She wears no shoes.

"Hello, honey," I whisper. "What's your name?"

The girl smiles, says nothing. She comes to the side of the bed in silence and crawls up next to me. She is missing a front tooth, the way small children lose them early on. She curls up on my lap and leans her head against my chest. I am winded by the gesture and wrap my arms around her, feeling her dress crinkle softly against my arms. She smells of meadows and rosewater. Her head nestles up against my chin and she whispers:

"You must remember…"

Sugarhouse

"Remember what?" I whisper back, but she doesn't reply. Her soft breathing puts the room into an eerie quiet. The rhythm of her breath calms me until I quickly fall back to sleep with her still cradled in my arms.

The Man (Morning)

I awake. I'm awake. I don't remember this place at all.

It's noon. A large bay window to my right lets a cool breeze into the room. A bird chirps, a cricket rubs its legs together timidly. Clouded sunlight spots the floor. The taste of foul morning coats my tongue and I instinctively reach for the water to my left. How did I know that was there? The glass shakes in my hand as I sip.

The sheets have been kicked unceremoniously to the end of the bed and lay draped over the edge like a cephalopod climbing down to the floor. I am clammy all over. My boxers, the only clothing on me, stick to my body. A nightmare. Daymare? A terror.

I scan the room; an ornate armoire against the wall straight ahead. By the open window, a slim stand holds a rotary phone. No pictures hang on the wall, no bric-a-brac clutters the corners. It feels sterile. To the left, an open closet and in the far corner, a door. Shut.

Like a dam collapsing, I am suddenly surrounded by pressure, a feeling of steady force closing in around me. A claustrophobic feeling making me incapable of doing anything but allowing it purchase on every inch of dermis. My skin prickles and rivulets of sweat drip from underneath my

Sugarhouse

arms before rolling down my sides. I have no concept of what day it is or, truly, what time it is. Minute-wise or year-wise. I don't know that this matters much, however. It doesn't feel like it does.

I empty the glass and rise from the bed, an incredibly comfortable place with an intricate, wrought-iron headboard. Matching dressers sit on either side and hold aloft two old-school hurricane lamps turned into electric ones. I turn one on and light spills out from beneath the lampshade and fills that corner of the room. Inside the base of the lamp, however, a soft orange glow bobs and weaves as if being tossed about by a violent storm. The effect is strangely calming.

I get up, stumble upon the bathroom and take a shower. When I finish, I find that my bed has been made and the window has been shut, though the shade has been lifted further to let in more of the dim light. A pair of jeans, a shirt, socks and shoes have all been laid out on the comforter. I assume they're for me and once dressed, I put the towel back in the bathroom and continue down the hallway.

The clattering of pans and metal lids comes from downstairs, so I head in that direction. The house seems empty, as if no one else lives here but myself and whoever is

Sugarhouse

in the kitchen. This doesn't make sense to me. But not much else does either.

I head down the wide staircase, noting the tiny sculptures holding up the railing. They are old and pockmarked with age. What may have once been a nondescript and emotionless cupid now appears to have evil intentions; his smile seems crooked and I imagine seeing an unnatural gleam in his wooden eye.

At the foot of the stairs stands the front door. To my right, a sitting room filled with furniture and curio cabinets filled with pictures and trinkets. To the left of the door, a den, a study, an office; a large oak desk sits like a boulder in the middle of the room. Behind it, wall to wall bookshelves filled with binders and awards, books and picture frames. To my immediate left, a hallway leading back along the side of the stairs and heading to the back of the house. I turn left down the hallway, towards the source of the noise, and pad gingerly into a kitchen the size of the room I just awoke in.

Cabinets, stained a deep, brownish-red, line the walls. There are two stoves, neither in use. Three convection ovens stacked on top of each other stand next to a refrigerator that blends in with the rest of the cabinetry. Had the woman at the sink not opened it as I stepped into the room, I'm sure I would've assumed it was simply more cabinet space.

Sugarhouse

The woman turns from the sink and is startled by my silent appearance. I don't know this woman. I don't recognize her at all. Her face shows only surprise, but she is pretty; shoulder length chestnut hair, thin face, little to no makeup. Her eyes are big and brown – true doe eyes – and seem to smile at me before she does. "Oh. Good morning, Martin. You scared me, sneaking up on me like that." She gave a nervous laugh and covered her chest with her hand before covering her mouth.

She called me Martin. I roll the name across my lips and nothing. This doesn't feel wrong, but it doesn't feel right either. If she had simply called me "man," it would have felt truer. I am Martin. "Good morning," I croak. My voice sounds strange, not my own. Though I cannot remember what my voice is supposed to sound like.

"Are you hungry?" she asks.

I nod. "Yes, thank you. Food sounds wonderful right now."

She smiles at me, wider this time, and wipes her hands on a dishtowel on the counter. "I think some fresh air might do you some good," she says, coming around to lead me out of the kitchen. Her fingers cup my elbow gently. I can smell pork on her apron, something sweeter on her neck and wrists. Her lips are glossy, moist when she looks at me. She almost puts me at ease without realizing it.

I let her lead me past the counter and through the living room out onto a large back patio. A large marble-topped table with built-in benches surrounding it takes up most of the space, but the view is immense. Not another house in sight for miles.

"I've almost got lunch ready. When it's done, I'll bring it out to you out here, is that okay?"

Lunch outside? It's a partly cloudy, but gorgeous, day, so it's not so bright as to be uncomfortable. Yes. Lunch outside is most definitely okay. I nod. I take a seat in one of the large chairs scattered about the porch and stare out across the rolling hills. I hear the screen door shut behind me gently, a pleased and creaky sigh, then the sound of lunch being made in the kitchen again.

Where the hell am I? *Who* the hell am I?

The Woman

[Memories are the ghosts of the past made present. They cannot be trusted. What we remember may not be truth; what we forget may not be truth. It is not what we were that's important, but what we are. The present is all that matters; it is the only thing we can control and even that small bit of control is not always up to us. Some claim divine intervention, others claim karma, while more still claim fate. We all end up in the place we're supposed to be eventually. A stray path here and there takes us off-course for awhile, but we always return whether we know it or not. Our final place of rest never changes. It waits patiently for each of us.]

Day 34
06/15/93
2:15am

I let him outside today for the first time. It was like watching a newborn testing the world to see if it was safe. He spent a half hour just sitting on the porch, looking out over the property. After that, he walked along the property line, putting his hands and fingers on everything with a texture. He fondled the petals of the blue wild indigos and dawny hawthorns, ran his palms over the wood railing fence as he walked. At one point he even stopped to watch a bird build a nest for at least a quarter of an hour. Martin would not have done these things before.

Sugarhouse

I didn't want to leave him alone, but I didn't want him to feel that I was lording over him either like some kind of unwanted caretaker…though I think a case could be made that's exactly what I am.

I worry that one day he'll just up and leave. One minute he'll be sitting on the porch and the next…he's gone in any one of a hundred directions from here. I worry that one day he'll wake up and a switch inside him will get flipped and he'll walk and walk and walk away. Through the fields out back, down the road out front…I wake up terrified that he won't be in his bed and as hard as I try, I won't see his figure on the horizon. He'll have vanished without as much as a note as to where and why and I'll be right back where I started while he was in the hospital.

I guess I treat his presence like a child's now because that's essentially what he is until he gets better. I need to stop thinking this way. It's not healthy for me and it won't be healthy for him in the long run. Dr. Sullivan says I need to keep fighting this parent/child urge that seems to be taking over, but I'm not sure how yet. He is my husband, I am his wife. This is the only balance of power I should be focused on.

The house is finally clean. Of course, now that I've finished the last room, it's time to start all over again. I don't understand this house sometimes; clean a room one day only to return to it the next to find a thick layer of

Sugarhouse

dust on nearly every surface while the linens stay pristine. Regardless, the cleaner and more organized the house becomes, the more I feel the stress of things lifting. I don't feel so claustrophobic or like I'm just going through the motions.

The Man (Night)

I awake. I'm awake. I remember this place.

The room is black; night has settled outside and it takes my eyes forever to adjust to the lack of light in the room. I feel the evening breeze pass through the room; I shiver briefly. I clutch the sheets tighter around my legs and realize that I have not forgotten the day's events. The images my mind is able to conjure up don't feel hazy or fuzzy; each moment is a tangible thing I feel my brain wrapping around and holding onto tightly. They are little life rafts floating along in my own mental sea of black.

I reach for the glass of water, full again, on the nightstand to my left. I gulp from the glass thirstily. The woman from earlier said my name was Martin and that she was my wife, but these concepts are still unsure to me. They feel like the wrong mathematical answers on a chalkboard problem. Erasable, changeable, but not quite right.

I put the glass down and rise from the bed. My joints creak and pop as I walk over to the window. It is a cloudless night; dark purple-blue and starry. The moon's corona is thick tonight and bathes the fields in ghostly illumination.

From the corner of my eye, there is movement in the front yard. I see a billowing bit of fabric, a dress, down below. A girl stands there staring right up at me. I think back to the day, but don't remember seeing her before. She has dark blonde hair that cascades down to the middle of her back, a porcelain face sprinkled with freckles, and a light green dress that falls just below her knees. She wears no shoes.

I raise my hand to say hello and she returns the gesture. I realize what time it is and how strange it is that this girl is out in the yard. Her mother must not know she's out there. No parent would let a child wander around so late at night.

The girl beckons me outside and I nod. Since I am only in boxers, I search the dressers for some clothing and find a sweat suit and a pair of soft-soled shoes I knew were in the closet. I make my way downstairs and out the front door, seeing the girl standing in the same spot.

She smiles at me as I get closer and holds out her hand, which I take in mine. She is cold. Not quite freezing, but enough to make me double-check that I'm awake since it's warm for early morning. Humid even.

"Hello, honey," I whisper. "What's your name? Why are you out so late?"

The girl smiles up at me, says nothing, and points to the road. She tugs on my arm and I follow, unsure of what

Sugarhouse

she wants or why I'm following. Our feet swish through the moist grass quietly, feeling it cushion every step across the lawn. We cross the dirt road, a firm wide thing made of hardened mud and red clay, to a ditch on the other side. We stop on the edge and I look down at her, curious. She remains silent.

"What is it that you want me to see?" I ask. The ditch is deep, perhaps seven feet down and with nearly vertical walls. It's not a place either of us should be exploring, much less in the dark.

She leans over, points down into the dark. Before I can stop her, she loses her footing and falls headfirst down into the ditch. I watch in horror as her body falls limp against the ditch walls, twisting her legs and arms into uncomfortable positions until she rests, unmoving at the bottom looking straight up at me.

I slide down the side of the earthen gash, feeling the rough earth scrape against the back and sides of my legs, and end up kneeling beside her. She blinks as I cradle her head against my chest. I am stunned by the moment and wrap my arms around her, feeling her dress crinkle softly against my arms. She smells of meadows and rosewater. Her head nestles up against my chin and she whispers:

"You must remember…"

Sugarhouse

"Remember what?" I whisper back, pleading, but she doesn't reply. So I hold her, trying to figure a way out of the ditch without causing her any more harm.

I look up at both sides of the gulley; steep and with no real way for me to climb out with her in my arms. I don't want to throw her over my shoulder for fear of worsening her condition, but I may have no choice. Can I climb out on my own and get help? Is it her mother in the house that's taking care of me?

I lay the girl's head down on the ground and stand up. Frantic, I try to find somewhere on the wall where I can find a foothold; if I can find one high enough, I can pull myself up and out and get help. After several agonizing minutes searching the dark walls by hand, I find an outcropping barely big enough to fit my toes onto. I step onto the jutting rock and hoist myself up to the edge, hoping to find something to grab onto and find purchase on nothing before losing my balance. I hop off the outcropping and jump as high as I can to see if there's anything near the ledge I can aim for. Nothing but weeds and flowers, nothing safe or reliable.

I put my foot on the outcropping, ready to spring again. I throw both hands up towards the ledge as my leg kicks me up, but I feel the outcropping loosen beneath my toes. Before I can right myself, I am falling backwards into

Sugarhouse

the ditch. My back hits the ground hard and knocks the wind out of me. I open my eyes and groan, seeing the stars above me start to blur.

Then the girl is standing above me. Her face is full of concern and sympathy. She kneels down beside me, lays her hands on my chest and leans down to whisper in my ear:

"You must remember…"

Before I can ask what, everything goes black.

The Man (Morning)

I awake. I'm awake. I don't remember this place at all.

I have no idea what time of day it is. A large bay window to my right is closed and rain pelts the panes hard. Dark thunderclouds swirl and move quickly in the distance. The taste of foul morning coats my tongue and I instinctively reach for the water to my left. How did I know that was there? The glass shakes in my hand as I sip.

I empty the glass and rise from the bed, an incredibly comfortable place with an intricate, wrought-iron headboard. Matching dressers sit on either side and hold aloft two old-school hurricane lamps turned into electric ones. I turn one on and light spills out from beneath the lampshade and fills that corner of the room. Inside the base of the lamp, however, a soft orange glow bobs and weaves as if being tossed about by a violent storm. The effect is strangely calming and helps to alleviate the pounding headache I've woken up to.

The sheets have been kicked unceremoniously to the end of the bed and lay draped over the edge like a cephalopod climbing down to the floor. I am clammy all over. My pajamas stick to my body. I'm not clammy, I'm soaked. There are mud and grass stains on my knees and little

Sugarhouse

bits of detritus cover the bed. I have made a mess of someone's bed, but whose? Where am I? And where did all the grass come from?

I scan the room; an ornate armoire against the wall straight ahead. By the open window, a slim stand holds a rotary phone. No pictures hang on the wall, no bric-a-brac clutters the corners. It feels sterile. To the left, an open closet and in the far corner, a door. Shut.

Like a dam collapsing, I am suddenly surrounded by pressure, a feeling of steady force closing in around me. A claustrophobic feeling making me incapable of doing anything but allowing it purchase on every inch of dermis. My skin prickles and rivulets of sweat drip from underneath my arms before rolling down my sides. I have no concept of what day it is or, truly, what time it is. Minute-wise or year-wise. I don't know that this matters much, however. It doesn't feel like it does.

I see a pile of freshly folded clothes on the dresser and immediately change into them. Once dressed, I rip the dirty linens off the bed and gather them all into a pile with the pajamas without trying to make too much of a mess; the scattered grass bits refuse to play nicely and find their way out of the sheets and on to the floor anyway.

Sugarhouse

I stumble upon the bathroom and jump in the shower. When I finish, I find that my pile of sheets and clothing has been taken from the room and the grass clippings have been swept up; though the bed is without sheets, the room is pristine again. This must be a hotel of sorts.

I wonder where the grass clippings came from. What kind of person goes to bed so filthy and ragged? Am I that kind of person that doesn't clean up after himself? That doesn't *feel* right, though nothing really does at the moment.

I reach up to scratch the back of my head and feel the bump again. I thought I felt it while showering, but now that my hair is dry, I feel how tender it all is back there. It must be bruised; my fingers touch it gingerly and black stars light up behind my eyes, momentarily fuzzing out the room. Woozy, I sit on the bed until it passes.

There is a room down the hallway – I saw it briefly before showering – that looks like a child's room. Toys and stuffed animals populate the miniature book cases and shelf space throughout. The tiny bed is empty and made; ruffled pink pillows and sheets cover it. A stack of quilts sits on the edge. An unsmiling stuffed monkey leans against the pillows as if standing guard for the child so that no one intrudes upon her slumbering place. A ceiling fan hangs, unmoving, in

Sugarhouse

the middle of the room. The only window is on the back wall. From the doorway, I can see a vast expanse of green — sparsely forested areas surrounding tiny glens — and further out, a pond. So this is probably not a hotel, as I first thought.

I sit on the child's bed, the sheets and comforter adorned in pink sheeting and frills. A dollhouse stands in the corner. It is closed and clasped shut on the side. Homemade, I think, knowing this to be true without knowing why. The closet doors at the foot of the bed stand open; more stuffed animals lay piled up on the floor below a rod full of dresses and shirts and pants in various shades of young girl. The room is untouched, clean. *Unused?*

I am compelled to open the doll house and crawl across the floor. I flip the latch up on the side and open the structure wide, seeing the house cleaved in two, right down the middle. Each room contains the appropriate furniture (some glued down, some not) and intricate decorations splayed across the walls. Someone definitely took their time putting this together.

In the kitchen, a woman figure (*mother*) stands at the sink looking out the window towards a non-existent yard. The man figure (*father*) stands in a library facing a bookshelf. I search all the rooms for other figures, moving from lower level to upper level until finally reaching the attic (*fifth floor*)

Sugarhouse

where there is a picture of me with a small girl taped against the wall. The child figure (*daughter*) stands staring at the picture.

In the picture, I am smiling and looking into the camera. The girl appears stuck in mid-laughter; eyes closed, mouth open in joyful scream, a missing tooth exposing the roof of her mouth. Her strawberry blonde curls rub against my neck as she reaches up beneath my chin and holds my cheek. Her hand is small, *so small*, against the rough skin of my aging face. We are happy; we are overjoyed. Who are we?

Am I a father? Is this my daughter? These ideas flood my aching head, pounding against the walls already being pounded on and I shut my eyes.

Sugarhouse

The Woman

[When Thomas Edison died in 1931, his friend Henry Ford trapped the inventor's dying breath in a bottle. If one is to believe a final breath could be ensnared as such, what's to say we can't do the same for a soul? Why would we want to? Like the wild animal, each of us has an ache to live the way we want, to be free of physical boundaries. Perhaps this is why man has tried so hard over the years in finding a way to make his feet leave the surface of the earth. Perhaps this is why he cranes his neck upward and risks injury trying to reach the moon.]

Day 62
07/13/93
6:17pm

I left him alone again. Two months in, and
I'm finally getting better about it, *allowing*
myself to get better about it. Trying to let go,
trying to let him do whatever he feels like
doing, but it's always in the back of my mind
that he isn't progressing. He's not on a
learning curve, so I worry that he could vanish
one day, poof, never to be seen again. This
rips me in two. He'd be gone, which would
devastate me, but it wouldn't be intentional
on his part. He wouldn't do it to hurt me.
Would he?

He woke up this morning with grass all over
his pajamas – again. And complaining of
headaches – again. This is the third or fourth

Sugarhouse

time both have happened in the last month
and I'm at a complete loss for any
explanation. The sheets were soaked and grass
filings were everywhere. I had to start the
laundry while he was in the shower. I don't
know how that all got there. I didn't hear him
get up last night, but then again…I fell asleep
pretty hard. But still, if he's sleepwalking,
maybe that's a good sign? I'll have to ask Dr.
Sullivan if that's possible. I can't imagine it
being progress though, especially if he seems
to be hurting himself while out traipsing
about in the dark.

I'm thinking about driving him around at
some point. I don't know how he'll react to
being in a car again. I wonder if the sensation
will trigger his mind back into a working
capacity. The photos haven't helped and
neither has walking around the property. If
something doesn't give soon, I might.

The Woman

[The house is almost quiet. A floorboard creaks, a wall shifts and sighs. The muted sound of a dishwasher running in the kitchen hums and echoes through the old halls. A breeze flows from one end of the house to the other, from screen door on the porch to open windows facing the backyard. Curtains flap in the wake, billowing out like the long lappets of jellyfish in no hurry to get anywhere in particular. The leaves of the potted plants and flowers in the den rustle in a gentle photosynthetic symphony. A ladybug explores a window sill in the den. If one listens hard enough, they can hear a dog barking from the closest house a mile away. Two birds chirp a conversation somewhere near the driveway. The cicadas make their presence known. A neighbor's cat, a country gypsy of sorts, leaps up on the railing of the porch and stalks imaginary prey on silent, padded steps.]

Day 91
08/11/93
10:15am

Martin shows no signs of remembering me. Doctor Sullivan said this would be a long process, but this has been the longest three months of my life. Sometimes I wish that I was the one that had lost all ties to the past. It would be so much easier – but then I get angry for thinking that way. Some days, the pain makes for a good anchor and keeps me grounded. Other days, I find myself walking the halls in a daze with no particular

Sugarhouse

destination in mind and no reason for doing anything but haunting this house.

Every day it's the same; he wakes and I become the teacher. There is a margin of instinct in him. He knows the water on the nightstand is for drinking, and he feels shame at nakedness around a woman he doesn't seem to know. He remains familiar with the use of kitchenware and toiletries, but the specifics of who and why are intangible concepts. Each day is a new one for him, but only for that day, and then his very "*him-ness*" gets erased. He is rediscovering himself every morning, but his identity remains out of reach. Perhaps there is some small consolation in knowing he can't fathom the irony of his own tragedy.

Those months he lay comatose in the hospital, he was trapped within himself, a prisoner of his own mind. His mind has now, however, given him complete and absolute freedom. I'm not sure which situation is worse.

My mother is no help, of course. She still believes that Martin is faking it all just so he can laze around the house, which is simply absurd. Martin would never have done that before the accident, so I can't imagine him doing it after. There is genuine confusion in his eyes when he wakes up and he wakes up at almost the exact same time every day. I see Hell inside his irises and it stares straight back

Sugarhouse

at me. It's Martin's body, but the man inside him is a stranger to us both.

I'm not asking for all of Martin back, I just want a small piece or two, something to attach my hopes to. For now, they remain untethered.

The Man (Morning)

I awake. I'm awake. I don't remember this place at all.

It's noon. A large bay window to my right lets a warm breeze into the room. A bird chirps, a cricket rubs its legs together timidly. Sunlight spills across the floor. The taste of foul morning coats my tongue and I instinctively reach for the water to my left. How did I know that was there? The glass shakes in my hand as I sip.

The sheets have been kicked unceremoniously to the end of the bed and lay draped over the edge like a cephalopod climbing down to the floor. I am clammy all over. My boxers, the only clothing on me, stick to my body. A nightmare. Daymare? A terror.

I scan the room; an ornate armoire against the wall straight ahead. By the open window, a slim stand holds a rotary phone. No pictures hang on the wall, no bric-a-brac clutters the corners. It feels sterile. To the left, an open closet and in the far corner, a door. Shut.

Like a dam collapsing, I am suddenly surrounded by pressure, a feeling of steady force closing in around me. A claustrophobic feeling making me incapable of doing anything but allowing it purchase on every inch of dermis. My skin prickles and rivulets of sweat drip from underneath my arms before rolling down my sides. I have no concept of what day it is or, truly, what time it is. Minute-wise or year-wise. I don't know that this matters much, however. It doesn't feel like it does.

The breeze from the window carries with it a creaking sound from outside. It is a slow and rhythmic sound that begins to soothe rather than annoy. I get out of bed and stand at the window, basking in the warmth of the sun rays. I hear robins, I hear cicadas. I hear the sound a day makes and the claustrophobic feeling dissipates slowly as I stand in front of the open window with my eyes shut. I have no idea where I am, but in this moment, I simply don't care. I am calm again.

I hear a knock and turn to the door. A small girl stands perfectly still in the doorway. She has dark blonde hair that cascades down to the middle of her back, a porcelain face sprinkled with freckles, and a light green dress that falls just below her knees. She wears no shoes.

"Hello, honey," I whisper. "What's your name?"

The girl smiles, says nothing. She comes to the window and leans her head against my thigh. When she looks up at me, I notice that she is missing a front tooth, the way small children lose them early on. She grabs my pinky with both of her hands and tugs gently. I kneel down beside her and smell…what? Meadows and rosewater? The sun beats down on both of us, blinding me to the point of turning her into a faceless glow. She is all corona.

She tugs on my hand again and then leaves the room. I stand to, not understanding this game. I follow her down a long hallway with that is well lit from a skylight at the end. I can see that it's cloudy outside, but only with those perfectly bright, white clouds that lay stark against the pristine blue around them. Six doors line the hallway, all open, all curious.

I pass the first and look in. A child's bedroom, but larger. Toys and stuffed animals populate the tiny book cases and shelf space throughout. The tiny bed is empty and made; ruffled pink pillows and sheets cover it. A stack of quilts sits on the edge. An unsmiling stuffed monkey leans against the pillows as if standing guard for the child so that no one intrudes upon her slumbering place. A ceiling fan hangs, unmoving, in the middle of the room. The only window is on the back wall. From the doorway, I can see a vast expanse of green – sparsely forested areas surrounding tiny glens – and further out, a pond.

I move to the next door and find a bathroom. Three of the doors lead to empty rooms. Wooden floors, bare walls, nothing save for a curtain-less window in the exact middle of

Sugarhouse

each back wall. The final door at the end of the hallway is ajar. I can see bookshelves, a file cabinet, a couch - a quiet reading room perched there at the top of the stairs.

I look down to the first floor and see the young girl smiling up at me, anxious and waving me on, wordlessly telling me to *hurryhurryhurry*. I head down the wide staircase, noting the tiny sculptures holding up the railing. They are old and pockmarked with age. What may have once been a non-descript and emotionless cupid now appears to have evil intentions; his smile seems crooked and I imagine seeing an unnatural gleam in his wooden eye.

At the foot of the stairs stands the front door. To my right, a sitting room filled with furniture and curio cabinets filled with pictures and trinkets. To the left of the door, a den, a study, an office; a large oak desk sits like a boulder in the middle of the room. Behind it, wall to wall bookshelves filled with binders and awards, books and picture frames. To my immediate left, a hallway leading back along the side of the stairs and heading to the back of the house. I turn left down the hallway, watching the child skip through the house, and pad gingerly into a kitchen the size of the room I just awoke in.

Cabinets, stained a deep, brownish-red, line the walls. There are two stoves, neither in use. Three convection ovens stacked on top of each other stand next to a refrigerator that blends in with the rest of the cabinetry. The back door is open and the nameless girl swings the screen-door wide for me. I'm to go outside then. At least the weather is good for it.

I hear the slow, rhythmic creaking again. She leads me around the side of the house and I'm stunned by the sight of the thickest, tallest tree I've ever seen. That I think I've ever seen, anyway. On the closest limb, a tree swing sits motionless. I walk around its gargantuan trunk, looking for the girl, but she has disappeared, outran me, hidden. I look up into the branches and it takes me a moment to realize there is a woman there, hanging from a rope. Her body sways in the breeze; the rope she dangles from is the source of the rhythmic creaking.

I don't know this woman. I don't recognize her at all, and were she alive, she would be pretty; shoulder length chestnut hair, thin face, little to no makeup. Her eyes are open, forever seeing; big and brown. True doe eyes. My skin crawls and prickles the child must not understand this moment, must not understand the severity of this *now*. Why else would she be smiling?

A note is attached to the cuff of her pants leg. The name *Martin* is scrawled across it in swooping, swirling letters and I wonder if I am Martin, wonder if the note is for me. I

Sugarhouse

unpin it from the cuff gently, and begin to read, completely forgetting about the girl for the time being. It doesn't even occur to me until much later to bring her down from the limb.

The Woman

[At the end, sometimes you forget how much others depend on you. Or perhaps it becomes that much clearer and makes the end sour a little more. A faithful pet will often sit by the body of its dead master and starve itself. Out of compassion or confusion, loyalty or something else, this is what loss does – it takes a part of something whole and refuses to give it back. You cannot fight loss with fists. You cannot beat loss with more loss. Sometimes we are just meant to lose.]

Day 113
09/12/93
9:37am

Dear Martin (yes, your name is Martin),

If you're reading this, then you have found me, your wife (yes, your wife), hanging like some skinny bird feeder blown about in the wind. I can't imagine what the initial shock will be like for you since I am a stranger to you every time you wake up. There is a certain kind of solace I take in the fact that you won't have to grieve for me the way you might have before the accident two years ago. You will forget about me as soon as you sleep and that is a kind tragedy in and of itself.

This letter is for you, husband that I have loved before, during, and after you came back from the dead (for your heart stopped in the emergency room for the longest minute of my life). You may never remember these things on your own, but mind the date at the top of this letter and keep it by your bedside to remind you

Sugarhouse

*every day; you are NOT a hollow man, you are NOT
a stranger, you ARE my Martin and you ARE a
good person, confused as you may be for however long.*

*You are/were a father — this is the truth.
You are/were my husband — this is the truth.
Our daughter, Elsie, is dead — this is the truth.
She has been dead for two years — this is the truth.
You were driving her home when it happened — this is
the truth.
It was an accident — this is the truth.
You awake every day in our home — this is the truth.
You may never come to remember me or Elsie — this is
the truth.
You will need to seek out Dr. Sullivan — this is the
immediate and most important truth right now.*

*You came home on May 15th, 1993. Like an infant
who could already walk and talk and eat on your
own, I took care of you and hoped (beyond any
rational means) that something would stir your murky
soup of a memory into something tangible and real,
into something you would wake up and remember the
next day, and remember the next day…and yet you,
through no fault of your own, are a blank slate every
morning. The sun rises and wipes your mind clean
when it shines through the window. Selfishly, I often
wished over the last few months that I had that same
luxury, that you and I could simply start each day
brand new over and over again. Together.*

*You're probably thinking I must've been a terrible
wife now, what with all this being laid out for you.
This must all sound like a terrible guilt-trip being put
on your shoulders and I hope that's not what you take
away from this. When you meet with Dr. Sullivan,*

Sugarhouse

there will be people who want to poke and prod you, run more tests on you, find out what is broken inside you that cannot make the memories remain fixed. This is fine, but they may not always tell you the truth and if I do one thing right in this last act of living, I want you to have the truth, and all of it, ugly as some of it may be.

I've kept a journal since Elsie's death. It was part of my therapy once you were hospitalized and I had no one in this house of ours. It is unfortunately raw in places, but it is the truth. The journal is in your desk in the study, along with a drawer full of albums of you and me and Elsie. These are all yours to one day, hopefully (oh so hopefully) cherish the way I cherish the both of you.

After four months of nursing you back to health, of trying everything to make your memories return, to unfog you, I cannot stand by any longer and watch another member of my family die while I figure out how to deal with it. I moved from room to room while you and Elsie were both hospitalized, but she passed mercifully quick while your brain erased itself. I wish you could've been awake to say goodbye to her. I wish you were "awake" so I wouldn't have to say goodbye to you now.

Know that she loved you immensely ("bigger than the sky," she used to say) and know that I love you the same, though I can never expect that feeling to be reciprocated.

I don't know what's worse — that tomorrow you will wake up and be unable to conjure up your lover's face

Sugarhouse

on a whim and a smile or that I have given up on you.
And myself.

All my love, my heart,

Christine

The Man (Mourning)

I awake. I'm awake. I don't remember this place at all.

It's noon. A large bay window to my right lets a warm breeze into the room. A bird chirps, a cricket rubs its legs together timidly. Sunlight spills across the floor. The taste of foul morning coats my tongue and I instinctively reach for a glass of water that is not there.

The sheets have been kicked unceremoniously to the end of the bed and lay draped over the edge like a cephalopod climbing down to the floor. I am clammy all over. My boxers, the only clothing on me, stick to my body. A nightmare. Daymare? A terror.

I scan the room; an ornate armoire against the wall straight ahead. By the open window, a slim stand holds a rotary phone. No pictures hang on the wall, no bric-a-brac clutters the corners. It feels sterile. To the left, an open closet and in the far corner, a door. Shut.

Like a dam collapsing, I am suddenly surrounded by pressure, a feeling of steady force closing in around me. A claustrophobic feeling making me incapable of doing anything but allowing it purchase on every inch of dermis. My skin prickles and rivulets of sweat drip from underneath my arms before rolling down my sides. I have no concept of

Sugarhouse

what day it is or, truly, what time it is. Minute-wise or year-wise. I don't know that this matters much, however. It doesn't feel like it does.

I hear a little girl's voice in the hallway and notice a note on the nightstand. The name *Martin* is scrawled across it in swooping, swirling letters and I wonder if I am Martin. I wonder if the note is for me.

The Memory of a Gypsy Moth

A forever sky the color of old blood on bandage was backlit by a sun hidden behind the opaque haze that had come and never left. The ocean seemed to burn eternal flames all the way out and past the shimmery horizon. All you saw were reds and oranges, yellows that lit up and stained the backs of closed eyelids. If you stared long enough, that horizon line burned itself across the retina for weeks, slicing through every visible thing. The sky seemed to be the only thing you could rely on anymore.

You were too young to fully understand then, but by the time you and your sister came to tossing chance in the air, the answers to your survival were laid out in front of you. Big chunks of truth too large, too dense to be swallowed.

Heads or tails? she asked. You looked up, saw her silhouetted against angry sky. You didn't understand the tremor in her voice, couldn't fathom the immensity of the choice. The glint of silver twinkled in mid-air as the coin went up and came down, flipped end over end, landing in the palm of her hand. She flipped it onto her wrist, kept it covered, waited for you to choose before looking fate in the eye.

What does it matter? you asked. *Why does one of us have to leave?*

A sniffle, a clothed arm slid across the bottom of nose, a snorting of sinus. It's not leaving, she said with watery voice.

The Memory of a Gypsy Moth

First father, then oldest sister. Mother passed from grief and then it was only you and other sister. Alone, with each other. They weren't here, so they left. No goodbyes. No farewells.

A breeze rustled her tattered skirt, wrapped it around her legs as you stared up at her. You came forward, wrapped your arms around her waist and felt your own hot tears stain the dirty fabric. You felt her dress stick to your face as your hands clasped each other across her back.

You remembered the meals together, meager but rich. The holding of hands for prayer. You never closed your eyes and always sneaked glances up, saw the sorrow in mother and father's faces, saw the looks they gave each other before doling out the largest portions to you and your sisters.

It didn't used to be like this, but you were too young to remember then. You had to rely on stories from everyone else, had to listen, confused, at how so much could have changed in so little time.

Heads or tails? she asked.

Father used to have a job and wouldn't always be at dinner, then he always was. First a foreman with a construction company, then a door to door salesman, finally settling into butchery right there on the property. When the townsfolk stopped paying for the heft of his blade, the family livestock dwindled down and became your meals. He taught you and your sisters how each blade served a different purpose. He taught you the slow hand of fat-trimming, the precision of separating the skin from the meat below. He wanted you prepared.

After the money was gone, after the livestock had all been carved up and served, the meals became sparse; unripe root vegetables from the garden sliced and diced into tiny, but equal, portions. Bellies rumbled, skin shrunk on the bone, father's face held the worry of the world in each crow's foot. Tempers held in check during the meal erupted when it was finished.

Your sisters took you for walks when the shouting came. You remembered scattershot dreams of blackened lakes and skies lit up by purple lightning and warm snowfall that smudged your clothing gray in spots.

A sniffle, a clothed arm slid across the bottom of nose, a snorting of sinus.

You remembered the sounds of sobbing coming from mother and father's bedroom at night while you slept between your sisters, their teenage warmth cocooning you until dawn. Some nights you'd awake sweaty, clothes clinging to skin. The savage smell of puberty hung in the air around you.

It's not leaving, Rory.

Once father left, it was you and the women. You knew nothing of the world that you couldn't see yourself and no one spoke about it in front of you. Not at meal times, not while playing, not even in whispered secrets. But when father left, you all ate well for awhile. Meat was plentiful and there was no shouting after dinner. You wondered often where he had gone and why he'd left you, but mother always said it was for the best, though she cried when she said so.

Heads or tails? sister whined. *Don't make me choose.*

You loosened your grip around her, felt your arms fall to your sides as she held the coin against her wrist, arms elevated above your head.

You remembered the notches carved out in the doorframe as you stood with your back against it, the many divots a history of your slow growth into manhood.

You remembered your father's arms above you, holding kite string tight while the flying colors sailed in bluer skies.

You remembered reaching up to lowest limb while chasing sisters up the tree. You remembered being nestled into the folds of mother's bosom as she helped you count the stars.

Rory, please.

You remembered oldest sister holding your favorite toy out of reach above you as she squealed with glee.

The Memory of a Gypsy Moth

You remembered younger sister pulling you up onto her bed, the one you couldn't climb up on your own.

You remembered watching mother cook while you stood at the counter, your head nowhere close to the counter's edge.

You remembered father's arms wrapped around your torso, hoisting you around the house as if you were flying.

It's not leaving. It's not, it's not, it's not.

A sniffle, a clothed arm slid across the bottom of nose, a snorting of sinus.

Where did they all go? Where will we go? What will we do? you asked. You could see her eyes brimming with tears, ringed in red. Her lips quivered behind her teeth, her face taut, stretched tight to show strength where none existed.

I can't tell you, I can only show you. But you have to choose.

No. Show me first. Then I'll choose.

A heavy sigh. An exaltation of larks took flight from the tree line beyond, spread out like an undulating black wave across the ocean of sky. You watched it fold in on itself, spiraling over and over, becoming hypnotized by the fluidity of their dance. Their wings seemed to beat together in a rhythmic precision, a living machine on display for those stuck on the ground.

Sister lifted her hand off her wrist, glanced at the coin before putting it in her dress pocket, and held out her hand.

The Memory of a Gypsy Moth

You took it, felt the tears drying on her young skin. Her fingers wrapped around yours and you followed her across the property.

The tree-line used to block their view of the road into town, but now stood ragged and broken, part ash and part petrified. A phenomenon your father had never understood or tried to explain. It simply was.

She guided you towards the shack you were never allowed to enter. It sat nestled at the bottom of a gently sloping meadow. Once green, the dead grass crunched and crisped beneath your shoes, flaked apart and stuck to your frayed shoelaces.

You remembered how oldest sister taught you to tie them when your fingers became nimble enough.

You remembered being pushed down the slope on sunny days by youngest sister. You remembered mother's warnings about playing near the shack, citing danger and tools meant for boys much older than you.

Show me. I will choose.

The shack was half the size of the home, built of rotting wood, peeling paint, and falling dust motes from every crevice. Sister opened the heavy, rickety door and led you inside.

Bruised sunlight filtered through the fractured slats of the walls, made the space feel like the inside of a diseased and withering heart. A stone butchering slab sat monolithic in the center. Stains the color of the sun covered it in waves and dried puddles, but you couldn't remember a time when the family owned animals. The room smelled of life gone, of sadness, of things you couldn't understand. The hiss of summer insects rattled loudly inside the shack, reminded you of when you used to play more and worry less.

You remembered the ripple of placid lake water when tossing in stones.

You remembered your sisters splashing water on your face and crying because the water blinded you.

You remembered pictures of you being bathed in the sink, still fresh from birth.

Sister looked down at the table, gripped your hand tighter. You could feel the strength in her fingers, the frailty in her palm. You imagined her heartbeat thumping deep and slow beneath the surface of her clammy skin. Outside, the wind lifted, whistled through the slats and tousled your hair.

Heads or tails?

What is this? you asked quietly, not wanting to shatter the moment. You didn't understand why you felt the need for whispers, why you felt a sense of strange reverence, but it was all-consuming. It felt right, in a way.

Rory. Please.

On the wall, five railroad ties. Three held darkened, soiled clothing while the others remained empty and unused. Above each, an inscription:

Nail One:

A pair of faded and frayed chinos, covered in patchwork and awkward stitching.

One belt strung through a single belt loop, hanging limp and almost touching the ground. On top of that, a single plaid shirt (faded dark blue), the back of which stuck out below (one) heavy brown coat, leather, coming apart at the seams.

The inscription: "The first sacrifice; the first and last love."

Nail Two:

One pleated skirt, stained with dirt where the knees would be, the yellow fabric dim in spots but stained dark beneath the arms.

On top of that, a pair of once-white leggings framed with canvas shoes hung by the shoestrings knotted together at the top of the nail.

One red hair ribbon flits in the breeze.

The inscription: "The second sacrifice; my eldest, the protector."

Nail Three:

Another pleated skirt, brown and not quite crisp.

The Memory of a Gypsy Moth

Darker stains lay splotched across its landscape in near circles and falling puddles.

A silken slip, a beige bra.

Heavy boots with toes worn through and the soles rubbed soft.

A tarnished locket hung low between them, swung and spun in the air.

The inscription: "The third sacrifice; from her came we all to this place."

You remembered the clothing, remembered burying face in all the fabrics at one point or another.

You remembered the figures that filled them, wore them daily.

You remembered the locket open and hypnotizing.

You remembered the hair ribbon slipping off during play, escaping on the wind of a spring afternoon.

You remembered the heavy lumbering of boots on the floor in the morning, waking you from deadest sleep.

A sniffle, a clothed arm slid across the bottom of nose, a snorting of sinus.   It wasn't leaving; you understood now, but didn't fully comprehend.

Heads or tails, Rory?

To the right of the nails hung father's tools, gleaming and bright in the dim light of the shack. Clean and silver, they seemed sharp and new. A hand hook, sticking knives,

The Memory of a Gypsy Moth

cimeters and bone saws. Node hooks, wire cutters, chop knives, a block brush.

It's not really leaving.

No, Rory. Not really.

A sniffle, a clothed arm slid across the bottom of nose, a snorting of sinus.

Will I see you again?

I hope so, I really do.

You stood there in the scattered light of the shack, stared up at sister who couldn't bring herself to look down at you. She clutched herself tight, as if she were cold or trying to keep the last bit of her humanity imprisoned inside her.

You reached out, slid your hand in her pocket and removed the coin. It felt heavy in your hand, big. A face etched on one side, a building on another. You turned it over and over, examining every facet, every divot made around the edge until laying it flat on the stone slab.

Tell me what happens, you said. *Tell me how it's not really leaving.*

She leaned down, whispered hard, sobbing the truth of your survival in your ear. When she was done, she cradled your face in her hands, wiped your tears away, then her own. You understood now. Your stomach roiled at the idea, turned and seemed to fight your survival instinct until you finally came to peace with the decision.

The Memory of a Gypsy Moth

Heads, you said, and sister flipped the coin again. The glint of silver twinkled in mid-air as the coin went up and came down, flipped end over end, landing in the palm of her hand. She flipped it onto her wrist, kept it covered.

*   *   *

Nail Four:

Another pleated skirt, hung from the neckline and wafting.

No necklace, no ribbons, but a coin, unseen, sat quietly in the right hand pocket.

Scuffed, black shoes dangled from the nail, brown soles pockmarked with rubbed color, showing the beige beneath.

The inscription: "The fourth sacrifice; she held my hand until the end."

Equity Lamp

They say God got lost in the satellites, as if He was some scrambled bit of signal transmitted by televised shepherds to a sofa-bound flock clutching remotes like rosaries. As if He were the culmination of our collected knowledge inscribed on shiny surfaces, sent out to those life forms that have already checked in on us and said "no thanks." As if God, our creator, would get lost in the objects of our primitive imaginations made real.

As if.

I don't know how much truth there is to that, God lost in the technology. What I do know is that if He was ever here at all, He's long gone now and left the world completely dark. Sure, there's a flicker of true faith here and there, but separating the devout from the fanatic is harder. They've got the same books, the same text – essentially the same basic dogma – but even they can't agree on the message. It's as if they all still stand at the base of Babel speaking past each other in foreign dialects and intonations. As if they didn't all have the same flames burning inside them. As if the name "God" didn't mean the same thing in every language.

As if.

*　　*　　*

Right or wrong, this is what I believe:

Equity Lamp

I believe that the sun wants to shine for longer than one quick hour of the day.

I believe the roaming gangs of armed teenagers are desperate to be held by someone, anyone, other than each other.

I believe the words coming from the television are dangerous half-truths.

I believe in the phony smiles of politicians and religious leaders because they remind me that capitalism doesn't die easily.

I believe in fate, but not luck.

I believe in ritual, but not superstition.

I believe in romance, but rarely show it.

I believe that burning the pages of a book keeps me warmer than the message scribed inside it ever can.

I believe in violence, but I don't agree with it.

I believe in the importance of expanding one's intellect, even in a time when intellect is vilified and made a second class citizen when placed side by side with the fist.

I believe a single bullet to the right person or idea can do more damage than several clips unloaded into a lowing crowd.

I don't believe we set foot on the moon. Or Mars. Or any other planet, crater, ring of sky dust, star, comet, galaxy, or black hole.

I don't believe we can do better, but we make an art of trying to do worse.

I believe the human condition is built to sink easily and struggle when on the rise.

I believe that touch is the most important of the senses; the other four are wonderfully overindulgent.

I believe that when the effigies of normal, rational men are burned from tree limbs and porches, civilization has jumped the shark.

I believe that I am stoic on the outside, but that I tremble on the inside.

I believe that I'm afraid and I cannot seem to stop that fear from spreading inside me like a cancer. I see where things have gone, I see where things are headed. I won't say we need a miracle, since I don't believe in them, but a huge leg up on a global scale would be a phenomenal step in the right direction.

*　　　*　　　*

Karlos and I sat on the 35th floor balcony of a vacant condominium. It's kind of a routine now, like back in the day when older folks used to post up on porches, smoking pipes and sipping coffee. We found some old plastic chairs in the lobby while out exploring one day and carried them around

Equity Lamp

with us. With no one living in the building anymore, we had the run of the place. Time was irrelevant now, so if we felt it was daytime, we'd choose a balcony on the west side of the building. If we felt it was nighttime (which now seemed perpetual), we'd find a balcony on the east side. The constant midnight colored sky could make you crazy if you didn't just give into its reality and roll with it.

Sometimes we'd make our way up to the roof, but it was better to be on a balcony. If someone happened to see us from down below, it'd be harder for them to figure out our exact position and sneak up on us. The problem was remembering which unit we'd left our chairs in last, but even the search for them became part of the fun, a sort of hide-and-seek for the day's comfort. The first time we came back, it took us several hours to find them. Neither of us had thought to remember the unit or floor number, so we agreed to never do it from then on out. It's the small things that keep us amused these days.

The wind wasn't so bad today. It could get so that we couldn't speak over it, and that was fine, but conversation made the time pass faster and I think we both wanted to fast forward to a different existence, a different *now* that suited us better. I don't think that's much different from before the blackout though. People in general are rarely happy with the present and assume the future will be better. I think we're

Equity Lamp

birthed with a sense of hope ingrained in us that life is meant to constantly chip away at until it's just a sliver of cynicism.

But something had changed in Karlos recently. He was never a dark person to begin with, but he seemed...lighter? There was more truth to his face now. He smiled more and the crow's feet around his eyes and mouth were more pronounced. Whatever had changed, he wasn't saying and I wasn't about to pry. At least one of us had a reason to have some kind of mirth and that was all to the good.

I stared out at the dark skyline, trying to remember the places from memory: the Oakfield Mall, Marty's Deli, the shoe store, the vast empty stadium where no games had been played as long as we could remember. We speculated that the decks and locker rooms had been populated by those wanting to feel more protected than a dark home could provide. But we didn't know for sure. I claimed the cement structure felt more solid. Karlos thought it was an act of nostalgia for younger days, for teenage years spent in physical education classes. I don't think either of us was completely wrong.

"Saw a blind girl walking around last week," he said, finally breaking the comfortable silence.

"Alone?"

I heard him uncork the bottle of rye, heard him spit it out and then the dull ring of cork on metal railing. I heard him chug twice and then the bottle was thrust out to me, rested against my arm. "Just out and about like a usual day."

I tipped the bottle up, drank, grimaced. Not the best of whiskeys, but we couldn't really be picky any more. Anyone else would be surprised that he even had any at this point, but I knew he sat on a hidden stash somewhere. While the rest of the city looted for supplies and furniture and electronics they assumed would work later, Karlos had pilfered a mountain of booze. I think he may have been the smartest of all of us by this simple act alone.

"How old?" I asked, passing the bottle back.

Karlos shrugged. "Old enough to still be called a girl, I s'pose."

"Think she knows?"

"What?"

"That we, the whole city, see things the way she does now."

"I think she's probably noticed there's no sun since it doesn't get hot during the day anymore."

"Hm."

"But I'm sure someone's told her. I can't imagine her being completely alone." He tipped the bottle again, licked his lips. "It's dangerous to be on your own these days."

I nodded, said nothing, tried to remember where the old hardware supply store sat, a big box of a building to the north. After all these months, it was still unnerving to not see the garish neon signs of fast food joints, retailers, bars. Not just unnerving, but disorienting. Strange how those most commonplace things become such easy landmarks for the city dweller.

"Heard anything from the outside world, lately?" he asked.

"Nah. I don't know that I'll hear from Sarah and the girls again. I just hope they made it somewhere with more life than here."

"Light?"

"Life. But light, too, yeah."

Another swig and a sound of satisfaction. The bottle tapped my arm.

"I miss reading. Is that weird? I liked reading before bed. The entire house would be dark except for the single lamp on my night table. Bad detective novels, wonky new fiction, fishing magazines. Anything."

I tipped the bottle, felt a rivulet escape out the side and run down my chin. "That's not weird, no. Why would you think it was weird? You've still got books, right?"

"Of course not. Had to burn them for heat. Burned the bad ones first, obviously, but no. They're all gone now. What do you miss?"

"My wife. My girls. A nice dinner. Picnics in the park on a sunny day. The news."

"The news?"

I took another sip and passed the bottle back. "The news."

"Why? It was never good for anything."

I stood up and leaned against the railing. Amazing that even the stars had plinked out, disappeared, been swallowed up by darkness. What had we done that wiped out an entire ocean of dead starlight beamed in from millions of miles away?

"I liked the clichéd morning coffee while reading the paper. I never did the sports or entertainment sections. Always the editorials. I guess it's not the news so much as it was reading the common man's opinion on things great and small. If I could get a paper delivered to me daily, just to feel a little bit of normal, that'd be alright."

"Why deliver news to the dead?"

"We aren't dead yet. This is interlude."

Karlos took another swig, set the bottle on the ground and joined me at the railing. He snorted, hawked a loogie, and sent it swirling end over end out into the dark.

"Well, at least there's one good thing about all this," he said.

"Hm?"

"I don't get electric bills in the mail anymore. I don't get nothing in the mail anymore."

*   *   *

I don't believe in the oft-promised happy endings of my childhood.

I don't believe that scientists make good politicians, or vice versa.

I don't believe we're going to get another chance. I don't believe we're going to get saved this time.

I don't believe in warning labels on mattresses, on toys for small children, or on prescription pill bottles. If you have no common sense, you should die a common death, something so unspectacular it barely registers a response much less an obituary.

I don't believe Karlos is the Luddite he makes himself out to be. His moments of true sophistication may be rare, but they are more profound than those of many academics I've known over the years.

I don't believe there is a blind girl walking through this desolate waste of a city. If she exists, much of what I do believe goes out the window. I believe I'm afraid to separate myself from my own dogma.

I don't believe we did this on our own.

Equity Lamp

I don't believe in free will, free advice, or the word *free* itself; I believe in the currency of a good and honest barter.

I believe in the unity of one and no more.

I believe my wife left for good reasons, but I don't believe my daughters are any safer for it.

I don't believe pushers have ever had the answers, but I believe that addicts have always asked the right questions.

*   *   *

Later, I awoke from a nap and instinctively reached for the watch on the night stand. The hands twisted and moved around in concentric circles. It hadn't worked right since the blackout. No time piece had, in fact. The digital clocks were obviously paper weights now, what with no electricity, but the mechanical ones fascinated me almost to the point of obsession.

The one on my table was a gift from my father's estate when he passed, a German pocket-watch of solid gold that opened up to a glass face exposing the cogs and spring wheels beneath. On the back, the words "Wind True" were inscribed. I could never decide whether the phrase was meant as instruction for the watch or the wearer.

Once Sarah left (and before the rioting), I went walking around the city more and more. I kept coming across piles of watches and clocks, which struck me as odd until I dug the pocket-watch out of its velvet case. When I saw the hands moving erratically, regardless of winding, I understood the leavings across the city. Not completely, but it seemed to make a little more sense. Who needed an obviously busted clock?

I began sifting through the piles, digging out time piece after time piece; cuckoos, grandfathers, desk types, old school alarms. All of them ran at different speeds and in different directions. I was fascinated by the phenomenon and carried as many home in my hands as possible. The living room and kitchen walls were quickly covered; family photos replaced and put in boxes. I never planned on trying to figure out the mystery, I just liked the inherent weirdness of it all.

I guess I'm not surprised that we never truly harnessed the wonder of time. Running ever forward even while we kept looking back, it laughed at us as we plummeted to some unknown depths. I think I liked this fact while the rest of the city shunned it and tossed it from view, tried to forget it. But time doesn't stop just because you stop believing in it. Even if the clock hands move erratically, they're still moving, still reminding you that something larger than you is always in perpetual motion.

Eventually I stopped collecting them on my walks. I should've stopped walking as well, what with the gangs of teenagers growing daily, but I couldn't help myself. Karlos liked to explore the abandoned museums now, and I had my walks. We both needed some kind of routine to adhere to so we didn't completely lose it altogether. We were restless, bored with how life, like the clocks, had lost all normal functions and put us on the defensive.

I slipped on some pants, a pair of boots, and a shirt that smelled like two months ago. I grabbed a water bottle and an old bag of stale crackers from the kitchen pantry and left the house. I don't know that I will ever get used to the constant feel of nighttime. I don't know how the Norwegians did it. Or was it Alaska that sees months of darkness at a time? I can never remember. I can never seem to remember to arm myself before leaving the house either. I may be subconsciously anxious for a true crushing of my routine. Like I'm waiting for the universe to make the first move.

The streets were empty. Once I was awake, I was awake for awhile. I spent a lot of time randomly napping, sleeping whenever I chose to and, with no sun hanging in the sky (sometimes it doesn't show up for weeks), my circadian rhythms had been thrown out of whack. I got my rest, I ate my meals, I walked. This was life in a dead city.

About an hour later, I came across a rusted bike leaned up against the side of an abandoned, boarded up home. This was good fortune as I had used my eldest daughter's pink bike to get around before it got stolen. The pedals creaked and cried as I propelled myself out of the neighborhood. It was more noise than I would've liked, but I was moving with good speed.

There was a park I used to meet Sarah and the girls at sometimes on my lunch break, back when people had jobs, back when jobs existed. It was a small place, but lush and green with a pond. The ducks and geese that swam there would often stop traffic as they crossed the street aimlessly. I steered the bike to our meeting place and leaned it against the tree. The pond had shrunk in size, turned brackish with tendrils of some dark green plant life crawling up out of the water and lazing about on the water line. I'd never been here at night, and despite the ruin that had occurred, the view was still calming in an eerie way.

I sprawled out on the grass and opened up my bag of crackers. The black sky above stretched out forever, starless. As if there was a black blanket separating Earth from Heaven. As if the world itself had gone blind from a terrible accident. As if the world had gone to sleep.

As if.

I don't know how I missed the procession of geese coming back into the park, but they never made a sound. They seemed like a funeral procession, quiet and mournful, as they waddled around the water's edge. It was then I saw the girl across the way. She was on her knees in the grass beyond and seemed to be staring right at me. My fatherly instinct wondered what she was doing out so late before I realized time was all relative now, time was unreal. I gave her a weak wave, but either she didn't see me or didn't care to engage in a wave back. She looked older than a school child but younger than a late teenager. Was this the girl Karlos had told me about? The coincidence was too great, especially this far out from his usual stomping grounds.

The geese pressed on in silence, waddled up to the girl who, without looking, stretched out her hand. The lead goose lowered its head beneath, allowed itself to be stroked while the girl continued to stare at me. She sent her hand down its long, graceful neck, smiling. The goose ruffled its feathers briefly before kneeling down beside her. The rest of the gosling procession found places around her, knelt down as well. She looked like an aviary queen, a bird woman of dreams and day mares.

I opened up my water and began to sip slowly, never dropping my gaze from the moment. Perhaps it was a trick of the night, perhaps I was tired, but she seemed to be bathed in a dull white light, an aura of something unexplainable. I would rationalize it later, saying the bright white plumage of the geese in the dark made it appear as if she glowed, but I don't believe that's the truth of it.

She pulled a piece of bread from a pocket of her apron, tore it into several pieces, tossed them out and about to the docile birds. Even when faced with food, they remained calm and composed, not at all like the fluttery, easily agitated birds from before. I was spellbound, fascinated, enraptured. There was something very ethereal about the vision playing out across the pond. I didn't want to disturb her, but I badly wanted to speak to her and find out something, anything, about her.

After several long minutes of tossing the idea around, I made a decision to walk the bike over to her and find out what she was all about. I stood up and moved towards the bike, but when I turned to look back across the lake, both she and the birds were gone – *poof* – vanished. There was no bread on the ground, no indentation or marring of the grass where she sat, not a single feather drifting on the wind. As suddenly as they had all appeared, they disappeared as mysteriously.

It wasn't a miracle, but I felt an overwhelming sense of calm, a soothing of my ambivalence into an easy peace. I felt warm and flushed all over. Something stirred inside me, like a fastened clasp, rusted over for so long finally coming undone, like an expansion of lungs with the first delicious breath after nearly drowning.

I rode home with a lightness in my chest I could not explain, as if I had been witness to some magically universal thing meant only for me. It was a feeling I had not experienced in many years. When I got home, I realized I hadn't looked over my shoulder in fear or worried about running into any gangs during my ride through the city.

*   *   *

Today, Karlos and I found a way into the penthouse suite. We'd been leery about breaking any of the doors down if they had been locked from the inside, some kind of leftover morality we still clung to, but we finally decided no one was around to really care. There were also two matching recliners in good shape that we pulled out onto the crumbling patio. A far better seating arrangement than the plastic chairs we were used to. I can't speak for Karlos, but I felt fancier just for sitting in them. We were at least more comfortable than we had been in weeks.

"I think about art more now. You know I was never the museum type, but I think about it a lot since many of the museums have been destroyed."

"What about it do you think?"

He passed the bottle to me. It was nearly empty and I wondered if we had enough to last until the end of today's musings.

"At first, I didn't care since it was never my bag. Now it feels like we're missing something, like we're the people that have been erased from the world and only the buildings and architecture remain."

"That's a little bleak."

"I know, but I can't shake the idea. No one makes music anymore either. No vinyl, no tapes, no songs played from rooftops or street corners on real instruments or shit found in the garbage bins. This is profoundly unsettling to me."

"Even though it was never your thing." I tipped the bottle up, sipped, passed it back.

"Yes."

We sat, not speaking, for a bit, watched a group of pigeons alight on the building across the street, coo at each other and then take off again. Things stayed relatively normal for some, I guess. Karlos guzzled down the last of the amber, tossed the bottle behind us into the thrashed living room, removed another bottle from his satchel and passed it to me.

"I think it stems from a walk I took a few months back. I stumbled across the front steps of the gallery downtown. There was so much graffiti all over the walls and doors that I probably should've left well enough alone, but what did I know? I've always lived by my gut feeling and it's done me well so far."

I shook the bottle in the air between us.

"Exactly," he said. "So I went in, fumbled through the dark. I thought it'd be scarier for some reason, like all my nightmares were hiding in the corners I couldn't see, but I was calm. Even when I got lost, since I'd never been there before, it was as if I were just taking a stroll. The walk was more important than the destination, so to speak."

"Mmhmm."

"So I take one of the stairwells up, come into this room of, I don't know, paintings of real things and places. Landscapes and ornate rooms full of people eating and lounging around and whatnot. Hedonist yuppie-looking types. Wouldn't have given them a second look before, but every one of the faces had either been cut out or spray painted over, like they didn't matter. That was when I realized that they do, it all does."

I uncorked the bottle, drank, passed it back. "All the faces?"

"Yup. At least in that room. I heard a noise deeper in and figured it was better to shake a leg and get to gettin' if someone else was there, so I just assumed the others were the same."

"Safe assumption. Did you ever go back?"

"Nah. What's the point of looking at something that's obviously been ruined?"

I nodded. We both stared out at the darkened skyline in silence.

"I think I saw your girl the other day, the blind one."

He looked over at me with eyebrows raised. "Yeah?"

"Yeah. I found a bike and rode to the park I used to go to on my lunch breaks. Sarah would bring the girls and we'd have a small picnic of sorts. You know, back when things were…"

"Yup." He kept the bottle wedged between his legs, the mouth of it glistening with liquor and spittle.

"I think it was her. I'm not sure. Hell, I can't even be sure I saw her."

Karlos grinned. "If you're not sure, you definitely did."

"I don't understand," I said. He passed the bottle to me and stood up. He swung his head about lazily, staring out at the skyline, but without really seeing any of it. He had turned inward.

"I wanted to keep it to myself. Thought I was crazy, so I just told you the bare bones facts, dig?"

"Okay."

"Remember back when I hurt my ankle? I was on the south side of the city, scoping out the old booze distribution center. Kinda hoped someone wouldn't have thought to look there for extra booze. They had, of course – the place was empty."

"Sure."

"So I head out to the back, figure maybe some of the trucks out on the delivery dock had been forgotten about and were still unfound. Of course they were emptied out too. Pretty violently from the look of things. Broken glass everywhere, trucks all banged up, tires flat. So on."

I sipped the bottle, held it out to him and he waved it off.

"So I took a powder, sat on the edge of the dock and just hung out for a bit. Nothing really to see out there. I mean, it's the industrial district, so it's all worn down fences, empty propane tanks, rusted metal grating everywhere. Crabgrass up to the waist and no scenery. I wasn't tired, but I must've fallen asleep. Maybe shut my eyes for a bit, I don't know. Hard to say, but not a good thing to happen when you're out in the open."

"God, no." The flesh on my arms goose pimpled a bit. I felt a tingle climb up my spine and make its way through my limbs. I shivered; not out of fear for Karlos' safety, but for fear that we had experienced something similarly eerie at different times.

"I realized I couldn't remember a fair bit of time and looked around, made sure there was no one else around. Understandably, I was a bit scared."

At this, he gestured for the bottle, which I gave up quickly. Despite the dark, I could see that his face had flushed, his cheeks gone a shade of rosy I'd never seen before. He chugged, licked his lips, and panted slightly.

"I thought I saw something move on the other side of the fence. I couldn't make it out, but I sat there, frozen. I figured if it was someone watching me, it might be better to make like I hadn't seen them. Then I knew there was something moving out there because I could see the grass move. Not like wind over all of it, but a small stretch of the stuff. I don't know why, but I jumped off the dock and headed towards the fence. The movement had stopped, but then I saw it further out and decided to climb up and over. Being all kinds of graceful, I fell on the other side. That's when I jacked up my ankle, but it's fine now."

"You chased after it?"

"Dumb, right?"

"Did you have anything on you? A knife or stick or anything?"

"No. The thought didn't even cross my mind, believe it or not. But here's where shit got weird. The deeper into the field I limped, the more my body tingled. Not out of fear, but something else. When I looked back behind me, the fence, the dock, the entire damn building…all of it had disappeared. There was nothing but tall grass everywhere as far as I could see."

I cocked my head up at him, confused.

"I know, I know. This is why I didn't tell you everything the other day. I kept hobbling through the grass. Didn't know which way to go now. I couldn't see the city, didn't see any trash, nothing. It was like I'd been transported somewhere else. I could see this, I don't know, a clearing? Further up ahead, so I moved towards it. When I came through the grass, I saw this girl kneeling in the middle, surrounded by roses. Redder than anything I've ever seen, like blood painted on petals, but nicer than that. Not creepy, if that makes sense."

I nodded and took the bottle from him. "Was she wearing a dress?"

"She was. Did you see her eyes?"

"She sat on the other side of the pond. I never got close enough, no."

"Well, they weren't there. She must've heard me come through the grass, so she looked up at me and smiled. It was

Equity Lamp

a nice smile, but her eyes had been smoothed over with scar tissue, all flesh-like. She motioned for me to sit in front of her. Weird thing was, I felt compelled to do it even before she waved at me to do so. I had this calm wash over me, made me feel whole. It was an odd feeling, like I was safe."

I nodded again. "Serenity."

"Exactly. So we sat there, staring at each other. Or me staring at her I guess. She reached out to one of the roses and began peeling the petals apart, tore them off the bloom and sucked on them, one by one. She leaned over and lifted my pant leg and put all the petals, still wet, against the bum ankle. At first they just stuck there, but then they seemed to melt right into the skin. It didn't burn, but they were hot when she put them on."

"Alright." This was certainly far stranger than my own experience, but I could see why he kept all the details from me. Neither of us really knew each other that well before the dark came. Neighbors passing every so often, is all. We recognized each other, but never knew the other's name until after we started sharing the bottle. Assuming mental illness with this kind of story would've been an easy thing to do, might have split our weird friendship down the middle, fractured us. He motioned for the bottle again, sipped, and continued.

"When she was done with the petals, she rolled my pants leg down, smiled at me, gave a brief wave and that was that."

"That's it?"

"I woke up back on the dock as if nothing had ever happened. Like the whole thing was a damn dream."

"Are you sure it wasn't just a hyper-realistic dream?"

He smiled at me and put his leg up on the arm of the recliner. As he lifted the fabric of his pants, I could see the discoloration of his skin. Not patchy, but full on bright red, the color of pealing newborn skin all the way up his calf.

"Oh my."

"I don't know what really happened out there, but I believe it happened. Since then, I wake up from restful sleep, sleep I've never been able to have since I was a kid, and I'm warm, fuzzy even. Blissed out, if you like the idea of that better."

"Blissed out. I do like that." I felt the same after my experience. Not exactly, but close enough.

"I keep feeling like I'm waking up in pure sunlight. Like something spectacular is coming and I'm supposed to be there for it when it comes."

I nodded, grabbed the bottle from him, drank. I realized we did a lot of drinking and nothing else these days. Post-chaos philosophers with no place to call our own, speaking just to hear ourselves speak. Maybe we had reached a point where we were forcing ourselves to believe in something better, something different than what this current reality was spoon-feeding us on a daily basis. The psyche can't cope with such bleak surroundings for long. Something inside breaks, either for good or ill, but it breaks regardless. Maybe we were just tired of being broken and didn't know how to go about fixing ourselves.

*   *   *

I believe she was a vision sent from a deity I never believed in.

I believe that I will never see something as lovely as I did that day, and I hope it is never outshined by anything else.

I believe that I am living inside a purgatorial morality play of sorts. I keep looking over my shoulders expecting Dante to crest the horizon or peer through a copse of trees.

I believe Karlos.

I believe the sun has left us for good, has given up on us prematurely, but that we've been gifted something else entirely that may take us a lifetime to unravel and understand.

I believe in the mirage that changes minds, the illusion that melts hearts, and the idea that sparks revolution.

I believe the green will return when the world finally thaws from the darkness.

Now, I believe.

*　　*　　*

They say faith is something deep within, a thing both frail and somehow intangible. As if it were smoke bottled up and captured, waiting to be released. As if it were some inner light that shines bright through veins and arteries, miles of skin and capillaries. As if a belief could be strong enough to outshine starlight a thousand-fold and still not blind those nearby. As if it were something easily tamped out, snuffed, blown on and scattered to the wind in little tufts of withering nothings.

As if.

Ruinous Bloom

It is said that when Elena Leranjo died, the smell of lilacs lingered in her bedroom for days, emanating from her corpse before tumbling softly out the window to smother the dirt streets of Sao Brunois for years after. The scent permeated the brick and mortar buildings in both directions: up the hill towards the rickety old church, where she was later buried, and down the hill towards the bay where fishermen and dock workers alike began to weave rumors into mythologies, mythologies into truths, that were carried out to distant currents and passed onto others. Whether real or imagined, men who had never seen a lilac before claimed to smell an army of its blossoms while their boats drifted slowly into port.

The saccharine odor soon came to symbolize the town, a place where the sun seemed to shine too brightly, the food too rich for outsiders to finish, the wine too sweet to get drunk on, the people too friendly to ever be completely trusted. The smell baked itself within the breads and pies, mingled with chimney smoke in the evening and spread yellow across the starry skies. It was a constant reminder of the impermanence of life and the permanence only found in death...

*　　　*　　　*

As a boy, I was told there was supposedly nothing special about Elena Leranjo; she was born like any other child and was treated as such. An unfailingly polite girl, she smiled at everyone when not transfixed by the slow-moving clouds

Ruinous Bloom

above. On any given day, one could pass her home and find her helping her mother with chores or picking flowers from the lawn. She held imaginary conversations with imaginary things, believed her dolls to be living, breathing things. She was, like the other young girls, being groomed to take over the duties of keeping our village running while the men were out at sea.

No one knew what caused her to suddenly slump over in death while playing with the other children. No one saw anything out of the ordinary; she simply stopped running and fell face-first into the dirt, the hem of her dress flapping in the ocean breeze. The village doctor, and another that had arrived on a monthly supply ship, examined her, found nothing wrong, shook their heads, bewildered. The funeral procession up to the church was a small one; her parents, her older brother, an uncle from a distant village, and her dog, a three-legged mutt that whimpered the entire way. So they say.

Now? Others in the village have her name stuck to their lips, as if she were the beginning of a curse that had turned our part of the world into something sickly and gangrenous, something to be chopped off and thrown away without a second thought. I don't believe in curses and I don't believe our current problems began with the mysterious death of a girl nearly half a century ago.

Ruinous Bloom

But this wasn't the only rumor, oh no. With every ship that arrived, news of the world came with it. Some in the form of print on paper and the rest from the slippery tongues of men in easy lies and half-truths that made it hard to sift for reality. We saw a change come over our scenery, odd bits of detritus washed up on shore. Over the years, talk of Elena changed into whispers of a floating sanctuary, an island that moved on the ocean's whim, full of tall buildings crammed tightly together and built deep down into its earth. The sailors who claimed to have seen it called it a castle on the horizon. I called it all nonsense until the sailors stopped coming to port.

One day, our wharf was a loud and bustling market place filled with foreigners and local tradesmen, harlots and wine sellers. The next, only the sound of seagulls could be heard flying through the nearly empty harbor. We pressed on, believing these changes to be momentary, but then pieces of vessels, thousands upon thousands of smoking and disintegrating slats of heavy oak, began washing up onto the beach. The tides brought with them questions about the missing sailors. They also, in their own strange way, brought answers.

For weeks they had washed up on the shores of our little ocean-side hamlet, looking like long and sun-bleached dominoes of the dead scattered across the sand. Femurs, tibias, ulnas, radii. Skulls both whole and caved in, lengths of

Ruinous Bloom

spine still intact like tiny ladders. The smell of dead marrow and rot overpowered the sea spray and salt blowing in from the west. We could no longer fish, for even their skeletal remains arrived picked clean by whatever had turned our water brackish and unclean.

The surface took on a marbled sheen; blood mixed into tidal pools and turned the water the color of fresh bruise. The waves, once high and mighty and full of power, lapped slow against the coastline, lazy and sluggish as if burdened by the phenomena too. Sunlight fell upon the surface and seemed to disappear or die within the thick fluid. Oars dissolved when sunk below the surface, came up smoking and missing ends. Some great unknown thing had poisoned our ocean, had turned it dangerous.

For the first week, packs of wild dogs had appeared in the mornings and disappeared by afternoon, carrying in their mouths the largest bones they could carry. Soon, they began coming at all hours of the day, snapping and snarling at anyone on the beach, as if worried their new treasure trove would be stolen away from them. And then one day, they too simply disappeared. Some villagers believed the dogs had finally filled their hidey-holes full with the chew toys. And while I couldn't say why at the time, I felt it was something else, something more sinister. Their sudden disappearance was a dark omen that trembled deep within my insides and kept me awake at night. And I am not a man of superstition.

The meadows beyond the outskirts of the village began to die. The grass withered to brown and then finally to ashy black. Our landscape looked like a shriveled organ, diseased and unusable. The wither spread closer and closer to our homes, large and spacious homes made of mudded stucco, bamboo and palm fronds tethered together with think vine lacing. Large windows cut out of the communal areas that opened up to views of the ocean, stairwells that spiraled up around the entire home. The more ornately crafted a home, the more respected the man who built it. I should say that my own home, built by my grandfather and later added onto by my father and me, began practically enough before I added several balconies and trellises for creeping seaweed vines and wild blossoms. It was a fine home to be in and one I had no intention of leaving.

But as the black crept closer, we had to choose: stay and possibly wither black ourselves or find a way to leave to make a home elsewhere. Elena Leranjo's name became an unspoken whisper on our lips again. Had her death so long ago brought us this quick and silent decay? Was our little coastal hamlet in some way cursed? I dismissed the ideas as quickly as it appeared.

Ruinous Bloom

I was the first to start collecting the bones, worried that the supply washing up on shore would dissipate and thin out. We could no longer trek out to the forests beyond the black for fear, real or not, of instant death in the meadows. Some believed it would creep up from the ground, slither between toes and find its way into our veins, soaking arteries and strangling us from the inside out the way the sea had done to our boats; we heard them fracture and crack loudly one morning. They fell apart and dissolved within the water before our eyes. Steam rose up off the black water's surface around the disintegrating vessels. What happened to the sailors now became clearer, but no less understood. The poisonous water was crushing in on us from all sides. It was only a matter of time now.

And yet, I noticed the washed-up bones remained strong and intact, floating in from every direction. They seemed to stand up to the strange nature of the ocean while the wood could not. I did not fall prey to wasting time questioning the strange nature of this phenomenon and instead began planning our escape. To where, I did not know, but the black would soon overcome us if we didn't act. The choice between staying and being swallowed up by the unknown or floating out into a greater unknown was a losing one, but I've always thought it better to be actively moving in a direction, even if it's the wrong one. Sitting around and

Ruinous Bloom

waiting to die seemed like giving up. It seemed cowardly and I could imagine my grandfather's face scowling down at me for even allowing the idea into my head.

And while I did not believe the rumors of a floating city that moved with the tides, we made a boat of bones and set ourselves adrift, hoping to find the water still blue somewhere. Hoping to find the rest of our sailor brethren safe and out of harm's way.

*   *   *

By the end of the first day, we had acclimated ourselves to the idea that we were floating on the remnants of people we may have once known, may have once broken bread with on a slow and drunken evening. I realized the idea hadn't occurred to me while putting the boat together, but necessity seemed more important than dwelling on revulsion or sentimentality at the time. The setting sun had gone all aflame, bathed the ocean in bloody light on the horizon. Behind us, we could make out the scraggly black outline of our island home. I wondered if I would ever see her coastline again. Or if I would ever want to after the ruin had its ways.

"How many of them made it, papa?" Giulia asked. "How many of them got off the island?"

Ruinous Bloom

I shook my head, unable or unwilling to speculate. I had hoped all but knew this wasn't the truth. My cautious optimism was one of the few reasons her mother, Adara, had married me in the first place. I didn't wear the constant scowl of someone staring into the sun like other men on the island. *There is a spark in you that has yet to catch flame*, she told me once. I always liked that particular memory and it was one I thought of often as we sailed to wherever.

"Here," I said, cutting a slice of papaya. "Eat. We will need our strength in the morning and there's not much to keep us."

She took the fruit from my fingers and bit into it gingerly, still afraid the blackness had left the island and somehow traveled with our supplies. She looked up at me, juice running down her chin, and I smiled back while holding the fleshy insides of the fruit up for her to see. "No black," she muttered.

"No. No black."

I knew the waves farther out would get choppy, so I had fortified the sides of the boat with multiple layers of bones. I had tethered it all together with lengths of tendon and ligaments that also washed up on our shores, looking like fleshy kelp strewn across the white sands. Why these did not disintegrate like the rest of the body parts, I could not say, but I was thankful for it. Our sea-faring transport looked more like a small ship than a raft, what with its closed-in roof and high sides.

There were four oars made of pelvic bones and femurs, a sail-less mast of sixteen incomplete vertebrae tied together and reaching up to the gods that created them, a rudder made of whale fins (a fortuitous surprise as they were the only ones that washed ashore), the transom and forward pulpits made of a small army of ribcages.

We had space to sleep without fear of being splashed on, but I worried whether we would survive our first storm. Did the rain also have the same kind of melting effect on the human body as the ocean? I couldn't be sure and didn't want to take the chance, so a tiny, windowless, cabin was built in the middle of the deck, large enough to fit us both. Giulia slept peaceful and curled up in my arms.

It took her hours to fall asleep and I…well, I lay awake most nights, body tensed and taut, ready to fight whatever wave tried to overtake us, ready to lift her high above my head if the ocean found its way into our walled-off cabin. I hoped that the gentle rocking of the boat would lull me to sleep, that the motion would cocoon me into slumber, but it only served to heighten my nervousness. They were small waves, but how much damage would they do if they spilled over into our ship? Would we melt away in slow screams? This was the thought that kept me from falling hard into dreams. Death did not scare me, but I was terrified of a painful death. I was terrified of having my skin sloughed off by some great unknown with only my bones to wash up on a shore where I remained unknown. No one to mourn my passing, no one to sing a hymn to my memory. I know not why, but it feels important that I be remembered long after my body decays. I've done nothing to earn this remembrance, it is simply an idea that vibrates deep within me.

We had been out to sea for several days, had gotten into a routine. Guilia would fix breakfast in the morning before waking me. She would take the first shift of ridding the deck of water that had washed over the railing while I struggled to wake up. Today, however, there was something in her voice that shook me to my core. Something inhuman, cold.

"Papa! The sun!" Giulia shouted from the deck of the boat. I untangled myself from the blanket and left the dark of the cabin to squint out into the daylight.

"Come away from the railing, darling. You're far too close," I said, hobbling across the awkward deck, my body protesting the aches and soreness of an awkward sleep. She didn't move, but simply pointed out to the sunrise. A haze of yellowish green sat atop the ocean like a layer of foam. It turned the birthing sunlight a sickly color, made the day look nauseous and foul. Not quite the color of sky before a storm, but something else.

"It's Elena Leranjo," she said, sleepily, as if in a daze.

"How do you know that name, Giulia? Where have you heard it before?"

She shrugged, never taking her eyes off the horizon. "But can't you smell it?"

I wrapped my hands around her chest and held her against my legs, sniffing the air. I smelled the static of coming thunder. I smelled the brine of ocean and the sweetness of deep ocean fish. I smelled other, unnamable scents that came on the breeze and then, as a landmass came slowly into view, I could smell the faintest hint of lilac. I inhaled over and over, hoping I had deluded myself into believing the fragrance was there, but it permeated, soaked through until it was the only thing I could smell. Giulia smiled up at me, but I could not return the sentiment.

The morning was long. We continued to drift, almost purposefully, towards the landmass as it seemed to grow larger on the horizon. We could make out its shape, see its colors. It had no trees, sparse vegetation jutting out from its rocky edges, but was instead like a large floating building set out to sea. Tall, brick walls lined its beaches and stretched their arm-like parapets up to the heavens. No birds circled it overhead; none sat perched along the wall's edges. No movement could be seen from the deck of our boat. I wondered what lay beyond the gates of this floating city, this marvel the fishermen used to speak of so often. As I've said, I'm not a man of superstition and blamed this vision on hunger, a possible mirage.

By high noon, we were close enough to swim to its shores, but knew better. We took our lunch on the deck, me slicing up fruit for the both of us as she tore bits of bread into pieces. We stared at the edifice, now blocking the horizon, the sun beating down on its browning façade from behind us, illuminating the cracks and the grouting. It was quite beautiful once one got up close to it.

By mid-afternoon, I realized I'd been wrong about there being no vegetation. What I'd believed to be cracks in the surface of the walls were actually lengths of leaf-less vines snaking upwards to the ramparts above. It was as if a great castle had come under the ruin of the world, succumbed completely and totally to nature. Its walls, easily hundreds of feet tall, were choked by the slithering vines, covered in them.

Beyond, the horizon remained soaked with yellowish-green fog, though it had been hidden by the castle before us. I could still smell lilac if I thought about it, but found myself too engrossed by the enormity of the island structure.

It was wondrous majesty and Giulia and I were completely spellbound. That there were stories of this place on the lips of sailors no longer surprised me. I could see how one might believe it to be a paradise, some kind of holistic kind of retreat from the world. For the briefest of moments, I thought I saw a man standing on the tallest ramparts, his clothes flapping in the wind, staring down at us until we drifted ashore. Then the sun flashed and blinded me. The vision was gone when I looked again.

Our little boat washed ashore, slid up along wet ground until it stopped. I jumped off the vessel gingerly, careful to stay out of the wake of the lapping waves, and carried Giulia on my shoulders. Once we were safely out of distance, I put her down and let her walk on her own. I was too old now; I would not be able to carry her like that for much longer.

"Welcome!" a voice called out from above. We both looked up in surprise, eyes wide and mouths open, to see an elderly, long-bearded man standing on the outskirts of the craggy beach. He wore sun-faded khaki pants and a billowing dress shirt. In his right hand, a walking staff as tall as he was. He held his left hand out to us, as if to offer his meager strength to us both.

"Hello," Giulia stammered. "Is this your home?"

The old man smiled and looked back over his shoulder at the huge edifice behind him. "I'm more like the caretaker," he replied. "No one owns this particular island,

Ruinous Bloom

and one day, I'll be replaced by someone who will take care of it the way I have for so many years. You both look famished. Please, come eat and drink."

Giulia and I looked at each other. I could see the hint of a smile playing at the corners of her mouth as I reached out for her hand. We walked up the beach to our host and I realized we had become part of the island's mythology, woven into the tapestry of its legend, though we would never know to what degree.

The sand slipped and slid beneath my feet as I stared up the face of the wall, saw the bright blue of the sky for what it was: illuminating and clear, piercing and calm. We clamored up the rocky shelf and stood next to our host, who smelled like clouds, like sunshine on hung clothing. "What is this place?" I asked through short, panting breaths.

He put his free hand on my shoulder and looked me right in the eye. I believed I could see the constellations in the gleam of his retina, the North Star imprinted upon his brow, the passing of time whispering through his bushy eyebrows. "We call this place *O Anjo*, my friend." He smiled and walked towards an opening in the stone wall, never motioning for us to follow, just assuming we would.

And then, I understood, but all too late.

Elena Leranjo had been a myth, a girl no one had ever known. A dream perpetuated by those in love with ideas they could never wrap their arms around. A superstitious man's way of explaining a grandfather's death to his child or a mother's way of explain the passing of a pet.

O Anjo meant "the angel."

Given enough leeway, Elena and O Anjo could sound similar, I thought. Over the years, one must have come from the other. I rolled the phrases over and over inside my head, moved my lips silently and felt the syllables dance across my tongue.

The island O Anjo.

Elena O Anjo.

Elena Leranjo,

There was no Elena; the island was *O Anjo*; the island was the angel; the island was death. It was so clear now that we were here, now that we heard the phrase fall like silk from the stranger's mouth.

And yet we continued to walk, hand in hand, following our smiling host who explained in the kindest terms that this was how he received everyone that arrived and that some day, perhaps, we too would welcome strangers into the fold. His voice was that of softened fabric, of light thunderstorms in the evening, of waves gently rolling and crashing into the open arms of landmass. And we continued to walk while, outside, the yellowish-green fog slowly surrounded the island as it floated out onto other currents…

Ruinous Bloom

*　　*　　*

It is said that when the village of Sao Brunois died, the smell of bones and rotted flesh smothered the crumbled, vacant streets for years after. The scent permeated what was left of the ornate homes, made them unlivable by those that found them later. Fishermen and pirates alike began to weave rumors into mythologies, mythologies into truths that were carried out to distant currents and passed onto others. Whether real or imagined, these sea-faring men claimed to have seen the lone survivor of this village, floating out on the ocean with his daughter on a boat they made of bones.

I Waited for You

Susan and I never had children. We couldn't, in good conscience, find a reason amongst all the violence that built up around us like so much white noise. I remember when the news had moments of clarity, random moments of something good and decent pock-marking the surface of the increasingly volatile headlines. The inconsequential lives of movie stars and rock gods gave way to a new kind of celebrity: growing pockets of slow, deliberate chaos that singed the edge of normalcy until they caught fire and lit up the mind with fevered, unshakeable nightmares. Until the televisions all went dark, we couldn't tear ourselves away from watching our new-millennial empire fall. After that, well…we as a population seemed to forget how to look after each other.

We didn't complain when the government wanted to get rid of the cemeteries; we understood the space was needed and the bodies were no longer the vehicles for memory anyway. We didn't mind that the headstones and mausoleums needed to be broken down and turned into new world ghettos of gray sameness; the names and dates were already carved into our hearts and those that weren't had long been forgotten. We didn't mind the stench of burning carcasses; oddly, the smell gave us hope, gave us something to look forward to since our past had been all but erased by the idiocy of the most recent present. Out of a need to call it something, many had called it the Global Crumbling.

I Waited for You

I suppose that's as good a name as any. My friends and I called it the Time of Madness, but soon realized the phrase was inadequate and vague. It didn't express how widespread the problem was; though no one reported it, I'm sure the natives of underdeveloped nations fell under the same spell of destruction. Even the Swiss, those great neutral bastards, ate themselves from the inside-out. Remove man's structure (his moral backbone, his faith in order) and watch how quickly he becomes an animal, how quickly he lets his devils loose upon the world.

I wondered what it all looked like from outer space, from the viewpoint of someone floating in orbit and watching. I imagined each country ringed in a glowing fire that illuminated the borders. The fact that Susan and I made it this far is certainly up for question as we were less prepared than others. Luck, fate, common sense...who knew? It doesn't matter now, however. We're of the generation (un?)lucky enough to watch the world sew itself together one slow stitch at a time.

Somewhere along the way, the American dream curdled; not just for us, but for those that depended on us to make their dreams a more attainable truth. Their dreams soured as quickly as ours, but I wonder if maybe some of them, those in previously war-torn nations, had a leg up in preparation for this. Most of us stateside just never had any

I Waited for You

experience with bullet-riddled storefronts or watching our family trees wither in the streets. What did we know about fighting to protect our homes from drone strikes, militias, and rioting crowds?

Susan didn't like me leaving the apartment then. The trek down the stairwell was dangerous enough, what with the addicts curled up in corners and the displaced in need of warmth. But when the stores and pharmacies got ransacked, I kept having to go farther and farther out to find a way to keep us both alive. I didn't tell her this, but I think she probably figured it out when I came back later and later every time with fewer supplies. She never admitted to knowing, never did more than play along with whatever story I gave her, but her embraces got longer and longer every time I returned. So, we kept on. As long as I came back, she never complained. She offered to join a few times, wanting desperately to help, but I refused. "It's my job as your husband," I'd say, or "My health is better," I'd say. Half-truths, but truths nonetheless.

Music was a hard thing to come by these days, what with everything having gone digital so many years before. Little to no power meant most lost the joy of vast caches of collected music, but not us. We had an old crank turntable, an antique from Susan's side of the family. We never played it too loud though. The sound of music was like a beacon for the more violent-natured. Music meant life and life meant victims, possibly food and weapons. Instead, Susan and I would sit in the glow of a single candle, listening until the record was over or she fell asleep.

Though she was still awake, I carried her to bed after our first listening session. I knelt before her chair and slid my hands beneath her thighs, felt how thin she had become over the last few months. "And what do you think you're doing?" she asked with a grin.

"Carrying my bride to her bed, of course," I replied, trying not to grunt at the effort. I picked her up and she giggled, wrapped her arms around my neck and nuzzled up against me as I walked her down the hallway. I felt her warm, shallow breath against my skin. From that day on, I carried her to bed every night. She protested at first, but relented when I told her it was what husbands should do in times like these. But really, I felt it important for us to have some kind of ritual that kept us close. I wanted her to know, *needed* her to know, that she was my everything in a world that seemed to have shrugged off sentiment in exchange for survival.

When the hand-crank finally broke and left us without song, left us with nothing but the silence two people can fall into comfortably after several years, I never let her shuffle off to sleep alone. I saw her struggling to stand with every day that passed; I had never practiced medicine, but I felt weaker in ways too and chalked it up to our increasingly meager diets. We were getting along to get along, as my father used to say, but neither of us could say why. Maybe it was just our stubborn human nature to fight off death until weary. Why we were afraid to die when living wasn't a much better option is hard to say. I think we just wanted to experience it all together, wanted to continue holding on to something that we knew was good and true between us.

Three months after the crank broke, Susan passed away. With no one to care for but myself, there was never a rush to return home from foraging for supplies. For two days, I had not buried her - she remained in our room, in our bed, until I found a place I could lay her to rest. If I stopped to soak in the realization that she was gone, I'd lose my will to hunt and forage. My wife was gone and I had no music. The only thing left to do was survive.

*   *   *

I read somewhere once that scientists tried to measure the weight of the soul by weighing the body of the deceased shortly after dying. I don't know how much a soul weighs, but I know the weight of a memory. I know the weight of an infinite amount of memories and I know of no one strong enough to carry each and every one to the grave. I

I Waited for You

think this may be why we feel the need to be coupled with someone else along the way; love isn't about finding your soul mate, it's about finding someone with the desire and strength to help you share the load.

I was not awake when she died. There was no grand emotional scene full of clasped hands and last words meant to comfort her (me?) when she drew her final breath. When I woke up, she was both wholly there and completely gone. I'd like to think she passed with the violence of a petal falling slow and graceful to soft earth below. This is my hope.

I knew the moment I awoke. The feel of the room was different, thicker and quieter somehow. I rolled over to rest my hand on her stomach the way I did most mornings and felt nothing, the purr of her body silent and stilled. She was cool to the touch like sheets unslept in. It was unfair that she died first, having never left the building, but it was better that it happened in her sleep and not at the hands of some roaming stranger. I'm glad she didn't die alone or hungry. I'm glad I was by her side at the end. I'm glad I was able to give her that little bit of solace.

For months I'd been preparing for this moment, hoping it would never arrive. I'd act normal around her until she fell asleep, but some nights I'd stay up and ruminate on the what-ifs while fashioning a harness I kept hidden in the ceiling. What I did during the day was easier to hide since I was always on my own outside the apartment.

The harness was a pastiche of material I came across randomly during my foraging trips: shredded linens, strips of unmolested canvas, even a bit of sail material blown inland somehow. There was no way I would leave her to rot inside our home, no way I would tarnish her memory in such a way.

Near the outskirts of the city, I'd found an empty burial plot. The graves were dug out, but never seemed to fill, like someone had simply forgotten about their existence or died themselves before finishing the job. It was easy to remember the spot since a large weeping willow had taken root there and remained. I remember thinking that its heavy curtains of limbs and leaves felt like a good hiding place when the time came.

When I finally pulled my hand away from her body, I got out of bed and spent the day completing the harness. There was food enough stocked up for two, maybe three days and there was no need to work in secret anymore. By nightfall, I had re-stitched and sewn every strap, making sure they held steady for the walk the next morning. I tore the cardboard off the windows and stood on our balcony. For the first time in many years, I could actually hear the quiet of midnight. No bombs, no gunshots, no shattering of broken windows. It was as if the city knew how close it was to being rebuilt, to being reborn into something worth living in again. I wished she had made it a little longer just to help me count the stars even though they had fallen out of their constellations.

In my sleep, I had stolen the sheets from Susan and left her uncovered. It seemed wrong somehow and I felt guilty, as if I'd left her defenseless while she slumbered. I rose and spread the sheets over her before readying the harness and packing up some supplies.

The harness lay on the floor like some great beached octopus, the slots for arms and legs splayed out and open. The light of dawn spilled through the newly open windows and filled the room, covering the thing in bright glow, revealing the grime on the walls. We had been here too long. I had kept us cooped up and now her death was my punishment. I should've looked for a better place, a healthier place, to keep her hidden away from the violence that had become the world. That such a place even existed was doubtful, but still. I could've done more. Should've.

After packing the last of the supplies I could carry, I returned to the bedside and stared down at her. Loose skin gripped her thin bones, but her hair had turned a regal shade of silver over the years and remained full. She was beauty. I tried not to think about her eyes suddenly opening and staring up at me, at her mouth proclaiming her love for me, at her frail hands holding on to mine. I tried not to think of her at all as I finagled her limbs into the apparatus. If the tears came, I knew they would not stop.

I slipped my head and arms through the remaining loops of fabric and picked her up gingerly, felt her body settle against mine. I carried her through the apartment one last time. It took me an hour and a few stops to get down the seven flights of stairs.

*   *   *

Ten years ago, Susan and I had met at a ration station back when they were still teeming with the hungry, the confused. You could smell the desperation, the false hope, on people as they clustered around the supply trucks and pressed in on one another anxious just to eat. No one was rich, there was no class system; there was simply the government controlling all forms of commerce and product on one side and the swarm of populace with outstretched hands on the other, happy for even the moldiest of fruits or breads.

"Number 037893, step forward!" I heard over the mumbled din. The number was mine. I had run it through my brain so often that I knew it better than my social security number (long defunct and unused by then). I stepped forward and our arms brushed against each other; I smelled the faintest hint of soap, a near luxury, and looked down at her. Our moment was brief, but I saw her clearly: dingy gray overcoat faded yellow and orange scarf, eyes the size a man could drown in happily.

"Excuse me," she said. Her face crumpled in immediate understanding. "It's…it's you they called, isn't it? Not me."

I held my ticket out to her, the number printed black and thick across the parchment. "Afraid so," I replied with what I'd hoped was an apologetic smile.

"No, I suppose it wasn't 073893 they called, though they sound so similar. I must have misheard. Tomorrow, maybe," she said, dejected. I watched her turn and walk back through the crowd.

I grabbed my rations bag from the officer and tried to follow her. She had given up so easily, had not tried to fight me for what everyone else also wanted. Too often I'd seen such instances before, a show of our basest desires on display – wolfish hunger beating back the lion of decency. But I couldn't blame them. No one could.

I slid the bag inside my coat and pushed through the throng of people. I always hated navigating my way back through the sallow faces, the eager, starving looks. I felt guilty for having my number called, as I'm sure others did too. It was the luck of the draw and nothing else, but I had been luckier than most that month having been called three times. That fact made me someone worth mugging then.

When I got to the curb, away from the shifting, wanting bodies, I stopped to breathe. Fighting my way back to the curb felt like fighting a rising tide. And then I remembered the woman again.

I pivoted my head to look around the street, hoping to find her. I scanned the faces of every man, woman, and child until I saw a brief bit of yellow scarf take flight in the wind near the stoop of a walk-up. Her face was taut, thin. My gaze did not waver as I moved closer, instinctively clutching the bag tighter beneath my coat.

I stood in front of her, watching her rub the tears that came (strangely) from just her left eye. She looked up at me and that was it; I became softened heart.

"It's not much," I stammered, pulling the bag out and holding it between us, "but can I make you dinner?"

"I couldn't possibly. It wouldn't be right. They'll call my number again soon enough, I'm sure of it."

"How long has it been since they last called it?"

"Two weeks," she whispered. She looked at the bag. Her mouth tightened and I knew she was fighting another batch of tears. I held out my free hand.

"Join me. *Allow* me to share what I've got with you." I smiled down at her, she sighed and took my hand. From

I Waited for You

then on, we shared what rations we could with each other, an unspoken survival agreement between two strangers. It was only after a long while that something feeling like more than survival bloomed between us. Something richer and deeper, an affection neither of us seemed to be able to shake off as passing interest.

*   *   *

It was sometime past noon when I finally made it to the willow tree. I was slathered in sticky sweat. My back and arms ached. Susan seemed to get heavier the longer I carried her, but I knew it was simply my old age and the distance working against me. Had I not made the harness, it would've taken us much longer.

The adrenaline of sneaking through the city was wearing off as I passed through the heavy boughs. The sun shone through in small places on the ground, but the shade was otherwise thick and cool. I worried that I might have been overtaken by harriers or worse, the crazed, but by some grace, we were left alone and arrived unscathed. I don't remember seeing anyone, but I was also trying to walk quickly without stopping. It was dangerous to be that oblivious of the surroundings for so long a journey. I've seen men get killed for being less obtuse.

I knelt down and laid her on the ground gently. I slipped the harness off and leaned back, felt parts of my back pop and crack in relief. We had made it.

I had hidden a shovel up in the limbs the day before, deciding to dig my own hole rather than use one already made. It seemed right that I oversee the entirety of Susan's burial.

I looked up and saw the wooden handle still blended into the tree. It would be a few hard hours of work, but easier with the tool. And with night arriving by the time I was done, I could forage in peace and darkness. I did not have time to mourn yet, could not mourn yet.

I reached up and brought the shovel down. I marked off a flat patch of ground and hoped the root system wasn't too expansive below. I figured I'd have to chop through some of the roots, but I'd take the hunting knife to them when the time came. I slid the shovel into the dirt and heard the slick separation of soil as it sunk deep. I smiled and hoisted the first load out, the second, the third.

It didn't need to be too deep; I hadn't seen scavenger animals in months. It didn't need to be overly wide as Susan was a tiny thing to begin with. After an hour of toil, there was a divot in the earth two feet wide by six feet long; barely deep enough, but I wanted to go deeper. I stopped, rested against the trunk of the tree and nibbled on some dry rice and water from my bag. Susan's nightgown shifted in the lazy breeze, exposed a milky, veiny thigh. I reached over and pulled the fabric back down. She had always been modest and it just felt right to preserve her that way too.

Sweat ran down the bridge of my nose and I wondered what, if any, sounds were happening inside her now? The *thump-thump* of flowing blood and beating heart were quiet, but would her other organs sigh into silence the way she had? Did her nerves ever crackle with the sound of potential? Had her soul left an echo on the wind when it left? I realized these were the thoughts of a delirious grief pounding at the wall I badly wanted, badly needed, to stand firm for awhile.

I scooped out the remainder of the dirt, threw the shovel out onto the mass of soil above and climbed out. The willow shifted and swayed, allowing the coming sunset to peek through in a deep and burning red. Susan's face glowed in the dying light as I picked her up and stepped down into the hole with a grunt. I laid her down, ran my fingers along the tufts of hair along each ear and pushed them back. Her cheeks were cool and porcelain against my dirty fingers.

"I would carry you the rest of my days in this waste of a world if you would open your eyes one last time," I whispered. "I would gladly trade you places if I knew you'd be taken care of."

I Waited for You

I stood above her, legs straddling her body and finally let the tears come. I let the grief and anger seep through before righting myself, before letting it completely overtake me.

"I'm sorry I kept you locked up like an animal in a place that so badly needs more people like you in it. I wish I could be there to carry you the rest of the way. Wherever you're going, wherever you are, I wish we could've gone together."

I steeled myself, slipping shovelfuls of dirt around the edge of her body, careful not to spill a single grain or loose pebble on her until absolutely necessary. I knew how it would all play out in the end, but it felt wrong to do it quickly, to cover her up as if she were some deceased family pet. I started with her feet and made my way up, using my hands instead of the shovel. I spread the soil across her gently, as if this were a more respectful thing to do. It shamed me to cover her face, and I paused for awhile, stopping to stare at her one last time. By the time I could see no more of her skin, no more of her hair or nightgown, my eyes had glistened over, gone wet with grief.

Hate and anger have a way of withering the brightest bloom and it pleased me that Susan's petals kept unfurling until she died. It is a tragedy more people didn't get to see it the way I did. I don't know how much a soul weighs, but I do know the weight of a memory.

Acknowledgements

No one achieves their goals purely on their own – we've all had a little bit (or in my case, a lot) of help along the way in some form or another. Anyone who says otherwise is either a liar or simply chooses to ignore reality.

To my mother who, for many years, put up with my less-than-ideal aspirations of becoming an over-educated writer, but continues to support my passion.

To my father who has become the biggest fan of my writing, constantly asking for new work whenever it's finished.

To Surya, for his beautiful foreword and the many weekends spent with him and his family in Los Angeles and Napa engaged in culinary delights, heady patio conversations beneath starlight, and finding our way to the bottom of more than a few bottles in the process, hoping to, as he says, "put a shine on the night."

To the fellow classmates, fellow writers, and selfless professors who have read and critiqued previous incarnations of this collection (and other writings of mine), I say thank you. Through countless workshops, days spent both writing and critiquing alongside other writers, these pages are the culmination of many years of schooling and long, long hours of tweaking sentences, phrases, and narratives to be just right.

To my friend Rob, who I've known a ridiculously long time through music. He was patient with my constant, protean ideas for the cover art and came up with something that I believe gives great context to the stories within its borders.

To the list of publications at the beginning of this collection where these stories have previously appeared; without the validation of other literary journals and magazines accepting and publishing the utter weirdness found within these pages, I may have fallen into frustration and left this project largely unfinished. So, to them, I also say thank you for the opportunity to be seen and read by large swaths of new readers.

To the writers that came before me, the ones whose truly imaginative words dripped off the pages like so much influence as I read, firing up the once quiet synapses inside my head: Amber Sparks, Amelia Gray, Ben Marcus, Blake Butler, Carlos Ruiz Zafón, Donald Barthelme, Don DeLillo, Gabriel García Márquez, Haruki Murakami, Italo Calvino, Jorge Luis Borges, Margaret Atwood, Mark Z. Danielewski, Matt Bell, Roberto Bolaño...the list goes on and on. Thank you for showing me that there are no boundaries to fiction and that rules are sometimes meant to be broken, even if we may not fully understand the finished product ourselves.

- Adam "Bucho" Rodenberger

About the Author

Adam "Bucho" Rodenberger is a surrealist writer from Kansas City. He earned dual bachelor's degrees in English and Philosophy from the University of Kansas City-Missouri in 2009 while minoring in Political Science. He earned his MFA in Writing from the University of San Francisco in 2011 and continues to work on short stories and novels-in-progress.

He has been published in Agua Magazine, Alors, Et Tois?, Aphelion, Bluestem Magazine, BrainBox Magazine, Cause & Effect Magazine, Cahoodaloodaling, Crack the Spine, Eunoia Review, Five Quarterly Magazine, Ginosko Literary Journal, Glint Literary Journal, The Gloom Cupboard, Hamilton Stone Review, The Heartland Review, L'allures des Mots, Lunch Box, Meat For Tea: The Valley Review, Offbeatpulp, Penduline Press, Phoebe, Poydras Review, The Santa Clara Review, Serving House Journal, Sheepshead Review, Slice Magazine, Summerset Review, Up The Staircase, Fox Spirit's "Girl at the End of the World: Book 1" anthology, and was shortlisted for the Almond Press "Broken Worlds" fiction contest.

He blogs at:
http://triphoprisy.blogspot.com.

You can find his DJ mixes, specializing in hip hop, trip hop, funk, soul, techno, house, and retro at:
http://www.mixcloud.com/bucho/

Made in the USA
Middletown, DE
05 August 2019